AFTER & BEFORE

A NOVEL

TED M. ALEXANDER

GREYFIELD MEDIA

Greyfield Media

Printed in the United States of America

Published by Greyfield Media, LLC
Asheville, North Carolina.

Grateful acknowledgment is made for permission to reprint lyrics from the song "You Tell Me Your Dream and I'll Tell You Mine" by Seymour Rice, Albert H. Brown and Charles N. Daniels, © 1908, renewed 1957 Warner Bros. Inc. All rights reserved. Used by permission of Alfred Music, and courtesy of the Charles L. Blockson Afro-American Collection, Temple University Libraries.

Library of Congress Cataloging-in-publication Data

Alexander, Ted M.
After & Before

1. General—Fiction. 2. Fantasy - Contemporary—Fiction.
3. Thrillers/Psychological—Fiction. I. Title
Library of Congress Control Number 2014931889

ISBN-978-0-9914237-0-5
eBook ISBN 978-0-9914237-1-2

Cover/Book Layout & Design: Kim Pitman, FireflyInx.com

First Edition

10 9 8 7 6 5 4 3 2 1

Contact Author: TedMAlexander.com

For Paige

After & Before

Dark Matter

Prologue

Pale fingers emerged from the mist, toes inching forward below them. The feet halted and the hands slowly lowered, allowing the forefingers to mechanically glide moist leaf flecks backward from the toes and across the top of each foot.

She ached for the rest of the body to emerge, but it remained hidden except for the hands hovering over the feet, the forefingers sliding, sliding the autumn-colored specks across the dull skin.

She demanded that the remainder of the body move forward to identify itself, but instead, the scene slowly bobbed away—a bottle with message disappearing between gray waves. She stared after it, longed after it, when suddenly a black curtain crashed down, leaving her awash in darkness and freeing a lone bird to wing through her consciousness.

Trapped inside an airport terminal, the terror-stricken sparrow flew through a labyrinth of corridors, lunging at the glass for an opening, searching for the outside where it should be, yet unable to gain access. She could feel the bird's terror, the pulsating heart, the desperate need to break the glass and be free. She wanted to scream, but instead mumbled to herself, her eyelids fluttering.

"Jane, Jane, come back. Come back." Someone was tapping her shoulder. "Come back, honey." The voice was insistent, dragging her toward it. "Come back."

Jane's eyes flashed open and she stared into a blitzkrieg of color: black mascara, violet eye shadow, rose blush, vermilion lips.

Twyla.

"Where were you, honey?" Twyla asked from her sitting position on the edge of the couch, her hands clutching Jane's shoulders. "I lost you for a second back there. Where'd you go?"

Jane thought for a moment, her breath slowing. "I'm not sure where I was."

"Well, think about it." Twyla paused. "Go ahead and think hard and tell me where you were, honey," she said. "I have to know. If we're going to make progress, I have to know."

"I'm . . . I'm . . . " Jane's voice trailed away.

Twyla released her hands from Jane's shoulders. "We've got to talk about what you saw, Jane." She waited.

Jane hesitated. "I can't remem—"

"Of course you can."

"I'm not sure what to tell."

"Then enough of this. Do you think this is a game to me?" Twyla shook her head. "This is a partnership—you and me. I hypnotize, you travel to the past lives, wherever your mind leads you, and when you return, we interpret the voyage."

"Twyla, it was just fog and feet and hands."

"Tell me." She stared at Jane. "Explain to me."

Jane rose to a sitting position on the couch, then described the hands, the feet, and the forefingers scraping at the bits of colored leaves.

"Were they your feet or your hands?"

"No, no, they weren't," Jane murmured.

"Whose were they?"

"I don't know."

"And what else?" Twyla asked, her tone softening.

"That's all," Jane answered as she leaned over and reached for her shoes. "Except that I wanted to see who was coming out of the mist and I never did." Tears, surprising tears formed.

"That happens occasionally," Twyla replied. "Do you have any idea who it might have been?"

Jane thought. "Someone I love?"

"Perhaps, perhaps not," Twyla said, her interest waning as she stared at herself in the mirror over the couch. She twisted a curl and pushed it behind her ear. "We shall see."

Jane nodded and rose to her feet. "Thank you, Twyla."

Twyla nodded. "Until we meet again."

CHAPTER 1

"The saddest part of my sister's romance was that her husband was diabetic." Carrie glanced up from her spinach salad. "And it wasn't sad for the reasons you think," she said, spearing another leaf. "He could achieve an erection, or so she says, by controlling the amount of insulin he took—so the apparatus worked, even if it did need a little firepower from pharmaceutical America. The only problem was that it was possible for him to inject too much insulin and then pass out. And what good is the last of the red hot lovers if he's flaccid and suffering from insulin shock?"

Jane sipped from a glass of sparkling water, then pushed a lime wedge around with the straw.

"But, no, I tell you, Jane, it wasn't the sex that was the problem, it was the eyesight. Know what I mean?"

"You're saying he began to lose his eyesight because of the diabetes," she answered.

"That's right," Carrie responded, "and you forget what that means. Losing your vision can be more intimate than losing the sex."

"How's that?"

"Because all the little loving things disappear with the eyesight loss. He couldn't tell his wife if she had a piece of spinach stuck in her tooth. He didn't notice if she was wearing the earrings he bought for her on a vacation in Bermuda ten years before. He wasn't able to see the smile on her face when he said something funny, and he couldn't watch as the years aged the woman he had chosen for life." She placed her fork next to the white ceramic bowl. "Does that make sense?" She frowned. "You're not eating. Why?"

Jane shrugged as she stared at her friend. She loved Carrie's brashness and her sensitivity; an unlikely combination that had attracted Jane and enabled their unusual companionship—a boss and subordinate—to flourish. Corporate America frowned on an unpolished confidant from a lower echelon associating with a member of the management team, but Jane didn't care, they just clicked together and she needed a good friend.

Carrie stared. "What's the matter with you today? You don't look so good. You sick?"

Jane found it hard to communicate—to even begin to talk.

Carrie started for her. "I'm willing to bet big money this has got to do with you answering that ad in the *Village Voice* for past-life regression therapy." She held up her hand. "Don't tell me no, because it's got to be yes. How many times did I tell you not to answer the ad?" She frowned. "Oh, well, hard to believe, but I make mistakes too." She glanced about the room. "Dessert or no dessert, always the question. I wouldn't mind the calories, but I hate people staring at me eating something like chocolate mousse when I'm thirty pounds overweight. Know what I mean? Who are they to judge? The bastards." She pushed the salad bowl away from her. "So what's going on, baby? When did you go?"

"Actually I've had a few sessions before the one this morning."

"So that's why you were late. Talk to me."

Jane hesitated. "I don't know, Carrie, it's confusing. I seem to be feeling worse and worse. Did you ever believe you were a twin—a part of something—but you couldn't find the other piece of the puzzle?"

Carrie grinned. "You think there could ever be two of me? Howard would kill himself!" She hesitated. "I'm sorry, Jane, I'll shut up for a minute and I won't mention him again, as much as he loves being the center of attention."

"I don't know if that's the whole thing. I just feel distant and removed—like nothing matters."

Carrie hailed a passing waiter. "Cappuccino, please. I'm being good."

"And you?" The waiter directed his gaze at Jane.

"Black coffee is fine."

"Got it." He scooped up the plates and disappeared around a corner.

"I'm sorry, Jane, I promise you now have my full, complete, unadulterated attention." Carrie smiled and folded her fingers together on the table. "And I mean it this time."

Jane nodded and related her experiences with Twyla during the past weeks—some of the different lives she had encountered, but omitting the hands and feet emerging from the fog. She wasn't sure why.

Carrie listened as the waiter returned with the coffee and cappuccino.

"Actually that sounds kind of interesting," Carrie said when Jane finished. "Maybe I should try that too. What's her name, Twyla?"

"Yes."

"What's she like?"

"I don't know—she's different. She thinks she looks like Dolly Parton."

"Perfect."

"There's more," Jane said, now thinking she would feel safer if she mentioned the hands and feet.

"Okay," Carrie answered. "Let's hear it."

Jane explained about the mist and the pendulum hands

scraping the feet using only the forefingers. "I'm afraid, but attracted at the same time, Carrie, like not being able to stop staring at an accident."

Carrie studied Jane. "You're starting to scare me."

"Scare you. Why?"

"You're talking about weird stuff now. And you're acting as if it's real, as if it's actually there."

"It seems very real."

"What does Twyla say about some ghost playing with his feet in the fog?"

Jane hesitated. "She doesn't see anything unusual about it."

"Of course, she wouldn't." Carrie paused. "But you know, Jane, maybe there are some places we're not supposed to visit. You know the old saying, 'You can't go home again.'"

"Then why do I feel the pull to go back?" Jane asked.

"You tell me."

"I don't know, Carrie. I almost feel like I have no choice—like it's . . . inevitable."

"This is all done in your mind, right?" Carrie asked. "She's not drugging you and showing you movies."

"No, I'm hypnotized and visit past lives," Jane said, sipping her coffee. "It's incredible when it's happening."

Carrie studied Jane for a long moment. "Do you mind if I say something? I mean, we're friends and all, but you're still the boss and I'm your assistant, so I have to be at least a little careful."

"You don't have to be careful. We're friends before anything."

Carrie thought for a second. "Okay, here's the story, pal. You have two postgraduate degrees from great schools, indicating you're brilliant. You run the marketing department of DSRR, the fastest growing division of a multi-billion-dollar corporation, and everyone loves you. The ad agencies would even kiss your ring if you asked." She leaned into the table. "Forget about hands and fog, and forget about feet with leaf shreds too. She's ripping you off, setting her price after checking out your handbag and shoes."

Carrie slumped back in her chair, thinking, before edging forward again. "Jane, you've got too much going for yourself—you would have to be really, really nuts to continue this type of off-the-wall thing." She shook her head. "I mean, honestly, it makes no sense. I don't mean to be rude, but I wouldn't be caught dead going to a place like that—never in a million years. I've done some stupid things in my life, Howard being far and away the stupidest, but even someone like me is not simpleminded enough to go to some regression therapist in Greenwich Village, of all places."

"Will you come with me?" Jane asked.

"When?"

"Tomorrow after work."

"I thought you'd never ask."

CHAPTER 2

"You're home, Jane," Jimmy said. He stood in the kitchen stirring a martini with his forefinger. "Trains running late?"

"No, I just took the 8:17 instead of the 6:30. I had to catch up on some work."

"Want a glass of wine?" Jimmy stared at her.

"No. I'll just have some tea." She twisted the burner dial and placed the kettle over the flame.

"You go to see the witch doctor again and that's why you had to catch up?" He sipped the martini. "We both work too hard to pay for that kind of garbage."

"I like it."

"I like NASCAR too, but I don't drive one of the cars," he answered.

"You could if you wanted to."

"No, I couldn't, Jane, I couldn't."

She had been down this road before and knew it was a one-sided, dead-end conversation. "You're right." She crossed the kitchen to the living room, turned on the TV and sat down.

Five minutes later, Jimmy walked in, refilled glass in one hand and Jane's teacup in the other. He placed the cup on the coffee table in front of her, then picked up the remote and switched off the TV.

Jane offered no response, continuing to stare at the dark screen.

"We don't need to spend our money on witch doctors." Jimmy sat opposite her. "If you've got something physically wrong with you, of course, go to a real doctor." He sipped his drink and studied his wife. "You don't have anything wrong with you, right?"

"No, Jimmy, there's nothing wrong with me."

"There you go," he replied. "Nothing physically wrong, no need for a fortune teller."

"A past-life regression therapist," Jane answered.

Jimmy laughed out loud. "Do you hear yourself? A past-life regression therapist? What you mean is a quack!"

Jane looked away. Where had he gone? Who was the man ridiculing her?

"Where's the practical girl I married?" Jimmy asked. "Come on, Jane, we have better things to do with our money."

On chilly afternoons in the fall, he would unzip his down jacket and as she hugged him, he would wrap it around her back, allowing a return to the womb.

She measured her words. "Money isn't an issue, Jimmy." She hesitated. "And I like it."

"To visit some crazy gypsy bitch who has no license to do anything except steal from people with big bucks?" Jimmy gulped the remainder of his drink and rested the glass on his knee. "Does she have a neon sign in her window that says, 'Fortunes Read For Losers?' Give me a break."

Ignoring his comment, Jane thought of the fingers and toes protruding from the mist. "I feel like I'm exploring the past and I get a sense that I belong there."

Jimmy stared at her and shook his head. He stood and headed back to the kitchen. "You're a whack job," he called over his shoulder.

Jane heard ice being dropped into a glass, the top of a

bottle being unscrewed, the liquor being poured and the top being twisted back into place. During the next half-hour, alone in the dark, she listened to Jimmy gulp.

She knew the pattern. His first drinks enabled a quick and clever wittiness that had a lilting symmetry with the world, especially in group settings. The mid-game of the nightly ritual resulted in a lagging sense of humor with the abrupt ignition of flames that could rage to grand heights, consuming him and anyone who dared travel near, or burn in cool isolation, non-responsive, hostile, and supremely alone. The endgame left him passed out with the evil spirits slaughtered for another day.

She sat, unmoving. Hopeless.

The door from the kitchen to the garage opened and moments later Jane heard his car back out.

She used to worry whether he would come home. More than once, she had nightmares of fiery wrecks billowing out of control, enhanced by the alcohol rushing from Jimmy's bloodstream.

But all that was before. Now, at night, in nearly every dream, she was alone and unencumbered. Sitting on a velvet-cushioned bench in a sunny cupola, she reflected on pure thoughts while cradling a stuffed doll in her arms. It was an unburdened dream, a time before college, before Jimmy, and it remained lodged in her memory—a refuge created decades before to brighten the life of a child growing up with a drunk, intolerant father and a mother who baked bread and hummed the days away.

∞

Jane heard the garage door close. She glanced at the bedside clock. It was 1:35 a.m.

Jimmy lumbered up the stairs and entered the bathroom. She waited in the dark.

The bedroom door creaked open and he crawled into bed next to her. "You awake, Jane?" he whispered.

She pretended to be asleep, her torso turned away from him.

"You asleep, Jane?"

Alcohol, mustard, cigarettes, surrounding her—collapsing her.

He slid his hand down her side until he touched her thigh. His fingers reached for her panties. "You asleep, Jane?" he whispered. "You asleep?"

She didn't answer. What he was doing was irrelevant.

"What do you say, Jane," Jimmy whispered. "How about we fool around?"

Not speaking, not acknowledging her husband's presence, she obediently lifted her hips so that he could slide her panties down across her knees and past her ankles.

He pushed her nightgown up to her neck.

She had never understood the millions of words written describing the magic of sexual intercourse. She viewed it in pedestrian terms—one body part inserted into another—an elementary anatomical process that occasionally broke up the monotony of a twenty-four-hour period.

And afterward, the gray grew grayer, the black, bleaker.

Jimmy labored, and Jane wondered if this was the night of the heart attack—the night when she would have to call the ambulance, the night she would stand in the doorway draped in a robe, surrounded by darkness, a red light circling her face as four EMTs struggled with a two-hundred-and-seventy-pound body bag.

He rolled off her and was immediately asleep.

The perspiration from his chest began to cool and she remembered swimming in a lake, the ripples of water covering her breasts and skipping up to her mouth. When had that been? She saw oaks and bleached Indian birch near the shoreline, and the lake water was so clear that when she looked down, she could distinguish her hands, and below them, her toes. She would lean forward, her eyes open, her arms extended, momentarily silent in a dead-man's float.

When had that been?

The image crept back. Her parents had rented a cabin on a lake in New England for a week. A teenage boy lived next door. From the screen porch, she would watch him as he lay sleeping on the dock in the sun, shirtless, barely stirring. She was young. He was eighteen and beautiful. Jamie. That was his name. He'd smile when he saw her. She'd look away, embarrassed, but his blazing green eyes had accompanied her for years—for decades.

Jimmy began to snore and Jane rose from the bed. Reaching in the dark, she slid into her underwear, picked up her robe and walked from the bedroom, softly closing the door behind her.

Minutes later, in front of the picture window in the living room, she sipped from a cup of Earl Grey.

She measured the darkness outside and saw no movement: no cars, no lights . . . no movement.

She stared at her reflection. No movement.

And against the moonless night she was hollow and disconnected, and knew that a stiff wind might pick her up and toss her away.

Perhaps that was what she was waiting for.

She stared.

No one was awake but her.

No one was alive but her.

Moving her free hand across her breast to the opposite shoulder, a one-winged sparrow inside the glass, she bowed her head.

CHAPTER 3

"You feel relaxed . . . comfortable and relaxed from your head to the tips of your toes . . . relaxed . . . completely . . . relaxed."

Jane could feel the tension melting away—her home life, her career, now mere pinpricks on the outskirts of her consciousness.

"Imagine a white, fluffy cloud. It's under you, around you—embracing you. You're floating on this white, airy cloud and you are very comfortable. You can feel the sun and you are very comfortable."

As Jane hovered, Twyla's voice radiated through her, warming her, cleansing her.

"Push up a small piece of the cloud and shape it so that it's a comfortable pillow for your head, making you even more relaxed," Twyla continued. "Now just ease your head down into the pillow . . . and unwind."

At first, Jane was able to measure the intervals between Twyla's suggestions, but increasingly she was having difficulty keeping track of the prompts. Still, she was warm and in harmony with herself.

"You feel totally calm," Twyla soothed, "relaxed, unworried and unburdened."

Jane was on the brink of sleep.

"Totally relaxed," Twyla intoned. "From the very top of your head to the tips of your toes—just very relaxed. Relaxed and floating."

Jane never wanted to leave the cloud and the luxurious serenity that surrounded her.

"Now, from your cloud, I want you to raise your head."

Jane murmured.

"Lift your head and view the beautiful world below.

At once, Jane could see massive green, fertile fields, with the occasional dots of automobiles crawling down tiny roads that branched in all directions. Far in the distance, beyond the fields, stood the occasional clumps of skyscrapers, gray and forbidding. The sky was cornflower blue and she was part of the only visible cloud. If she wanted to, she knew she could select any field to visit, or any home, or any place she desired. Her heart was filled with optimism and joy.

"In a few moments, Jane, I'm going to encourage you to use your mind and wonderful imagination even further. I'm going to ask you to tear a piece of the cloud away and hold it in your hand, then roll off into the lovely blue sky that surrounds you. The cloud you're holding will be a canopy, a mushroom-shaped parachute, letting you drift to earth. On your way down, you will continue to be able to see for miles. And as you descend, you will look around and feast on all the beauty that surrounds you. It will become part of you. You will be relaxed and feel great comfort."

Twyla paused.

"When moving downward toward the ground, Jane, once your toes touch the earth, you will be in a different lifetime, one that was your very own. You will feel as if you've been there before and you will move about with ease and comfort. Your mind will allow you to visit any of your past lives, and you will be able to describe to me what you see and what you hear. You may feel unusual emotions within you, Jane. They are not to be feared, but rather understood as feelings you have experienced before. Nothing will harm you. Nothing will cause you pain. You are very relaxed and comfortable, and visiting one of your previous lifetimes will be enlightening and pleasurable."

Twyla's voice droned on, genuine, soft. "Now, Jane, use a piece of the cloud for your canopy so that you may drift down toward the ground. Take a handful of the cloud and slip into the beautiful blue sky. Come to the ground, Jane, and examine a previous lifetime. Move to the earth and discover what you never knew or understood about yourself."

Jane rolled into the blue, holding part of the cloud as a canopy. She was enveloped by color and felt it seep through her as she slowly descended to the earth and approached a former life. In total silence except for her own rhythmic breathing, she was unlocking time.

"You are now drifting closer and closer to the ground, Jane. Take one more look down, then close your eyes." A pause. "Your feet are on the ground now, Jane," Twyla whispered. "You have arrived at a previous lifetime."

Jane could feel solid earth beneath her shoes. She released the canopy that had accompanied her on the trip. "I wish I still had the cloud," she said.

"The cloud will be there for you whenever you desire," Twyla soothed. "Now open your eyes slowly when I count to three . . . one . . . two . . . three."

Jane opened her eyes.

"Now visualize what is before you. You are relaxed and comfortable and unafraid to discover what is in front of you."

Jane allowed her eyes to focus.

"You will accept what you see, knowing you are secure and safe, and that nothing will harm you. You are relaxed and willing to accept whatever is in front of you."

Jane looked around at her surroundings.

"Where are you?" Twyla asked.

"I'm not sure," Jane softly answered. "I'm not quite sure."

"What are you wearing? Can you tell me what you're wearing?"

Jane stared. "A black... habit... with rosary beads hanging from my belt."

Twyla waited. "What else?"

"High-buttoned leather shoes."

Twyla paused. "What more can you tell me, Jane?"

"I'm watching myself. I'm not part of my body, but I'm watching myself like I was on a screen."

"What are you watching? Can you explain what you see?"

"I'm walking with two other nuns," Jane answered. "We're moving along a cobblestone street. We're in a hurry and not talking."

Twyla waited. "What else do you see?"

Jane didn't respond.

Twyla whispered again, "What else do you see, Jane?"

"We're in a hurry," Jane mumbled. "We must move quickly. Our Mother Superior is angry."

"Why is she angry?"

"Because we're late," Jane answered, her voice low, then tense. "Don't you know we're late?"

"For what?" Twyla asked.

"The boy. The boy will die if we don't arrive on time and we're not sure which house is his. Mother Superior is very upset with me because I was supposed to know." Her eyes glistened. "I'm sorry, Mother. I thought I knew."

"Are you—?"

"We're inside, next to the boy's bed. He's very young and very sick. I see myself placing my hand on his forehead. He's burning. And he's afraid of us, but too sick to hide." She hesitated. "Mother is taking medicine from the leather bag she carried. I am holding the boy's head up so that he might swallow some of the elixir she gives him."

"Go on," Twyla prodded. "What happens next? What do you see?"

"We are at his grave days later," Jane murmured. "We were too late to save his life and it was my fault because if I had known where he lived, we might have been on time." Her eyes glistened again. "I should have known where he was."

"Look around. Who else is with you at the funeral?"

"I'm leaving the funeral. It's moving away."

"Where are you now?"

The tempo of Jane's breathing increased. "I don't want to go here."

Twyla hesitated. "Go where?"

"I don't like it here. It frightens me. I don't like it here. I don't want to be here."

"Where are you?" Twyla asked.

Jane was staring through the fog again, watching as pendulum forefingers mechanically slid specks of colored leaves backwards from the toes of each foot. Before, she wanted to see the whole person, not just the hands and feet. Now she wasn't so sure, no, not sure at all! Fear rippled across her shoulders. "I don't want to be here," she whispered. "I don't think I should be here."

"Where are you, honey? Tell me where you are."

The mist began to lift. Now Jane was able to see a dark profile, one she thought she recognized.

She had to get away, but the harder she tried to escape, the closer the profile moved. She was just yards away from the black silhouette. "No, no, no—"

"Jane, come back. Jane, do as I say. Come back."

The head was beginning to turn, twisting toward her, the dark face growing lighter. Who was it? Who was it? She was terrified to find out.

"Jane, come back. Jane, come back."

Silence except for her heart hammering against her ribs as she attempted to surface from an underwater dive where she had descended too far. She looked upward and could see the water growing lighter, but had no breath remaining! Her periphery grew black, narrowing her field of vision as the lack of oxygen began to shut down her brain.

"Jane, Jane." Twyla's cry was urgent. "Jane!"

She burst through the water, gasping for breath, her eyes wide open. "I don't want to be there," she cried. "I don't want to be there!"

Twyla wrapped her arm around Jane's shoulders. "It's okay, honey, you don't ever have to go there again. You're back now." She helped Jane to her feet. "Maybe this regression business isn't for you. It doesn't work for everyone, you know."

∞

Twenty minutes later and more at ease, Jane sat opposite Twyla at an antique parlor table sipping herbal tea. She wished Carrie had joined her instead of canceling at the last minute—she needed her rational perspective.

"Frankly, honey, I don't want you to continue if it's going to cause this type of anxiety," Twyla said. "As I said when you started, by coming here, you have the opportunity to learn from previous lives and adjust and evaluate your current existence through a type of catharsis—but believe me, regression therapy is not absolute." Twyla smiled. "Maybe there are some roads we shouldn't travel."

"But I have to go back again," Jane said. She wasn't sure why.

Twyla shook her head. "No, no, you don't. No one has to go back. This therapy is optional."

"But it's different for me," Jane answered. "I feel that I'm drawn to it. It's very powerful."

"Jane, honey, if you want my opinion, you look tired—like you're working too hard, like this life is bearing down on you just a little too heavily. Maybe you need some other kind of help, like a week or two in Hawaii, or maybe a psychiatrist. Not that I think there's anything wrong with you, of course."

"You don't understand," Jane said, not understanding

herself.

"How's that?" Twyla asked.

Jane could feel her lower lip twitching. "I feel alone . . . and trivial." She looked at Twyla. "Do you see what I mean?"

"I'm trying to."

Jane hesitated before continuing. "By traveling through these past-life regressions, I seem to be getting a better sense of myself. Isn't that what I'm supposed to do—learn from past patterns and apply that knowledge to improve my current life?" She was growing stronger as she reasoned aloud.

Twyla nodded. "Yes, that's right."

"I've visited several lives already, including the two today." She looked directly at Twyla. "I believe the process is helping me—I'm not sure how, but I think it is. So what if certain objects or people I see scare me. So what?"

"Honey, I'm not used to clients having fearful regressions during a session. My only experience is with people who gain a more positive sense of themselves by understanding what happened before."

"And that's what's going on with me, Twyla. I have this sense that I understand more and more, that I'm making progress—even if it does frighten me a little." She offered a tentative smile. "I need to come here."

Twyla unconsciously tucked a curl behind her ear. "Let me think about it. I don't want to get involved in a situation that I can't control. Your reaction of such fear is new to me. I have to evaluate what it all means."

"I'll be back next week," Jane said. "Monday is still good for you?"

Twyla hesitated. "All right. What could happen? This is about hypnosis and hypnosis only works if the mind is willing to accept the process." She stood up. "Okay, next week."

Jane rose to her feet.

Twyla stared absently at herself in the mirror. "Don't you think I look like Dolly Parton?" she asked. Not waiting for an answer, she added, "If I had big hair and bigger boobs, I figure

I'd be the spitting image. Don't ya think, honey?" She turned to Jane, waiting.

Jane realized an answer was required. She nodded. "You could be sisters."

Twyla was pleased. "Just my sentiments," she said. "You're exactly right."

CHAPTER 4

Jane stayed home Friday. She was weary. Her auburn hair, usually tied in a knot to accommodate corporate life, reached down below her shoulders.

As DSRR's vice president of marketing, she had just completed a massive fifty-million-dollar media launch of a lipstick branded *Scarlett!* All TV, radio spots and print ads assured the buyer that after one application, "He'll Give a Damn!"

America's women were listening and spending.

Jane was a superhero.

She slid her finger around the lip of a Lalique bowl that rested on the desk in her home office. A low-pitched drone emerged from the frosted maidenhair ferns etched on the crystal, or was it a distant ship signaling its whereabouts in a fog?

Like Jimmy, her father had been a big drinker, and she now thought that her mother would have even accepted it if, just once, he had shown a preference for her instead of the bottle. But he never did. Instead he would take his cigarettes and lighter and walk across their tiny backyard in suburban

Chicago, step through the gate of the chain-link fence onto the street, and walk fifty yards to the shopping-strip bar called Ed's Skipper Inn. And there he would sit each evening, flirting with the barmaid.

Once when Jane was small, he took her with him. She sat on a stool and drank Coke through a tiny black straw while she watched his nicotine-stained fingers run around the edge of a dime-store ashtray, recreating the sound of a drifting ship lost in smoke, whispering the echoes she still heard today—"I'll have time for you soon, Jane. Very soon, I'll have time for you."

And always the private tears when he didn't.

Jane stretched. She was beyond burned out from spearheading the *Scarlett!* campaign. Yesterday she had tried to make an appointment with her physician, Barbara Greenman, but hadn't heard back.

Two landlines ran into the house, and occasionally Barb's assistant got confused and called on Jimmy's business line. Jane stood and crossed the hall to her husband's office. She could see three messages on his ancient answering machine and pressed the "play" button.

The first two were solicitations, the third, a female voice: "Jimmy, what happened last night? Where were you? I know I'm not supposed to call you here, but I'm worried. Call me."

Jane replayed the last message. "Where were you?"

She played it again. "Where were you?"

What a non-surprise. She had suspected his philandering for years, and now with the verbal confirmation, she should have been devastated, or outraged, or both.

Instead she felt only relief that with another woman on the scene, he wouldn't be around as much.

Jane moved back across the hallway into her office and leaned against her desk.

It was all the same.

Her father had returned home late one evening after spending several hours at Ed's. He discovered his wife reading at the kitchen table, and for no apparent reason other than her presence infuriated him, he backhanded her to the floor.

Jane heard the commotion, but by the time she arrived downstairs, her mother was back at the kitchen table pretending to read, her trembling hand covering her reddened cheek.

Jane's father was nearly passed out in the bedroom.

It took years of random bits and pieces from her mother's conversations before Jane discovered what had happened that evening, and by then her father was long gone, having moved out and gone public with the blonde-black-roots barmaid. After his exit, the slide downhill had been swift. Within two years his liver grew to the size of a football causing him to whimper and sniffle like a child, and when it ruptured, his last view was a bloody mosaic left on the hospital sheets. His five-thousand-dollar life insurance policy barely covered the cost of his funeral and the debt he had incurred purchasing a used pickup for Blondie.

Her father's name had been Jimmy too.

One night in college, years later, a student who had drunk too much beer made a remark to Jane in her future husband's presence. It had been a brainless and innocent comment by a freshman only two months out of high school, yet it took two bartenders and three fraternity brothers to pull Jimmy off the pitiable drunk.

He was suspended for a semester and placed on probation while the student who had been severely beaten never returned. She recalled the commotion, the shouting, the knocked-over chairs, but mostly she remembered a glimpse of the boy's fine, blond hair matted with blood.

"Where were you?"

If she were to confront Jimmy, would she get the same kind of treatment her mother and the drunken student had received?

She wasn't afraid to take a beating—it would just hasten her departure.

Jane stared down at the Lalique bowl, an extravagant gift

to herself for being promoted to vice president of marketing. It was filled with potpourri, but only the scent of lilacs emerged.

She looked at her watch—late morning. She should call Barb Greenman again, but instead she stood, walked into the kitchen, lifted a bottle of white wine from the refrigerator, along with a stemmed glass from an overhead cabinet.

The phone rang, but she ignored it.

Jane kicked off her shoes, walked across the living room to the back of the house, then through the French doors onto the deck. She pulled a white wicker chair past the trunk of the towering maple tree that grew through the deck's center and sat with her feet straight out, heels on the railing.

The colored leaves reminded her that it was fall. She'd forgotten.

She stared into the trees surrounding the Connecticut home. A bird chirped, then silence. The sun struck and an electric orange leaf drifted down, landing on her leg.

A breeze ruffled the branches overhead, and as an hour passed, more leaves floated down; vibrant, day-glow yellows, reds and oranges, alighting around her, on her, until she too was a mosaic.

Just as her father had been when his insides burst over the crisp hospital sheets.

Just as the student's bloody scalp had appeared after Jimmy sprang to her defense.

Just like always.

CHAPTER 5

"Jane, I can't find anything medically wrong with you," Dr. Greenman said. "You do appear to be tired, and we have to wait until the blood work returns, but I don't anticipate any problem."

Jane nodded from her chair in front of the doctor's desk.

The physician shuffled through Jane's file. "When did you have your last mammogram?"

"Six months ago." As an afterthought, she added, "Barbara, I know how busy you are. Thanks for taking me on such short notice."

"We're both busy." She stared over her bifocals. "How are things at work?"

"Crazy, like always."

"Decided to take a day off?"

"Yes, my boss told me I looked like I could use some rest."

"It's smart to take some time every once in a while. You're still with DSRR, right?" Barbara glanced into Jane's file in front of her. "From what I read, DSRR is one of those companies that keeps on growing." She removed her bifocals and tossed them on to the desk in front of her. "Things at home all right?"

Jane meant to nod again, but unexpectedly, her eyes brimmed. She looked away and focused on the ticking of the wall clock.

Barbara waited a few moments. "You know, sometimes if problems do exist it's better to get them out in the open. It never hurts, at least in the long run. You know what I mean? I've been all through an ug-lee divorce, so I know."

Jane didn't respond.

"Maybe that's something to consider. I mean talking with someone," Barbara said.

Jane swallowed, then managed to speak. "Actually, I was thinking I might be a candidate for some kind of antidepressant."

"Why do you say that?"

"Sometimes I have a lot of difficulty getting through the day. I don't have the strength or desire to move forward. I'm a robot."

"Those sound like pretty good reasons," Barbara said.

"Is that something you could prescribe for me?" Jane asked.

Barbara folded her fingers in front of her on the desk. "Jane, I'm conservative when prescribing medication. In most instances, I tend to under prescribe. With mood-altering drugs and with narcotics, I'm especially cautious."

"I'm not clear what you're saying . . ."

"When someone exhibits or talks about depressive symptoms, and there's medication involved, I like to have the other railing in place."

"Other railing?"

"I like to have a psychiatrist involved. He or she can regulate the medication while at the same time working on the issues that are involved. To just prescribe meds can be helpful, but it's not necessarily the total solution. A trained physician—a psychiatrist—can make that determination by working with you."

"You think I should see a psychiatrist?"

"Couldn't hurt. Worst case scenario is that it doesn't help and you stop."

Jane hesitated. "So you really think I should see a psychiatrist?"

"Let me put it this way, Jane, I wouldn't be comfortable prescribing medication for you without having a psychiatrist, or at the very least, a psychologist, as part of the equation." She shrugged. "Maybe another doctor would consider it, but I don't recommend it."

"I don't know any psychiatrists."

"I can give you a referral. You don't have to make a decision right now. Sleep on it. If you decide that's something you'd try, I'll be glad to make the initial call for you." She glanced at her watch and stood. "Sorry, I'm running a bit late. I've got a tennis class in a half hour."

"Thanks, Barbara," Jane said, standing. "I'll let you know."

∞

Darkness was closing in as Jane crossed the parking lot to one of the two remaining cars. The overhead lights cast an artificial glow, stretching shadows across the asphalt. A good night for Halloween, she thought, a good night for flocks of children moving through the streets dressed in orange and black and white.

Juvenile impostors, but like herself, impostors nonetheless.

CHAPTER 6

Women loved Jimmy. His lively brogue, created and perfected for maximum public effect, combined with his ruddy good looks and sense of humor, got their attention. He understood the right thing to say, and women who had never entered a Catholic church or had any understanding of the meaning of "Erin go bragh," giggled like schoolgirls when Jimmy targeted them.

It was all fraud. He wasn't even Irish. Both parents were Polish immigrants. Upon arrival in New York City, his father discovered that to get a job working the Brooklyn docks, he had better be from the Emerald Isle. He changed the family name, perfected his accent, picked a county in Ireland to claim as his own and worked his way up to foreman.

Jimmy waited until after they were married to tell Jane the truth. His ease with misrepresentation was just one of the red flags she had chosen to ignore.

Jane watched the young woman behind the bar at the country club light up as the interaction with Jimmy began.

Moments later he was back. "And here's to the loveliest lady in all of Connecticut," Jimmy said, placing a glass of wine in front of her. He took a sip from his drink, sat, and focused on his wife. “Dinner seems to get better every year. Of course, I’d rather have corned beef and cabbage.”

“Of course,” Jane answered.

“How many of these country club dances have we been to, Jane? I’ve lost count.”

“A lot. Fifteen, maybe.”

Jane saw Katy Rockland approaching the table. She stopped and leaned over Jane’s shoulder, offering Jimmy a sprawling cleavage shot.

“Jane, Jane, Jane,” Katy said.

“What? What? What?” Jimmy answered, an impish grin covering his face.

“You stop that, Jimmy McBride,” Katy answered, a smile appearing. She turned her back to Jimmy. “We’ll just ignore that smart-guy leprechaun of yours.” In a stage whisper, she asked, “Jane, I have to ask, is that new *Scarlett!* commercial yours? It’s fantastic!”

The lowered tone exposed Katy. "Where were you?" Jane offered no hint of recognition. “Right, Katy, *Scarlett!* is one of our products.”

“I have to tell you,” Katy replied, “it’s one of the best commercials I’ve seen in a while. And the actor looks just like Rhett Butler.”

“Now we’ve just got to be sure we don’t get sued. It’s been cleared by legal, but you never know,” Jane said, staring at Katy. “Where did you see the commercial anyway?”

“On TV last week. I loved it.”

“Up here, in Connecticut?”

“Yes, I think so,” Katy answered.

“That’s odd,” Jane replied, “the flight with the Rhett Butler look-alike isn’t scheduled to run up here for another month.”

“Oh,” Katy stammered, the synthetic smile cracking, “maybe I saw it on one of those news shows.”

“I don’t know, Katy, I haven’t authorized any affiliate broadcasts.”

"Well," Katy said, "I saw it somewhere. Maybe a TV show pirated it." She paused. "Is that the correct word, Jane, pirated?"

"That must be it," Jane answered. Or maybe you just watched a copy of it in my house while I was working in Manhattan, she thought. Jimmy had viewed the spot and loved it.

"Good to see you," Katy said, righting herself. "Great commercial." She turned to Jimmy. "And you behave yourself, Jimmy McBride." She turned and crossed back to her table.

"Nice gal," Jimmy said.

"Well preserved," Jane responded. "I wonder if those breasts are real." She stared over at her husband.

Jimmy placed his two hands in the air, palms straight out, while he shrugged his shoulders. "Who knows?" he asked. "They look real."

"You would know," Jane answered, then paused as her husband watched her. "You're an observant man. Most men can tell."

Why did she even care? Why did she try to trick Katy about the commercial? She should just throw her cards on the table, tell Jimmy she knew what was going on, stand up and walk out. She'd be able to maintain her dignity and prove to herself that she was worth even more than a Lalique crystal bowl.

Her life had deteriorated into a series of surrealistic moments—one-sided sex with Jimmy, Katy and her prefabricated chest, Twyla, the fog in the regression—it was endless.

I wonder if this is what the beginning of a breakdown feels like, she thought. I wonder if I'm going off the deep end.

The band resumed playing, interrupting her thoughts. Across the table, she saw Jimmy staring at her, probably wondering if she knew about Katy. She smiled and focused her attention on the musicians—the same group that had been at the club for years—several locals, including a schoolteacher, a couple of wannabe rock stars, and a female bass player.

"Come on, Jane, let's get out there," Jimmy said, nodding to the dance floor.

"Later, Jimmy," Jane said, "not now."

"You sure? Come on, Jane."

"Maybe later."

"Okay," he replied, standing and looking toward the bar, "but I'm going to hold you to it."

Jane observed Katy walking into the club lobby. "You know a waiter will bring you a drink," she said.

"Too slow," Jimmy said over his shoulder. "Place is jammed tonight and I can't wait that long."

She watched him saunter past the bar and into the lobby.

The image of two middle-aged adolescents floundering, tugging at each other's clothes, and attempting to relive their wonder years amused her.

But no, it wasn't funny, it was pathetic.

Jimmy was pathetic. He had never even approached the superficial, like her favorite color or movie. She would love to be pregnant and tucked into a Victorian novel on a rainy Saturday afternoon, but Jimmy had no clue. He couldn't have been farther away from tapping her inner core, and now, sadder still, she thought that perhaps it wasn't even his fault, that he just didn't have the emotional capacity.

What a choice she had made.

She was struggling, yet Jimmy was doing just fine, selling insurance, having sex with Katy, and enjoying a high-end lifestyle, ninety percent of which she paid for.

Jane sipped her wine.

She was searching and knew it. That's how the past-life regression began. She had leafed through a discarded copy of the *Village Voice* she found on the back seat of a gridlocked taxi, and Twyla's ad was so foreign to her that she was attracted. She kept the newspaper for two weeks before making the phone call, then with the promise of being able to learn more about herself by visiting and analyzing past lives, Jane agreed to the first meeting. If nothing else, she figured it would take her mind off *Scarlett!* or Jimmy, the drunk, arriving home at one in the morning seeking sex.

And with each visit, the pull of past-life regression seemed to grow stronger, almost as if a former existence, a time she would one day fully grasp, was dragging her toward it.

Maybe she was closer to the edge than she had ever imagined—not caring about her husband sleeping with another woman wasn't normal. And visiting an unlicensed regression therapist, who fancied herself as Dolly Parton's twin, wasn't close to fitting her personal or corporate identity.

"Jane, I'm back," Jimmy said. "Time to get that dance you promised me. Come on, let's go." He pulled her to her feet.

As the band trudged through a flat version of a Tony Bennett standard, Jimmy took Jane's hand and pulled her to the dance floor, then wrapped his arms around her.

She could feel the weight of him pressed against her. He was huge, sweltering, and she was suffocating in his arms.

"This song was even before our time, Jane," Jimmy said. Then he added, "We don't do this often enough," as he led her around the parquet floor.

Jimmy's brogue was disintegrating which meant the alcohol demons were assaulting the faux Irish knight and gaining control of the fortress. He picked up the tempo of his movements so that Jane had difficulty following him.

As the final chorus began to crescendo, she sighed with relief.

"Just like college," Jimmy said. "We'll do the old dip. Think you can touch the back of your head to the floor?"

"Jimmy, no," Jane protested.

"Hey, we're not that old," he answered, spinning Jane to the center of the dance floor, his arm a steel coil allowing no escape.

As the final chords of the ballad reverberated across the dancers, Jimmy leaned forward, a sweat sheen coating his face, and pushed Jane toward the floor.

"Jimmy, stop it, you—"

He pushed her farther and farther backward.

"Jimmy, stop it right now."

Jane's head was just inches from the parquet when Jimmy lost balance and dropped her. He leaped over Jane's body and staggering forward, his arms flailing in an attempt to maintain his equilibrium, smashed headfirst into the crowd surrounding the dance floor. Two tables crashed to the carpet before he landed on top of Janet Hayes, the first female president of the Andover Country Club.

With the last note of the song completed, the female bass player held up a piece of sheet music. "A score of five-point-eight from the Russian judge," she said into the microphone, a disbelieving, but coast-to-coast smile crossing her face.

CHAPTER 7

"These stairs are tough," Carrie said Tuesday afternoon as she followed Jane up the steps to Twyla's apartment. "Smells like someone's been cooking with garlic." Breathing heavily, she added, "You gotta look on the bright side. It's better than a subway restroom."

"We're here," Jane said reaching the landing.

"I'm glad I could make it this week," Carrie puffed as she caught up. "What kind of name is Twyla anyway?"

"Not sure." The door was ajar, but Jane knew to ring the doorbell. "Southern, maybe."

"This is very, very crazy doing this," Carrie answered. "Trust me, Jane, it's very, very crazy."

"I know."

Twyla opened the door. "Jane," she said, before noticing Carrie. "Oh, and I see you've brought someone."

"Twyla, this is my friend, Carrie. She came along to observe."

"I'm so sorry, honey," Twyla replied. "I don't work with an audience. It's too distracting and I can't be assured that—"

"You look like Dolly Parton," Carrie interrupted.

"Excuse me," Twyla said.

"You look exactly like Dolly Parton."

Twyla smiled and reevaluated Carrie. "You do think so, don't you, honey? I can tell you're being honest. It's my business to be able to correctly read people."

"I'm blown away," Carrie replied. "The resemblance is amazing. Amazing!"

"Could you make an exception with Carrie?" Jane asked. "She's thinking of regression therapy, but first she wants to get a better idea of how the process works."

Twyla frowned as she glanced at Carrie. "I usually would never allow this." She thought for a moment. "You'll have to sit in a far corner and not say a word."

"I understand," Carrie said.

"It's rare that I would make this kind of concession," Twyla answered. "I hope it isn't something that I'll regret."

"I know I won't," Carrie answered. "I can promise you that."

∞

"I'm here watching the sick little boy on the movie screen again." She thought for a moment. "The Mother Superior keeps glaring at me. She is furious that I didn't know where the boy lived." Jane paused. "I can see there is little hope of recovery for the child. His face is gray and drawn."

"Can you describe the room you're in?" Twyla asked.

Jane hesitated before speaking. "It's small and primitive-looking," she answered. "There's a wooden chair against the wall and a crucifix over the bed. That's all."

She shifted on the couch.

"Now I'm at the cemetery again—just like last time.

The boy has died."

"Who's there?"

Jane hesitated. "Just a small group of people and the priest. They're knotted together in front of the grave."

"Knotted together?"

"Entwined," Jane answered softly, "their arms are entwined, and I'm sad and feeling guilty. If we had gotten there earlier, maybe I would have been in time to save the boy's life." She hesitated. "I'm sad."

"Are there more reasons for your unhappiness?" Twyla asked.

"I feel like I was related to the little boy, and now he's gone." Her eyes fluttered. "And it's my fault."

Twyla waited.

"They're lowering the casket into the ground. The mother is crying. She cannot control herself. She is being held by . . . I think . . . her husband. He's very big and strong, as if he were a laborer."

Twyla held off for several more seconds, then probed, "And?"

"That scene is fading," Jane responded, her voice calm.

"Where are you now, Jane?" Twyla asked.

The room was silent.

"Jane," Twyla said, "where are you now?"

Jane's breathing grew heavier. "I'm back," she whispered.

"Back where?" Twyla asked.

"I can see the fog. There's fog everywhere." She ran her tongue across her top lip. "It's all around me." She hesitated, and then added, "This is very strange."

"What's strange, Jane?" Twyla asked. "Tell me what's strange?"

"It's different," Jane responded. "I'm in the fog. I'm not watching it from a distance. I'm in someone's body in the fog." She turned, seeing nothing but the heavy mist surrounding her. A clammy sensation settled across her neck, her shoulders, her arms.

"What do you see?" Twyla asked.

Jane continued to revolve while attempting to peer through the gray. Twyla's voice was becoming distant, a radio channel with atmospheric interference—mariachi static—camouflaging words. "It's all around me," Jane whispered.

"What do you see?"

Twyla's words were now broken fragments of white noise. Looking down for the first time, Jane saw the bare feet from previous regressions were now her own.

As she leaned over, she noticed flecks of colored leaves scattered across the pale skin on top of each foot. The fragments made her feel pockmarked and unclean. Reaching down, using her forefingers, Jane attempted to move the bits of color. Sliding, slowly sliding, her forefingers bunched the leaf fragments together, creating tiny dams above her ankles.

To her left, the haze was becoming brighter. A beam of light aimed in her direction was attempting to penetrate the mist, transforming the fog into sparkling threads of Christmas tinsel.

Jane wanted to run, but her legs were leaden, as if each leaf bit was a tiny anchor. She huddled in her white nightgown, then heard voices far away. She began to tremble uncontrollably as she slid to her knees.

In the distance, a man's voice, "Where is she? She's got to be here somewhere."

Echoes: "She's got to be here somewhere. She's got to be here somewhere."

Another man calling, "I don't see her."

The sound of dogs barking, straining against their leads.

A female voice she couldn't place, called for her, the tone reverberating over and over again.

"Let's check over there under the oak trees, boys."

"Where are you, Jane?" A faint female voice spiraling from the darkness. "Where are you?"

"I don't see her, Russ," a man called.

"Over there, near the tall grass. The dogs smell her. Let's go."

Jane curled up in her nightgown, allowing the grass to scrape against her skin. She held her hands to her face.

The barking hounds were closer, hostile and anxious, yipping, held back by choke collars.

The female voice angled through the fog, this time louder, "Jane, where are you?"

"I think I see something over there, boys," Russ called.

Jane rose to her feet. She had to run. She was too afraid to stay still, but the weight of the tattered leaf bits on her feet held her hostage.

"Got her! Got her! Got her!" Russ yelled as the beam of light splashed through the mist, saturating Jane. "Under the trees."

"Jane, where are you? Come back, Jane, come back!" The female voice was emphatic.

"Got her now, boys," Russ called again. "Creep up, let's be easy about this. Hold them dogs back so they don't do nothin'."

"Jane, Jane, where are you?"

"You hold still, baby," Russ called from twenty feet. "We're here now. Hold still."

Jane saw the dark figures advancing crab-like, closer and closer, infiltrating the fog. She couldn't dig into the ground. She couldn't close her eyes. She couldn't run.

"Jane—"

"Easy now, baby. Easy does it." He attempted to keep his voice level.

"Jane." Twyla's voice.

"We're going to just . . ." The silhouette of a man jumped forward through the fog at the precise moment Jane shrieked.

Her eyes snapped open. Her heart was pounding wildly. She could barely catch her breath. "My God, oh, my God."

"Jane, Jane, where were you?" Twyla asked. "Why didn't you answer me?"

Jane glanced around the room.

"Why didn't you answer me?"

"I'm back," Jane answered, struggling to breathe, her eyes still scanning the room. "I'm back."

"From where?" Carrie asked. She was standing behind Twyla. "From where, Jane?"

Jane couldn't focus.

"From where?" Twyla asked. "Where were you, Jane? Why didn't you answer me?"

"I was . . . I was in someone else's body. I don't know where." She sat up on the couch. "It was dark. A spotlight came through the fog, making it sparkle." She paused. "I heard men and dogs searching and they were closing in on me." She attempted to calm herself as she looked at Twyla. "Where was I?"

"I don't know, honey," Twyla said, "but it sure sounds fascinating."

"I may not go back," Jane said, glancing around the room again. "I was afraid."

"Of what?" Twyla asked.

"I was being chased by men and dogs." She took a deep breath and looked at Twyla. "I wanted to hide."

"Relax now, Jane, relax, it's all part of your experience," Twyla soothed as she sat next to her on the couch. "It may be uncomfortable, but it's not real. Remember that. Fear is new ground for me too." She patted the back of Jane's hand. "Just so you know, being afraid during last week's episode pushed me to do some homework. Fear is unusual, but not unheard of. You must remain confident that none of this will ever harm you. There's nothing to be afraid of—that I know for sure. We're just in the midst of a learning curve."

Jane nodded. She was still anxious.

"A week will give you some time to reflect, and offer you insights," Twyla said. "Think about what happened and translate it into events you may be experiencing in your life today. The two will merge into a complete picture of enlightenment." Twyla ran the fingers of one hand across her blonde bangs, then stood and placed her hand on her hip. "This is a great opportunity, Jane. You're a natural. You ought to make the best of it. And the good news is that we can learn together."

Jane exhaled deeply and stood up. "I'm not so sure it's a good idea. Let me think about it," she said. "Or maybe, I've just got to get used to the experience."

"That's exactly right, honey."

"We're so out of here," Carrie said walking to the door. "Come on, Jane. Nice to meet you, Twyla."

Jane followed Carrie to the doorway.

"And you, Carrie. Are you ready to schedule a regression for yourself?" Twyla asked.

"I'm going to think about it. How does that sound?"

"Just fine," Twyla answered. "And Jane, I'll keep your appointment for next Monday."

Jane opened the door. "I think so," she said to Twyla as she stepped outside onto the landing.

Carrie followed, then before closing the door, stuck her head back into the apartment. "Question."

"Yes, Carrie." Twyla turned back to face the door.

"When you hypnotize someone, aren't you supposed to be in touch with them all the time?"

"Of course," Twyla answered.

"Well, I may be crazy," Carrie said, "but watching and listening to what was going on, I got the distinct impression that you lost communication with Jane—that you couldn't reach her for a couple of minutes."

"That's ridiculous," Twyla answered. "Jane didn't always respond, but I assure you, I was completely in control." She nodded. "Look, she's here. She's back. Jane was always within my grasp."

Carrie stared at Twyla, unspeaking.

"There's no need to be concerned, Carrie," Twyla added. "When handled by a professional, no danger exists. Remember that for hypnosis to work, the mind must be receptive. And if the individual wishes to become," she said, forming two fingers on each hand into quotation marks, 'unhypnotized,' that's what happens." She dropped her hands. "The mind itself is the ultimate safeguard."

Carrie nodded. "Ciao," she said and closed the apartment door.

The two descended the stairs and walked down West Eleventh Street until they reached Seventh Avenue. Jane flagged a cab and, stepping in first, slid across the back seat.

"Grand Central."

"So?" Carrie asked.

"So, what?"

"So what went on back there while you were in the ozone somewhere?"

Jane stared at her hands resting on her lap. "That's where I'm supposed to be," she said at last.

"Jane, look at me," Carrie said. "This is where you're supposed to be, right here and now in this cab heading to Grand Central. All the fog and feet and hands that you could ever want are right here in New York City."

Jane looked at her friend, but didn't respond.

"If you want, I'll even throw in a few drunks," Carrie said.

"You're right, of course," Jane answered after a moment. She turned and peered out the windshield, watching as the cab driver blew through six yellow-to-red stoplight transitions in a row. She looked over at Carrie. "Of course, you're right."

∞

That night, with Jimmy snoring upstairs, Jane stood at the picture window in the living room, far away from the field with the grass that had touched her arms and legs.

Yet the field remained near.

Jimmy was distant.

She measured the darkness outside, then her reflection against it, but could discern no movement: no cars, no lights . . . no movement.

No one was awake but her.

No one was alive but her.

Streaks of lightning flickered across the night sky, serpents' tongues fracturing the black, dropping poisonous crystal shards at her feet.

The Lalique bowl or her world fragmenting before her eyes?

Jane placed the cup of tea on a side table and walked to her office, opened the phone directory and dialed Barbara Greenman. "I need the psychiatric referral," she said to the answering service. "The name is Jane McBride." She hung up the phone.

Chapter 8

When Briggs appeared in her office doorway, Jane struggled not to smile. He stood in studied European pose, one hand tucked in his suit jacket pocket, thumb out, his perpetual suntan accentuating a Provence image. An abstract gold-and-orange necktie added punch.

"Jane, I couldn't help but notice that last week's numbers are down for *Scarlett!* Any reason?"

She looked up from her desk where she had been reviewing a media print schedule. "Momentary dip, John,"she replied to DSRR's president. We made a couple of strategic decisions to pull some of the TV and radio spots last week. We couldn't get the adjacencies we wanted at launch, so we cut and ran. I used some muscle with the affiliates and we're back in primo positions where we should have been all along." Jane offered a hint of a smile. "Nothing to worry about."

"We don't pay you enough," Briggs said.

"No, you don't," Jane answered.

"We'll talk at bonus time," Briggs answered. He turned in the doorway, then stopped and reversed himself. "I don't mean to meddle, Jane, but you still look tired." He lifted his hand

and with the forefinger pointed at her, his thumb straight up, simulating a revolver, Briggs added, "Vitamin C. Take as much as you can. What you don't use internally, you just pee away." He grinned, then turned and moved away toward a cluster of cubicles in the marketing support group.

∞

"What I don't use I can pee away," Jane said to Carrie as they were finishing lunch.

"He's a very, very strange duck," Carrie replied. "And he loves the young girls."

"How's that?"

"There's no mystery why he's walking around the floors most of the day instead of commandeering the conference rooms," Carrie said. "He knows fresh meat has come aboard and if anyone is appealing, he'll take a special interest in her."

"Oh, please," Jane said. "He's an old man."

"Old and rich," Carrie answered. "He's a dirty, old, rich man. He just plays the odds—you know, throw enough against the wall and something will stick—which means some young IQ Zero with dollar signs for eyeballs always takes him up on an overture so that she can get done in the back of a limousine." Carrie shook her head. "I just lost a great kid because of him."

"Who?"

"Alyssa Bankers. Her exact words were that she was tired of him leering at her. At least the young people today are honest. He was visiting her cubicle all the time or inviting her to his office. She said every time he walked away, she wanted to take a shower."

"But we have sexual harassment policies in place here."

"Sure. You going to turn him in? That's the problem. Nobody will call him on it. He's got Human Resources in his back pocket anyway. Even Alyssa didn't say anything. She was afraid that with his connections she might never land another industry job in town."

"How do you know so much?"

"I work with the little people, Jane. Little people gossip and there aren't many secrets. It's like a hospital—don't you think every nurse knows who the new intern is hooking up with? Plus, Patty Elders, you know, Briggs' assistant, is aware of everything that he does and gives me the details." Carrie shrugged. "DSRR is the same as any other organization. What surprises me is that Briggs' affairs aren't the best-kept secrets in the world, so from a PR point of view, I wonder why the board hasn't slapped his wrist." She thought a moment. "I guess as long as the company is profitable they look the other way."

Jane wondered how she could have been oblivious to what was so clear to others. "What does everyone say about me?"

Carrie shook her head. "Nothing bad. They don't know you. You're seen more as a loner than anything. And the marketing group is always ahead of plan, which means they get their bonuses, so there's nothing to complain about." She sipped her coffee. "Of course, everyone on my team may not be candid because they know we're friends."

"I'm a boring story," Jane said. "What's there to know?"

"Actually, I find you very interesting," Carrie said. "How many people in your position with your smarts would have weekly visits to a regressionist?"

Jane glanced away. She was tired of that conversation. "So Briggs is a dirty old man, huh?"

Carrie read the signal. "You heard it here first. Old and dirty. Reminds me of a boss I had when I was a sweet young thing. That guy wouldn't leave me alone, and then Carrie, Miss Naiveté, got involved with him. What I didn't know at the time was that he was jumping my bones for a reason. Somehow he knew my family had money and he had a plan to make some of it his own."

"What kind of plan?" Jane asked.

"He rigged a photograph of the two of us, shall we say

engaged in carnal activity, and sent me a copy with instructions to send fifty thousand for the negative."

"That's extortion," Jane said.

"Call it whatever you want," Carrie answered. "That's what he did. His mistake was being unaware I was from a traditional Sicilian family."

"What happened?" Jane asked.

Carrie thought for a moment. "We're a close-knit family, Jane. I made the obvious choice that any young Italian girl would have in that situation—I cried my heart out to my mother, begged forgiveness, made her swear she wouldn't tell my father, and gave her the picture. She slapped me three times across the face and then cried in her bedroom for two days. The following week my boss didn't show up for work. I never saw him again."

"What happened?"

"The problem was taken care of."

"How?"

"I received the negative of the X-rated picture and a copy of my boss's hospital chart in an envelope with no return address." Carrie stared into her coffee cup. "He had been beaten."

"Beaten?"

"Beaten to death, as a matter of fact. He died in the hospital." Carrie shook her head. "It was all over the news for at least a month." She looked back at Jane. "Under the miscellaneous section of the hospital chart, a notation was made that he had been discovered critically injured in an alley with a G-clef painted on his forehead. The cops tried to hush up the G-clef for their investigation, but it eventually leaked to the newspapers and became a huge story." She tapped the side of her own forehead using her index finger. "That was my uncle, who was a piano tuner, telling my mother that he had taken care of business with the man who had disrespected his niece." She placed both hands palm down on the table. "End of story."

Jane stared at Carrie.

"You have to take care of your own," Carrie said.

Jane didn't move.

"I think my uncle might be connected," Carrie added, a smirk on her face.

"That's an understatement," Jane replied after a moment. "And now I can assure you you'll get a raise anytime you ask for it."

"Isn't that wonderful," Carrie said with a wink, "the story has a happy ending after all. And now that you know about my uncle, Jane, he'll be at your disposal as well."

"What a generous gift."

"Obviously, this story is between you and me."

"Obviously," Jane replied.

"He lives in Terre Haute now. I suspect things got a bit hot here."

Jane laughed. She didn't know whether to believe Carrie or not. "How's Howard?"

"Some things never change," Carrie said.

"Still at Ashton's on Fifth?"

Carrie nodded. "It is a fun store. Terrific customer service, quality products, good buyers who look for unique merchandise—it's found a niche."

"I know, Ashton's on Fifth has a great reputation," Jane said.

"Which is good news for Howard," Carrie replied as she turned to hail a passing waiter. "Chocolate mousse cake, hold the moose by the horns." She glanced over at Jane, then back at the waiter. "Just kidding. Bring her a piece too," she said, nodding across the table. "What she doesn't eat, I will."

Jane smiled to herself.

Carrie hesitated. "Where was I? Oh, I know. You have to get to know Howard. I'm used to him. We grew up together—families across the street from each other in Brooklyn. I never thought we'd get together, but after college, one afternoon I ran into him. Carrie Binotti meets Howard Dreyfus, and the rest is history." She reached into her purse, took out a compact mirror, applied a shade of *Scarlett!,* then dropped both the lipstick and mirror back into the cosmetic bag in her purse. "I think I need to have my eyebrows done, and by the way, I hate the expression, the rest is history," she said. "Know what I mean? The rest is history. Everyone is always using the same phrases, think out of the box and the rest is history. I hate people who repeat themselves."

"Lunch is over and the rest is history," Jane said.

"Now that's thinking out of the box," Carrie responded, a smile breaking across her face.

CHAPTER 9

Jane was nervous. Fortunately, Dr. Alford didn't work in a medical setting, which meant she wouldn't have to be in a general waiting room crammed with other patients surveying her, all wondering how crazy she was.

Night hours. Her appointment was for 7:30.

Jane slowed the car to read street numbers and pulled off the road into a shadowy drive. In the distance, a clapboard house sat on the edge of the wooded property. She parked in front of a sign that read "Office."

The house struck her as a series of architectural afterthoughts—rooms added to rooms with no overall plan.

Inside, no one was waiting. She hung her coat on a coat rack next to the door, picked up a magazine from a coffee table, and flipped through the pages. She heard the faint ring of a phone, followed by a barely audible voice through a closed door.

Why was she here? Now, she wasn't sure. She had been certain it was necessary the other night when she had left a message for Barb's service, but now she questioned herself.

A sandy-haired man opened the door on the far wall. "Mrs.

McBride? I'm Eric Alford." He gestured to the room behind him. "Please come in."

Jane walked past him into an office.

"Sit anywhere you like," he said, pointing to a couch with a chair on either side.

Jane sat in a corner of the sofa as close to the arm as possible.

"Where you choose to sit isn't a psychological test of any kind," the doctor said, a friendly expression on his face. He sat in a chair placed a comfortable distance in front of her. "Welcome. How are you?" His words were slow, easy, with southern overtones.

"Just fine," Jane answered, her conference-room smile etched on her face. She knew it was the wrong answer.

"Good, I'm glad," Dr. Alford said. "Doctor Greenman says you're in excellent health." He thought for a moment. "A couple of quick questions, if I may. Married?"

Jane nodded.

"Children?"

"No," Jane answered.

"Doctor Greenman says you're interested in medication for depression issues."

"I think I might need it."

"That'll be fine," Dr. Alford responded. "We can surely take a look at that." He paused. "Can you tell me why else you're here, Mrs. McBride?"

Jane couldn't think of a response, but her eyes filled.

He waited, thoughtfully watching her.

She stared past the psychiatrist, to his diplomas on the wall. "I'm not sure."

"Well, that'll be fine," he responded. "Many people aren't sure about why they initially come in."

Jane nodded, then hesitated. "What do I call you?" she asked.

"Doesn't matter," Dr. Alford responded, a smile crossing his face. "Eric, Doc, Doctor, whatever you're comfortable with."

"Doctor is okay," she answered, her eyes still brimming. "I don't think I know you well enough to call you Eric."

"That's fair." He paused, then asked again, this time, his voice softer, "Can you tell me why you're here, Mrs. McBride?"

Jane hesitated, then reached into her purse and retrieved a tissue. She dabbed at her eyes. "I'm losing control," she answered at last.

"How so?" he asked.

"I'm slipping away," she said, her voice a mere whisper. "And I don't know why."

∞

Jane drove in the general direction of home. On a straight shot, she'd be there in twenty minutes, but she didn't want to be in the house with Jimmy right away.

As she approached the Whitman Mall, she glanced at the Cinema Multiplex sign bordering the highway and decided to see a movie. She parked the car, walked to the ticket booth and selected a show beginning in ten minutes.

In the lobby, a lone high school boy in an oversized maroon blazer was sweeping up popcorn that had spilled across the carpeted floor. She moved past and walked through the theater doors.

No one was inside. Jane selected an aisle seat and glanced at her watch: 9:00.

She looked around the theater again. Still empty.

She hadn't revealed much to Dr. Alford, but had mentioned her suspicions about Jimmy and Katy.

Over the theater sound system a group of men sang in an old-fashioned, but not unpleasant harmony. Jane gradually recognized the music in tandem with a little girl sitting at the kitchen table, her father standing in the doorway, his hands in his pockets, quietly listening—a rare, serene, unspoken moment between a man and his child.

The Mills Brothers. She remembered them now.

Why did he want to sit in a bar instead of being with her? What had she done to make him go away?

Nothing. She had done nothing. It's the way he was.

No. Somehow, some way, she was responsible. Fathers were supposed to love daughters, and he had never loved her, not even for one instant. Just like Jimmy didn't love her now. And how could that happen? When did Jimmy turn away? Was it during some secret moment that only he knew about? Did he go to work one morning and return at the end of the day not caring? Had she been a willing partner or even the initiator of the disintegration?

Or, had it always been quicksand?

The Mills Brothers began a fresh song and in seconds, Jane recognized it as one she recalled from childhood. As the brothers' sweet vocal blend eased through her, wheels within wheels within wheels turned, exposing angles of blue light and splashes of time, and Jane began to realize that she understood nothing except pain.

She stood and crossed toward the theater exit with the Mills Brothers treading behind:

Come, sweetheart, tell me,
Now is the time.
You tell me your dream,
I'll tell you mine.

CHAPTER 10

Later in the week, Jane pressed the remote on the sun visor to close the garage door behind her. She was going to soak in the bathtub, pull on some flannel pajamas and creep into bed.

Jimmy's car at home was a surprise. Jane rarely saw him at night anymore. When she walked into the kitchen he was standing at the counter, mandatory drink in his hand.

"Where you been?" he asked.

"Doctor's appointment," Jane replied. She filled the tea kettle with water, placed it on the stove and turned on the burner.

"A witch doctor?" Jimmy asked.

Jane ignored the question. "I'm going to get out of these clothes, then come down and get my tea. It's been a long day, Jimmy." She headed across the kitchen.

"I hope it wasn't the witch doctor again," Jimmy said.

Jane halted.

"I'll tell you why." He turned to face his wife. "I've done a little bit of checking on these witch doctors—the ones you call regression therapists, and you know what I found out?"

Jane didn't respond.

"You know what I found out?" Jimmy repeated, his voice louder. "I found out that it's all garbage mixed with hocus-pocus. These regression quacks prey on rich people, hypnotize them, listen to them discuss some nonsense from their subconscious, tell them it's profound truth bubbling up from their former lives, then charge an arm and a leg for the process. They're latter-day gypsies, Jane, without the hoop earrings and the crystal ball."

Jane moved toward the doorway. Jimmy stepped in her way. "Tell me I'm wrong, Jane, prove to me I'm wrong."

Jane attempted to step around her husband and Jimmy grabbed her arm. "Just talk to me, Jane, I'm begging you, just talk to me!"

He was huge. Staring up, she realized she hadn't objectively looked at him for months, maybe years. Only an occasional spark of emotion from his eyes was familiar. She was overcome with sadness. "What do you want me to say, Jimmy?"

"Talk to me, for God's sake. All you do is avoid me. It's hard to live with someone like that." He released her arm.

"I work hard, and there's not a lot of time left in the day when I get home." She rubbed her elbow. "And you're rarely here anyway."

"I get tired of your behavior, Jane," Jimmy said.

"I get tired of your behavior, too."

"At least I make the attempt to be civil," Jimmy answered, placing the glass to his lips and sipping.

"Like dropping me on the floor at the country club, knocking over a few tables, and landing on Janet Hayes?" Jane asked. "Is that what you call civil behavior?"

Jimmy placed the glass on the counter. "I was under the impression that you were able to recognize an accident when it happened," he said. "It was a mistake, Jane, an error in judgment. And I bet you were the only one in the club to hold that against me. Most people were concerned with whether I was hurt or not." He picked up the remainder of his drink and swallowed it down in one motion. "But not my tight-assed wife, Jane. No, concern is not part of her emotional makeup. Jane just didn't want to be embarrassed. And we all know she can never forgive—never, ever forgive!"

Jane stepped around her husband and left the kitchen. She stopped and crossed back. "It's not just a question of being embarrassed, it's also being humiliated by your relationship with Katy Rockland."

Jimmy eyed her. "What is that supposed to mean, I—"

"Oh, please, Jimmy," Jane interrupted. "Stop lying. It does neither of us any good."

"Shut up, Jane," Jimmy said. "You don't have a clue."

"Am I wrong, Jimmy? Aren't you sleeping with Katy?"

Jimmy stared at her, then began to chuckle, immediately igniting Jane.

"Come on, Jimmy, tell me how I'm so stupid!" She could feel her voice rising. "What is it that I'm saying that you find so amusing?"

The grin disappeared. "You women never get it," he said, his voice hoarse. He was hovering over her. "Most don't, but you, Jane, never even came close." He shook his head. "Never even close!"

"What the hell are you talking about?" Jane screamed.

Jimmy threw his glass against the wall, spraying crystal sparks across the kitchen floor. "I'll tell you what I'm talking about! I'll tell you exactly what I'm talking about, Jane. I haven't had sex with you in over a year, and even then it was lousy, and you complain because I have an affair! Give me a break! You're lucky I don't have more affairs. You're lucky I don't have an affair with every woman that looks at me." He glared at her and then turned away. "Forget about it, you're so uptight celibacy is a victory for you."

"Just one question, Jimmy. If we haven't had sex in a year, what were we doing a couple of weeks ago when you came home at one o'clock in the morning?"

"I don't know, Jane," Jimmy answered, his voice mocking

her. "What were we doing?"

"You went out," Jane said, "and came home very late. You got into bed, and we were intimate." She looked at Jimmy. "That's what I would call a recent sexual relationship—good, bad or indifferent."

Jimmy stared at his wife. "What are you talking about?"

"Just telling you what happened."

Jimmy bent over and picked up several pieces of glass from the floor and tossed them into the wastebasket beneath the sink. "When I come home late, the last thing I want to do is have any kind of dialogue with you, sexual or non-sexual." He bent over and picked up more glass. "I don't know what you're thinking, Jane, because I haven't touched you in over a year, and even then, it was pretty damn rare."

"Well, then what am I doing, hallucinating? Was I dreaming I was having sex?"

"Sounds that way."

Jane took a cup from the cupboard, poured in hot water from the kettle and submerged the teabag. He must have been in an alcoholic blackout. What else didn't he remember?

"Seeing as sex has been a problem all our lives, Jane, believe me, I'd remember if we had done anything recently."

"I'm surprised you even remember where you live considering your condition when you arrive home at night, Jimmy," Jane said as she was leaving the kitchen. "Much less what you've done once you get here."

She crossed the living room and climbed the stairs. Minutes later, after filling the bathtub, she sprinkled lilac bath salts on top of the water and slid down until her head rested against the porcelain.

The tension gradually slipped from her shoulders and she could feel a gentle relaxation seep into her emotional wounds, the hot water, the lilac scent, a salve for frayed nerves, melting the icy aura surrounding her.

The door creaked open into the mist of the bathroom. She could make out only the hands and feet. "Some things I forget, Jane, but I guarantee you, if I had sex with you in the past two weeks, or two months, I would have remembered. I don't know what your stupid game is, but nobody wins." He left, closing the bathroom door before she could see his face, before his words could register.

Jane slid further down until her chin was underwater, until all she could hear were the soapsuds crackling and exploding around her.

CHAPTER 11

Jane studied Carrie lying on Twyla's couch.

"You are totally relaxed," Twyla said, "and when I count to three, I want your feet to touch the earth and then slowly, very slowly, I want you to look around."

Jane watched with interest. As a first-time spectator to the regression process, she recognized a tempo in Twyla's voice that she was unaware of as a participant. Twyla spoke in a rhythmic, soothing pattern that would leave the most agitated at peace.

"Look at your feet and tell me what you see."

Carrie sat up and began to chuckle. "I'm sorry, Twyla, I just can't do this. As they say in Brooklyn, 'It don't work on me.'" She stood. "Hey, I tried, but the old mind doesn't like to be roped in."

"Quite to the contrary, honey," Twyla responded, her voice on edge, "it's through hypnotism that the mind is freed and able to journey to places never before dreamed of. Hypnotism is merely a very primitive stepping-stone."

"I've heard of hypnotism before, but this regression stuff, I—"

"And it's all about dark matter," Twyla interjected.

"Excuse me?"

"The mind is its own universe and like the universe surrounding us, it contains its own dark matter."

Carrie frowned. "I don't mean to be impolite, Twyla, but what the hell are you talking about?"

"You know so little, honey," Twyla snapped, and then in a calmer tone added, "*we* know so little. The potential of the human brain is virtually untapped." Her voice became a stage whisper. "But it is alive with possibility." Theatrically holding her forefinger in the air, commanding attention, she continued. "Imagine you open your eyes after sleeping, only to discover that you cannot see. It's so dark you're unable to view even your fingers placed an inch from your eyes, and it's impossible to maintain your balance as you attempt to stand up because you have no point of reference in the pitch black." Twyla offered a satisfied grin, aware she had hauled in her audience. "And I'm there with you sharing the darkness. You have an old tattered book of matches in your hand, and after striking each one, you trigger a brief burst of light that teaches you more about your surroundings. You are alone, you are level, odd shapes and shadows dance nearby, and walls appear and disappear depending on which direction the light faces. Until . . ." Twyla paused, "you're out of matches and have seen enough to know you understand nothing. To learn more, to discover more, you must have a brighter light to engage the pitch-black room which is the dark matter that is embedded in our brains."

"Now I don't understand," Jane said.

"The dark matter that scientists are just discovering, the material that represents most of the mass in the universe, is also a part of the human brain. It remains an unconquered territory that leers at us, taunting us to move forward, to learn more about ourselves and our capabilities, to domesticate our personal darkness." Twyla's eyes widened, burying most of her violet eye shadow. "Dark matter is one piece of the brain that attempts to reach and teach another part. You must learn how—"

Carrie began to speak. "I don't—"

"Think," Twyla interrupted while pointing to her own temple, her voice now a stage whisper: "White light, black holes, time travel, relativity, Einstein, Nostradamus, and yes, Merlin. They're all shafts of light attempting to stab meaning into the blackness inside and out. And as the human brain evolves and continues to grow inward, deepening the crags and folds, the dark matter, the unused portion of the brain, expands, awaiting further investigation, waiting to reveal what is currently unexplainable." She paused. "We are novices. We know nothing. Our purpose on earth is to learn how to brighten the light and illuminate the dark matter. We must learn to formulate the questions about ourselves and seize answers that the dark matter, our own brains, will provide."

Jane tried to speak, "Twy—"

"There are new worlds to be charted, vast corridors of time, both forward, backward, and sideways, hidden in our brain's dark matter." She stopped, her eyes wide, her finger pointing in the air again. "But are we capable of navigating our own ship? Are we cap—?"

"I'm sure you're right, Twyla, I'm sure you are," Carrie interrupted, "but all that mumbo jumbo just doesn't work for me. Can't tell you why, it just doesn't cut it."

"It's hardly mumbo jumbo," Twyla responded quickly. "Maybe you would prefer to wait for Jane downstairs if this is uncomfortable for you."

"No," Carrie answered, backpedaling, "just because all this stuff doesn't work on me, Twyla, doesn't mean I don't appreciate what you're doing. And, of course, I'm going to pay you." She moved to the back of the room and sat. "I'll just watch and won't speak. I think it would be fascinating to see the process in action."

"Is that okay, Jane?" Twyla asked, still irritated.

Jane nodded. "Sure, I don't care." She stood, walked to the

couch Carrie had abandoned and lay down. "I'm ready when you are."

"One last point," Twyla said, "before we begin." She gazed at Jane. "I've mentioned this before, but it makes sense to repeat—once the process of perception alteration begins, you will never view anything quite the same way again."

"I remember," Jane answered. "But I'm not sure, is that a good thing?"

"I believe it to be," Twyla answered. "It's growth."

"Well, then I'm ready."

Though Twyla's dark-matter explanations sounded rehearsed, they made sense in an oddball way. From basic science classes in high school and college, Jane knew that the majority of the human brain lay dormant, untapped. She'd never heard of that area referred to as dark matter, but she'd never known anyone like Twyla before either.

∞

Minutes later, Jane was on the cloud and, in what seemed mere seconds, was back to a new arena, a new life she'd never seen before.

"Where are you, honey?"

"I'm on a hill that overlooks fields," Jane responded. "I'm in someone else's body."

"Are you alone?" Twyla asked.

"Yes, I'm alone and the sun is intense. But I don't know why I'm here."

"When you look around, what do you see?" Twyla asked. "Tell me what you see."

"I'm sitting in the grass now," Jane answered. "I see bees circling Black-Eyed Susans. They won't hurt me."

"What?" Twyla asked. "What did you say?"

Jane felt the urge to move, to walk through the grass. She crossed down the side of the hill and up the next. In the distance she saw a farmhouse with a red roof and began to move in that direction, but was unable to close the distance. Sitting once more, she briefly watched bees encircle the flowers again. She smiled and lay back in the grass, allowing the sun to first stroke her, then absolve her of all sins.

Jane realized that once she got to the farmhouse, there would be an apple pie cooling on the window ledge. If she concentrated, she could smell the cinnamon in the breeze. And somewhere near, she knew there was an apple orchard with lush trees bending with fruit. As she exhaled, listening to the rush of air from her lungs, Jane could sense the simplicity of life, and knew the hand of the old woman who had baked the pie would reach out to her and stroke her cheek, signaling that she was special. Raising her own hand, she touched her chin, then her cheeks, then the lids of her closed eyes.

This is where I need to be, Jane thought, alone in this grass with this wonderful sun. Yes, this is where I need to be.
Moments later, she was drifting, dozing, wondering all the while why she didn't live in the field forever.

"Jane, where are you?" Twyla's voice echoed across the horizon, bleeding through the serenity of the moment.

Baby.

"Jane, I'm asking where you are." It was no longer a gentle, prodding voice, but instead a terse command. "Where are you, Jane?"

"Here," Jane answered sleepily. "In the sun, on the grass, and I'm very happy."

"When I count to three, Jane, you will return, remembering where you have been, but you will return. One. . ."

Jane heard the voice, but couldn't move herself from the sun.

"Two . . . "

Two, that comes after one, she thought.

"Three."

Jane opened her eyes. She was staring at Twyla. In the background, Carrie watched, her face ashen.

"I think we've had enough for the day," Twyla said. "Maybe

forever."

"What do you mean, maybe forever?"

"Jane, you were not responding to me."

"What are you talking about? I just did. I'm here." She sat up on the couch.

"Honey, you were somewhere and you didn't answer me. When that happened, I tried to bring you back and I couldn't."

"That's ridiculous," Jane answered. "I'm here talking to you."

"Jane, you didn't answer Twyla for almost fifteen minutes," Carrie stated.

Jane shook her head. "I heard every word."

"You're not even hearing me now, Jane," Twyla replied. "Listen carefully. You were not interacting with me for fifteen minutes. I was unable to bring you out of the hypnotic state even by command." She shook her head. "That's never happened before and I don't want it to happen again. I don't want to be in that position, nor do I want you in any kind of jeopardy."

Jane looked at Twyla, then at Carrie. "Jeopardy? Fifteen minutes?"

Carrie nodded.

"Well, there's an easy solution, I'll just tell myself to respond to all commands—that will solve the problem." She smiled. "The brain is one unit and I'm running the show." She looked at Twyla. "You know that's true. You've told me so yourself."

"Yes, but this has never happened before," Twyla answered. "I don't like it, Jane, not at all."

Jane wasn't sure that she liked it either. She had no recollection of being out of contact with Twyla, and that was disturbing. But she considered the rolling meadows and the apple pie cooling on the window ledge, and even the hands and feet in the mist from previous regressions that had turned out to be her very own. It was the beginning of a tapestry—one that she didn't understand, but one compelling enough to arouse her interest further, even if that meant risk.

"This has never happened before," Twyla repeated.

Jane fixed her stare on Twyla. "Then to new beginnings," she said, holding an invisible glass aloft in a toast.

"I don't think so," Twyla responded. "I think we have gone as far as we should go."

"I thought it was our duty to domesticate our personal darkness," Jane said.

Twyla stared, and then turned away.

Chapter 12

"What I don't understand, Jane, is that over the past weeks, I've learned that in most situations you're extremely competent, but dealing with your husband, you seem . . . intimidated." His words were slow, thoughtful.

"My work is by rote—there are certain strategies and business models that perform when integrated properly. Focus groups, test markets, and common sense go a long way."

"Correct me, but didn't Johnson & Johnson have all that in place when they created the Tylenol capsule, and the product was still compromised?"

Jane shrugged. "That's different. It was about package tampering, not marketing." She briefly looked down at her hands resting on her lap. "Anyway, it's business and unemotional."

"And Jimmy is?"

Jane studied the psychiatrist. "Of course. He's my husband. How could it not be emotional?"

"Forgive me, Jane, but I just can't sort out why you would tolerate his excessive use of alcohol in light of the repercussions for you. It surely doesn't strike me as being part of your character."

"Eric, I've been married to Jimmy for a long time. He's always been a big drinker. What am I supposed to do, confront him?"

Eric didn't respond.

"Is that what you think I should do?" Jane asked.

"I don't know, should you?"

"I know what you're doing, Eric. It would be easier if you would just give me an answer."

"Confrontation doesn't have to be unkind. It can be done in a loving manner."

Jane felt the familiar sadness sweep across her. Seconds later, her eyes cast away, she said, "I also have a problem with the physical part of our marriage."

"How so?" The psychiatrist's voice remained even.

"It's never been right."

Eric hesitated. "Ever?"

Jane looked at the doctor. "Pretty much."

"Why do you suppose that is?"

Jane stared at her hands again. "I don't know why."

Eric waited. After several moments, he said, "Well, Jane, it's not an uncommon phenomenon. You're not alone with it although many people think they are." The psychiatrist shifted in his chair. "Sometimes, with all due respect, I think intimacy has too much Madison Avenue involved in it. Advertising often sends false signals and folks assume what they see, hear, and read is absolutely true."

"I suppose." Jane knew he was correct about Madison Avenue. Sex sold product. Her message for *Scarlett!* screamed that one application would lead to a steamy romance. Perhaps, but the reality was that the lipstick probably played zero role in any kind of relationship. She knew it, but couldn't say it in the advertising. Image was everything.

"You know, Jane," the doctor said, "it might make sense to bring Jimmy in here so that the three of us could work together."

"He'd never do it," Jane replied. "He'd never come here."

"Does he know about these appointments?"

"I think he suspects."

"Why don't you tell him? Sometimes when one spouse comes in, the other gets curious and wants to be part of the process." The psychiatrist smiled. "It can't hurt to try, and it might be the beginning of some sort of recovery."

"If I loved him, I would," Jane responded.

Eric paused.

"I would."

"So you're suggesting to me that you don't love him."

Against her wishes, her voice trembled. "I did once. That much I know. As trite as it sounds, he was everything to me." She glanced at the psychiatrist. "That's hard to believe, isn't it?"

The doctor shook his head. "No. Folks change; people grow. Just because the two of you began together doesn't guarantee you'll finish together. It would be nice, but it's not always the case." He considered his statement. "What's important is deciding what works for you."

"This isn't the way I wanted it to be."

"But you don't love him which is why you're not bothered that he's having an affair?"

Jane nodded. "When we were young, it was wonderful. I was madly in love once." She looked at the psychiatrist. "Do you know what I mean?"

Eric nodded. "I think so. Young love, first love—nothing is ever quite the same. Everyone wants those original feelings to remain."

"That's right. But it's all long gone. I've lost all respect for him and now I don't care if he has one or twenty affairs. It's hard to believe I feel this way, but I do." She stared at the clock on the doctor's desk. "It's sad, isn't it?"

"Yes. It is." He tapped his pen on the legal pad resting on his lap. "So what does all this tell you?"

Jane stared at the psychiatrist. She knew what the

words were, but saying them aloud, admitting what she now presumed to be true—that there was no future with Jimmy—was tantamount to the renunciation of her lifetime belief that one man would stay and love her forever. As their relationship had deteriorated, she had simply assumed that someday Jimmy would return to his previous self—to the man she had married, but it had never happened. Instead, everything between them continued to disintegrate. "I guess all this tells me that we're not going to finish together."

Eric crossed his leg over his knee. "Could be, Jane. It happens."

"I wish it wasn't that way."

"I understand," the psychiatrist said.

"Do you?" Jane countered.

"I do," he said, nodding solemnly, "I surely do."

∞

As she drove home, Jane barely noticed the divided white lines in the road flashing by her. She could feel anger uncoiling inside her, but wasn't sure why. Was her frustration directed at Eric for helping expose Jimmy? Maybe she was just upset with herself for staying with her husband too long.

One thing she did know—she was glad that Twyla had called and ended their relationship. She initially had been angry at that too, but now realized it was the right thing to do.

She stared ahead. The broken white lines in the middle of the road continued to stream in front of her in rhythm, hypnotically passing in cadence.

One . . . two . . . three . . . four . . . monotonous, yet like Twyla's voice . . . penetrating.

One . . . two . . . three . . . four . . .

One . . . two . . . three . . . four . . . hypnotic, soothing.

Twyla's voice, invading her consciousness.

Relax . . . two . . . three . . . four . . .

Relax . . . two . . . three . . . four . . .

The lines swept past her, faster and faster.

The road suddenly vanished and the hands and feet from the fog emerged into Jane's field of vision. She watched, horrified, as the fingers and toes crawled across the hood of the car, then slipped inside and morphed into her own hands and feet. She immediately felt the need to cleanse herself, to reach down and slide colored particles from the top of each foot, but instead kept her fingers locked on the wheel.

Above the headlight beams, in the dark distance, she saw a floating image of a woman sitting in a field of wild clover and Black-Eyed Susans.

Jane's hands began to shake on the steering wheel. Panic ricocheted through her.

The broken white lines hurtling past her in the center of the road were now a single stripe. As the car began to drift, Jane glanced at the speedometer and realized she was traveling at nearly ninety miles per hour. She moved her foot from the accelerator and allowed the wailing engine to wind down.

The woman in the field disappeared, and with the overhead light switched on, Jane identified her own hands and feet.

She glanced into the rearview mirror, seeing eyes that were ghost-like—filmy gray, preoccupied.

The blue had disappeared.

The eyes were not her eyes!

Whose, then?

An insane question.

Jane checked again in the mirror.

Blue. They belonged to her. She was positive.

Then she was calm; strangely composed despite what had just happened.

The images could have only been due to stress—job stress. That much she knew.

Jane began rethinking her conversation with Eric. Everyone

in the world was searching for the Fountain of Youth and its miraculous, accompanying energy and emotion. As a result of her marketing programs, her own company, DSRR, was telling women in America that cosmetics would transform them back to their teens or twenties, with the excitement returning right before their eyes.

Who was she kidding? She had been drinking too much of her own Kool-Aid, expecting all the old feelings for Jimmy to be identical no matter how much time had elapsed.

That wasn't fair.

Her thoughts turned to DSRR. With a large portion of the aging population considering retirement, it could be time to position more of the company's assets toward the graying of America. It made sense because of the vast market potential. Although the manufacturers of cosmetics were only mildly interested in that demographic, and continually stressed the twenty-one to twenty-eight-year-old group, maybe it was time to shift. The retiree population numbers were there for the taking—she just had to convince Briggs to go after them.

She glanced in the mirror. Same old blue eyes.

She stared at the road ahead.

Jane knew she hated change; anything new in her personal life scared her.

Maybe she'd give Jimmy another chance. It wasn't his fault she'd grown older and evolved. Maybe there was still hope for the two of them. Maybe beneath the surface, the man she once loved, remained.

She tapped her fingers on the steering wheel.

Yes, maybe she'd give him another chance after all.

CHAPTER 13

Flanagan's Pub looked the same.

"Jane, remember this place? It's like old times. We used to have lunch here a lot on Saturday afternoons." Jimmy was pleased. "I'll bet it's been at least ten years." He pointed to a table in the corner beyond the bar. "How about over there? We're the first ones here, we get the best table."

She was allowing him to hold her hand. It was a strange feeling, one she had forgotten, her hand buried in his. "That's fine, Jimmy."

She was trying.

"I can't believe you wanted to come here after all this time," he said. "Murph," Jimmy waved to the bartender. "Look who's back."

The bartender, in a starched white shirt, green plaid tie and floor-length white apron, looked as if he had just worked the boat from Dublin. He placed his hand above his eyes, pretending to block out the sun. "Do my eyes deceive me, or is that the lovely Jane McBride with you, Jimmy?"

"You got that right," Jimmy called back. "Just as beautiful as the day she was born." He pulled out a chair for Jane, then sat opposite her before calling to the bartender, "A white wine and the hair of the dog that bit me."

"Which dog, Jimmy?"

"Usual dog, Murph. Brown mutt."

Jane watched the interaction. The words between Jimmy and the bartender had been honed to an exact science. Like a husband and wife that had been married for decades, one could anticipate the other's next comment.

"Hello, Jimmy." A waitress appeared behind his shoulder. "Menus or no menus today?"

"Eileen, darlin', this is my wife, Jane. We used to come here together, but that was before your time." He looked at Jane. "Menus, right?"

Jane nodded to Eileen. "Definitely."

The waitress handed a menu to Jane, then Jimmy. "Specials of the day, corned beef and cabbage, prime rib sandwich, fried chicken with cottage fries. Everything else is listed."

Jane perused the menu and hoped for a surprise—something green beside the smiling shamrock, river-dancing on the cover.

Eileen walked to the bar and returned with a tray holding a pint of Guinness, a shot of Irish whiskey, and a glass of white wine. She placed the glasses on the table. "The whiskey is with Murph."

Jimmy picked up the shot, and shifting in his chair so that he might face the bartender, he raised the whiskey in salute. "'And wasn't he lucky,' said the good Father," he called.

"Indeed, he was," Murph responded, "though he was waving his wooden leg out the priory window."

Jimmy downed the Bushmills, then slammed the shot glass on the table. "Good stuff," he said, turning to face Jane again.

Jane began to realize she might have made a mistake. "Jimmy, I wanted to come here so we could talk. You said the other night that we haven't done that in a long time."

"True," Jimmy said, gulping the Guinness, then wiping away the foam using the back of his hand. "That's very true."

He lowered his voice. "What do you want to talk about?"

Jane hesitated, and then shrugged. "Well, I thought we could talk about us."

"What about us?"

Jane touched the stem of the wine glass, then lifted it and sipped. "Look, I know things haven't been the best between us, but it wasn't always that way."

"And?" Jimmy asked.

"I was hoping we could try to put the pieces back together. What we had together was special once. It was a long time ago, but it was real."

Jimmy held the Guinness with both hands, ten fingers wrapped around the pint glass.

"Does that mean you don't want to get divorced?"

Jane was surprised. "I never said anything about divorce."

"I thought that's what we were doing. Get me fired up and then lay the bad news on me." He looked at Jane. "That's not happening?"

Jane shook her head. "No."

"Really?"

Jane nodded. "Really."

Jimmy eyed his wife and a grin crept across his face. "You don't hate me?"

"I've never hated you, Jimmy. I just think that the two of us can do better together."

Jimmy stared into Jane's eyes. "You know Katy Rockland means nothing to me." He reached out and touched Jane's fingers with his own. "You know that, don't you?"

"I believe what you tell me."

"Is this happening because you're seeing a psychiatrist?"

Jane didn't respond.

"I'm just guessing that's what's happening," Jimmy continued. "Am I wrong?"

"You're not wrong about me seeing a psychiatrist. Barbara Greenman recommended I try it. Whether this is happening because of that, I don't know."

"Do you love me?"

"Yes," Jane answered.

Eileen appeared. "Have we decided?" she asked, placing a fresh round of drinks on the table. "I brought the drinks because Murph is getting backed up and I know you don't like to wait."

"Perfect, darlin'," Jimmy said. "Give us just thirty seconds and we'll be ready to order."

"Just want to warn you," Eileen said, "we're about filled up, and that slows down Jimmy in the kitchen too."

"Thirty seconds is all we need, darlin'."

The waitress turned and left.

"How come you don't want to know if I love you?" Jimmy asked.

"I know you love me."

"You're pretty confident."

"Is that wrong?" Jane asked.

"No, it's just that it wasn't always like that. I used to run the show." He knocked back the shot glass of Bushmills, then plunged into the Guinness. "You weren't always that confident, Jane," he said, wiping the foam away.

"Time alters things, Jimmy," she said. "I don't know why."

"You want some more wine?"

"No, the second one Eileen brought me is more than enough."

"And here I am," Eileen said, her pen poised over the pad. "What's for lunch?"

"Ah, yes, what will it be, Jane?"

"Chef's salad for me," Jane answered. "Oil and vinegar on the side."

"And you, Jimmy, my love," Eileen asked.

"It can be none other than the corned beef and cabbage, Eileen darlin'," Jimmy said.

"Good choice," the waitress replied. "I'll be back in a few minutes with the food and refills." She turned and headed for the kitchen.

"Hey, Jane, remember when we were back in college and I busted up that guy who got smart with you in the bar?" Jimmy asked. "I'll bet he still regrets opening his mouth that day."

"That's what I would think," Jane answered.

"You're damn right," Jimmy said, staring at the Guinness. "I took zero crap in those days." He shrugged. "And look at me now."

∞

Jane picked at her salad and listened to Jimmy snarl as he devoured the corned beef and cabbage he had coated with mustard. She watched every movement he made as she spun her own meaningless brand of small talk. She studied his focus on the food, the Guinness, the horseradish, the Irish soda bread, much as a baby boy would shark-eye his bottle as he drank, fearful it would be taken away.

And she knew that he was no longer listening to her though he would occasionally nod, or say yeah, no, maybe, or who cares.

He was a punch-drunk fighter caught on the ropes.

Jane's hopes that had spirited her through the morning were disintegrating. Maybe there was no way back home. Perhaps all those sweet memories with Jimmy—the very early days of kindness—that she now wanted to pick like wild flowers and save as the foundation of a new relationship, had died long ago in fallow fields.

Before they met, they had each been shoved from their sorry nests where neither had been coveted. And they had entrapped each other in free-fall, grabbing, clutching; a grim battle for self-preservation.

Their resulting marriage had been bland and passionless, and she realized now, again, never a particularly good match. Maybe it was just that simple.

"So, Jane, you never answered me. What about that guy I

busted up in college. Remember that? What was his name? I think he had the same first name as me: Jim. I'll bet he never got over the ass-kicking I gave him."

"I remember," Jane said.

"Kicked his ass," Jimmy said, his eyes still locked on the corned beef. "Kicked his ass, big-time. Remember?"

"I remember," Jane answered. "I didn't remember his name being Jim."

"Yeah, that was his name, all right." He looked over his shoulder. "Eileen, darlin', when you get a minute."

"A lot of Jimmys around here," Jane answered, now figuring how she could backtrack from what her husband would want to do after lunch.

"Only two," Jimmy answered. "Me and the cook."

"And the boy you had the fight with," Jane answered.

"Yeah, but he's not here now," Jimmy said. "That doesn't count."

"Oh, right," Jane replied. "That doesn't count." She had to be careful, a tinge of sarcasm had crept into her voice. With Jimmy drinking that was a recipe for disaster.

His eyes were on her. "What?"

Controlling her voice, keeping the sarcasm in check, she said, "He's not here so we can't count him." Continuing her maneuvering, she asked, "What was his last name anyway?"

"I don't remember," Jimmy answered, his fork stabbing the last pieces of corned beef. As he pushed the meat into his mouth, he mopped up the juice on the plate with a slab of the Irish soda bread. He chewed and swallowed and reached for the Guinness. "Good meal," he said, "damn good meal." He glanced over his shoulder. "Eileen, darlin', a little Baileys for the two of us."

"Not for me, thanks," Jane said, holding up her hand. "I've had enough."

"See that over there?" Jimmy asked, pointing to the fifteen-foot mirror behind the bar.

Jane nodded.

"See how it sticks out about six inches from the wall, and all three sides are closed off, but not the top, so it's kind of like a big, open envelope?" He grinned. "Know why that's there?"

Jane shook her head.

"So people sitting at the bar back in the eighteen-nineties could throw pennies and nickels and dimes, and sometimes silver dollars, and try to get them to bounce off the wall and down into the mirror."

"Why would they do that?" Jane asked.

Jimmy shook his head. "Probably because they were drinking and bored and unhappy." He grinned. "Anyway, one of these nights, Murph and I thought we'd take a hammer to the mirror and make a fortune. Maybe it wouldn't be a million dollars, but we think that some of the coins will be so rare that the total take will be close to a million."

"Interesting," Jane answered.

"Problem is," Jimmy continued, "we don't own the bar, so we could get into some serious trouble."

"Makes sense," Jane answered.

"Well, it's an idea," Jimmy said, "if we ever run out of money."

Eileen returned with Jimmy's drink. "Let me know when you're ready for the check, love," she said.

"Any day now," Jimmy answered, taking a sip. "Soon as I finish this up and have one for the road."

∞

Jane tried to talk Jimmy into walking around town following lunch. She hadn't shopped in downtown Andover in months and suggested it might be fun to look through the antiques shops and art galleries. She was desperate to prevent an increasingly blue afternoon from darkening further.

"Come on, Jane," Jimmy said, "I've never explored the town before, why would I want to do it now? Let's go home."

"Do you really want to, Jimmy? It's such a beautiful afternoon and this will be a new experience."

A smile crossed Jimmy's face. "No, let me tell you what will be a new experience. . . ."

∞

With each thrust inside her, Jane retreated further from her husband. Buried beneath the bulk of Jimmy, she could barely breathe, barely think. Her vision grew cloudy, her hair stormed across the pillow, and after each of his inward plunges, beads of colored fire short-circuited before her eyes, exploding across the ceiling before spinning downward in a star shower that turned to colored leaf flecks resting on the tops of her feet.

Then he rolled away, leaving her exhausted.

My feet are tainted, Jane thought as she struggled to breathe, and for that I can thank Jimmy. Yes, for that I can thank Jimmy.

She was too tired to reach down and brush them clean.

"How was it, Jane? It's been a long time."

Jane struggled to be civil. "It was fine, Jimmy, but I don't think the last time was all that long ago."

"Over a year is a helluva long time to not have sex," he answered from the far side of the bed, his breathing labored.

"Maybe a month, not a year."

"Yeah, right," Jimmy smirked. "Someone as smart as you with an answer like that," he paused, "maybe isn't so smart after all."

"You're right," she answered moments later, feeling the familiar tension returning, knowing he was wrong again, knowing he had one-sided sex with her a month ago—not a year, knowing he didn't remember anything due to his alcoholic blackouts, knowing she had been sick of him at lunch and was disgusted with him now.

A heavy silence permeated the bedroom, round bales of wet fog unrolling from above, encircling, individually isolating.

"I tell you one thing I know for sure," Jimmy said at last, his voice low, "you were never as sure of yourself as you think you are now."

CHAPTER 14

Jane picked up the Sunday newspaper from the stack next to the cash register and paid the owner. She moved to a stool at the rear of the counter and ordered coffee. Maybe I'll speak to three people today, she thought. The owner had said "Thank you," when he returned her change for the newspaper, the boy behind the counter said "Okay," when she ordered. One to go.

As she flipped through the magazine section, Jane sipped her coffee, not sure whether to stay and read an article or just head home—probably to the back deck if the sun stayed warm. Out of the corner of her eye, she saw the front door open. Eric Alford entered with a youthful trophy wife, striking and self-confident in her quiet elegance. His hand was briefly on his wife's shoulder and the two laughed lightly together while he waited to pay for the newspaper.

Jane lifted the magazine up to eye level.

"More coffee, ma'am?" The teenager behind the counter asked.

Jane shook her head. She watched the two leave the coffee shop.

"I'll take more now," she said, continuing to study the psychiatrist as he opened the passenger's side of the convertible for his wife, all the time talking. Jane focused on the woman, and from fifty yards, even through the coffee shop plate glass littered with advertising decals, the genuine contentment on her face was obvious.

Genuine contentment and immeasurable self-assurance.

A world away.

Maybe it was that entitled look of happiness, or perhaps the capillaries on Jimmy's nose, or the fact that she had only spoken with two people the entire morning, that sank Jane. Maybe it was because Katy Rockford was phonier than her artificial breasts, or because she knew *Scarlett!*'s production cost was a little over three dollars per unit, with a retail price point of twenty dollars, and somebody other than herself was becoming very rich.

She wasn't sure.

And she was tired of having to drink black coffee to keep her caloric content down. How many calories could skim milk have anyway? And what would they mean in terms of body fat? And who cared?

Eric Alford didn't know anything about her. He had no idea how alone she was. He had no comprehension of how much she wanted to return to the sunny field with the farmhouse in the distance and all the serenity it offered.

He knew nothing.

Jane left a five-dollar bill on the counter, grabbed the newspaper, her purse, and headed for the door.

When she got home, she reached for the phone. "Hello, Twyla," she said, "it's Jane, Jane McBride."

∞

"Yes, Jane, come in," Twyla said, opening the apartment door wider. She was dazzling in black and tan western gaucho gear—a fringe vest, suede skirt, black boots, with turquoise chandeliers dangling from her ears. "I didn't think you'd want to come to the city on your day off, honey." She glanced at the sweat suit. "And so quickly too."

In the background, Dolly Parton's sweet voice rose above dueling mandolins.

"I want to regress again," Jane said entering the apartment.

"Sit," Twyla said, indicating the couch. "I thought we had already discussed that when I called you last week."

"We had," Jane answered, sitting, "but I'm not comfortable with that decision."

"I'm sorry to hear that," Twyla said as she sat opposite her.

Jane struggled with her thoughts. "You allowed me to visit a place where I became content, or at least have the idea that I could be."

"And that place is where?"

Jane shook her head. "I don't know where it is, Twyla, but someplace in the regression I became at ease, like I was home."

Twyla picked up a notebook from the coffee table and thumbed through the pages, then stopped and read. "Among other lives, you seemed to spend time as a very early Sister of God, perhaps in Ireland." Twyla read further to herself, then continued, "You visualized yourself immersed in fog more than once, with the original hands and feet you were initially fearful of, eventually becoming your own. You were hiding in a field at night with men searching for you, and later, you were in a field that seemed very comfortable, perhaps the same place." Twyla looked at Jane. "And that's where we got into trouble."

"Because I didn't respond right away."

"Exactly, honey."

"There are ways around that, Twyla," Jane answered, her tone anxious. "I'll just program myself to your voice before I get hypnotized. I've mentioned before that I would be willing to do that. You know, the brain controlling the brain. That has to solve the problem."

"Honey, let me explain something," Twyla said. "I'm not a

psychologist, a psychiatrist, a social worker, a nurse, a nurse practitioner, a midwife, or a witch—nor am I registered with the state of New York for anything, including a driver's license. Friends who share common interests taught me about regression therapy many years ago. I believe it to be a psychological branch of an untapped science, but nonetheless, nothing has been, or can be proven legitimate." She smoothed the page of the notebook. "And that's not good in some situations."

"I accept all that," Jane answered. "I'm not looking for a PhD, or an M.D. framed on your wall."

"I know, and I believe you, Jane, but this has got to be fun and safe too, for both of us," Twyla said. "If I feel there is danger or unknown hazard in the regression, I don't want to be involved in that process. And now I believe that's a possibility."

"I thought you had done your homework and there was no risk."

Twyla shook her head. "This is different."

"I need to do this, Twyla, I need to do this."

Twyla halted and her face grew serious. "The reality is that I can't, honey. There are too many lawyers looking to make a living out there, and if you have a problem with me, and go complain to one of those ambulance-chasers, they'll come and take everything I own, even if it isn't much."

"I'll sign a release," Jane said. "It will leave you blameless."

"Maybe you should see a psychiatrist if you're this uncomfortable," Twyla answered.

"I am seeing one and it's not doing a damn thing except making me feel worse," Jane blurted out, her voice rising. "I feel worse, Twyla. Worse!"

"I'd like to help you, honey . . ."

Jane started to cry. And Eric Alford had a wife, too. She hadn't realized that made any difference to her, but it did. He was the only man who had shown any genuine interest in her for as long as she could remember, and though she was paying for that attention, as a pitiable, painted old hag would engage a gigolo, she liked being with him.

"Jane, can you understand what I'm saying?" Twyla asked.

Jane didn't respond, she looked away, then reached for a tissue in her purse. "I've never sued anyone in my life."

"I'm sure you haven't."

"And I would never be a trophy wife either, even if I was twenty years younger. It's not in me."

"Excuse me?"

"Never mind." Jane crumpled up the tissue and pushed it into her purse. Low gray skies, fallow fields. No one understood how fragile she was. No one could reach her; she could reach no one. "I'm sorry to take your time, especially on the weekend like this," Jane said, standing. "You were very good to see me, Twyla." She started for the door.

"Wait." Twyla held up a hand in resignation. She paused and then sighed. "I won't make you sign a release." Quietly, she added, "I'll just take your word that we're friends and that we'll take care of each other."

Jane turned. "I wouldn't hurt you, Twyla."

"And I recognize that now, watching you, listening to you. Part of my job is to be a good judge of character. That's how I knew your friend, Carrie, was sincere when she told me how much I looked like Dolly." She stood. "But if we're going to attempt another regression, Jane, you must remain in contact with me. I can't have it any other way." She walked over, placed her hands on Jane's shoulders and stared into her eyes. "Do you understand that, Jane?"

Jane stared back at Twyla.

"Do you understand that, Jane?"

"I do."

"Well then, let's get cranking," Twyla answered. "I've got a date with a cowboy tonight." She paused and chuckled. "We go to a club over on Tenth Avenue called Sweethearts of the Rodeo. That good old boy always takes me there, works to get me liquored up, and then later tries to get me to take off my clothes back here in the hayloft. We've been going together for at least twenty years, and he's sure not the young buck he used to be, but you'd think the poor, dumb rodeo clown would've figured out by now he doesn't have to get me drunk, he just has to ask.

∞

Jane was in the field with the sky locked around her. In the distance she saw the farmhouse, and now she realized the sense of contentment had returned. Comfort spread through every portion of her body—tiny, heated mink gloves massaging, probing, then massaging more—and she understood how a heroin addict felt as the drug seeped into the bloodstream.

"I'm back," she said to Twyla.

"Where, Jane?" Twyla asked.

"In the field, and the farmhouse is in the distance."

"What kind of shoes are you wearing?"

"I have bare feet." I can feel the grass and it's warm.

"What else are you wearing?" Twyla asked.

"I belong here," Jane murmured to herself.

"What else are you wearing?" Twyla repeated.

"And I'm in someone else's body again."

"Whose body?"

"I don't know, but it's a woman's body and she feels younger than me." Jane hesitated. "But I have no control. I'm watching. I'm in the body, watching, but I feel like I have limited control."

"That's fine," Twyla said.

"It's strange," Jane replied.

"Enjoy the experience. Learn from it."

Jane quickly grew comfortable in the woman's body, watching, not interacting. In the background, she could hear Twyla's questions ambling over the hills—annoying questions—and it grew difficult to respond. Gradually, she shut out the voice and moved toward the beckoning farm until she found herself in the front yard.

She heard the mumble of voices, a call, and a backdoor slam shut. To her left, in the distance, she saw the apple orchard that she knew would be there.

Baby in the air!

A gunshot echoed. "Stay the hell away from here," a man's voice bellowed from the backyard. "Next time I'll aim and nothing good's going to come when that happens. I promise you that!"

"Jane, are you there?" It was Twyla's voice, abrupt, clear, crisp.

"I'm here, Twyla."

"You're calm, Jane, and you know nothing can harm you."

"I know," Jane answered.

"It's time to return now," Twyla said.

"But I've just gotten here," Jane protested.

"It's time to return now," Twyla repeated. "When I count to three, you will be back, invigorated, refreshed. One . . . "

Jane stared at the farmhouse.

"Two."

She longed to go inside.

The screen door opened and a silver-haired man carrying a rifle stepped outside. "Jane," he said.

"Three."

She was back, staring into Twyla's eyes. "Someone called me Jane," she said immediately. "Someone called me Jane."

"I don't think so, honey," Twyla said, standing, her voice tense.

"I was recognized," Jane said. "A man called me."

"What time is it?" Twyla asked, her eyes flashing.

Jane glanced at her wristwatch. "A little after five . . . oh, my gosh, it's after five."

"Exactly," Twyla said. "A little after five. We started the regression somewhere around two o'clock."

Jane stared at Twyla. "That makes no sense. I was only back there for a few minutes at most."

"Honey," Twyla said, her voice still on edge, "I spent over two hours trying to get you to respond."

"That can't be," Jane answered. "That's impossible."

"Jane, I like you," Twyla said, "but I can't do this anymore. It's too nerve-wracking for me, and God only knows what it is for you."

"It's like going home," Jane said.

"Understood," Twyla answered, "but for every reason we discussed before, I can't do this again."

"I'll pay more money," Jane offered.

"The money is irrelevant. I've lost control. As I've mentioned, that's something that has never happened before, and I can't be involved with anything I can't regulate." Her smile was tense. "Jane, I think we could be friends, but we can't do business together. I should have never gone ahead with this last session. I'm sorry."

Jane sat up on the couch. She could see Twyla was serious. "Never again?"

"I'm sorry."

Jane rose to her feet. The thought of never returning to the farmhouse was beyond sad. To be stuck with Jimmy, Briggs, and a psychiatrist leading her down emotional pathways she had no interest in traveling, was a deadly formula.

"I hate to rush you, Jane," Twyla said, "but Tex is due here soon, and I need a few minutes to become even more enticing if he's going to undress me later."

Jane nodded, barely hearing Twyla. She placed three one-hundred-dollar bills on the coffee table. "Okay," she said softly, crossing the room. She opened the door and stepped into the hallway, then proceeded down the stairs.

If I ever got the chance, she thought, I'd go inside that farmhouse.

CHAPTER 15

Monday morning, Briggs stuck his head into Jane's office. He flashed his perfect white veneered teeth. "Any chance of lunch today?"

Jane was surprised. Rarely had she ever had lunch with the president, and never alone. "I can clear my calendar, John, if it's important."

"You might want to do that," Briggs answered. "How about we meet in the lobby at twelve-thirty? Carl will have the car waiting for us."

"Very good, John," Jane said. "That'll work."

"Excellent," Briggs replied. He moved away from her office.

Jane thought for a minute then called Carrie. "Are you free for a minute?"

"Not free, not easy, but a sexual dynamo when deployed," Carrie answered. "I'm on my way."

Jane was increasingly uncomfortable. A lunch meeting with Briggs—he was either going to promote her or fire her.

"You're forgetting one other possibility," Carrie said after she heard about the invitation, "maybe he wants to engage in a—how can I say this delicately—a quickie show-and-tell encounter, if you know what I mean."

Jane stared at Carrie. "You've got to be kidding."

Carrie shrugged her shoulders. "Just looking at all the options here, Jane. Stranger things have happened."

"Stranger things have happened? That's very flattering."

"My pleasure," Carrie said.

Jane stared past Carrie for a moment, then looked back. "I don't know how long this luncheon is going to run, and I have a meeting with the agency creative team at two in the Three B conference room. Can you get it started if I'm late?"

"Of course."

"What I will need is your objective opinion on their preliminary treatments for the *Arabesque* campaign. It's going to be diametrically opposed to what we've done with *Scarlett!*. Similar markets, different message, same goals. I want to make sure the agency is headed in the right direction. Keep them busy until I'm back."

"I know what you're looking for," Carrie answered, "we've reviewed it often enough. I'll be all over them."

"I'm sure you will be. Save the storyboards for last. With a little bit of luck, I'll make it back by two."

∞

"I hope this didn't disrupt your afternoon plans," Briggs said to Jane as he slid into the back seat of the limousine next to her.

Carl closed the door, then walked around to the front of the black Mercedes and climbed in behind the steering wheel. Through the intercom, he asked, "Versailles Club, Mr. Briggs?"

Briggs nodded to the driver. "Have you ever been there, Jane? You can see for miles, assuming it's a clear day."

"Never have," Jane admitted. "I've heard of it though."

"It's elegant, actually," Briggs said, "and a civilized restaurant that serves as a retreat from the corporate battlefield."

"I'm looking forward to it," Jane said.

"Good, me too," Briggs replied. "How's the family?"

"Thankfully," Jane lied, "my husband is fine."

"I'm glad to hear it." Briggs' eyes rested on Jane for a moment. "You're looking more at ease," he said. "Did you take my advice and overindulge on vitamin C? You never have to worry, you know, what your body doesn't absorb, you pee away."

∞

The Versailles Club turned out to be far more impressive than Jane could have imagined. They were seated in the middle of a private dining room at a table with crisp, white linen. Above the fireplace was an oil painting of a mother and child. An inlaid rosewood clock rested on the mantel. A vintage Waterford chandelier hung directly overhead and a rich crimson and gold Persian carpet covered the floor. Against the far wall, a personal wine steward and a waiter, both in white gloves, stood attentive, awaiting Briggs' signal.

"The painting," Briggs said, motioning to the canvas, "was completed in the 1850s by Thomas John Hughes. He exhibited at the Royal Academy."

Jane nodded. "Interesting."

"You're probably unaware of my personal artistic background."

"I am. Tell me more, John."

Briggs chuckled. "When I was young and free, I viewed myself as an abstract expressionist with talents similar to de Kooning's mature work."

"And?"

Briggs raised his forefinger to the steward, who took cocktail orders.

"And I struggled for several years trying to sell my paintings and concluded that I better find a way to make a living if I planned to eat." He shrugged. "So my artistic struggles became a hobby and not a vocation."

"I had no idea," Jane said. "Do you still paint?"

"If you want to call it that. I do organic, geometric work on silk which my tailor crafts into neckties. You may have noticed I have a wild variety of ties—so many that I can pick one that matches my temperament each morning." Briggs grinned. "And now I've given you my poker player's 'tell,' you'll be able to read my daily mood by the color I'm wearing."

The steward promptly returned with a chilled Chardonnay for Jane and single malt scotch, neat, in a crystal tumbler for Briggs.

"Enough of the poor, struggling artist talk." Briggs lifted the glass in a toast. "Here's to business, to life, and to you, Jane." The glasses touched and both sipped. "I took the liberty of ordering lunch for you. I hope you don't mind."

Jane broke eye contact first. "Not at all. Thank you."

After the salad and small talk, Briggs leaned back in his chair. "I expect you wonder why I wanted to meet with you today, Jane."

"I can't say that I wasn't curious."

Briggs thought for a moment. "Jane, as you know, or at the very least, should know, I think you're doing a marvelous job for DSRR. Market share is up, profits are up, and we're meeting our financial plans—goals that are not easy to achieve. I believe you deserve much of the credit."

Jane could feel her face becoming warm. "Thank you, John, those are kind words. I certainly am trying to do a good job."

"And that is precisely what is happening. The board is pleased with our balance sheets, and that makes my life easier." He smiled. "In a great many ways, I have you to thank for it."

Jane nodded again. "I'm pleased that I'm able to contribute to the company's profitability."

The steward brought Jane a fresh Chardonnay and Briggs

a new tumbler with two fingers of scotch. He picked up their original glasses though neither had finished. "Just a moment to freshen your drinks," he said, bowing as he backed away.

"As I was saying," Briggs continued, pausing to savor the scotch, "I think it's time the company gave back a little, which is unheard of these days in corporate America unless someone like me, of course, is driving the bus."

"And you do a remarkable job of leading the company, John," Jane responded on cue.

"Thank you." Briggs leaned forward. "Jane, I won't do this without your permission, but I would like to redesign the company organizational chart to create a new title for you. What I'm thinking is executive vice president of marketing."

Jane smiled. "I appreciate this very much, John. Based on our profit margins, I almost have to say, 'What took you so long?'" She laughed. "But I won't."

Briggs patted the top of her hand. "I've given this considerable thought and it's the right thing to do." He sipped the scotch. "But believe me, this is not just to help Jane McBride. I have the company in mind as well. I'll insist you sign a five-year ironclad contract with DSRR. That way I won't have to worry about you being stolen from me by the competitive wolves."

"So much for the glass ceiling," Jane said. "Thank you, John."

"Indeed," Briggs responded. "Finally, and perhaps most importantly, if you agree to this opportunity, your salary will increase by twenty-five percent beginning the first of the month, and I'll see that you receive a bonus of two hundred and fifty thousand dollars, as well. Additionally, as part of the DSRR executive package, you will be guaranteed annual salary increases of no less than fifteen percent, and you will be tied into the stock-option programs that are designed exclusively for the executive level. You will also have access to the company apartment on Park Avenue and use of the DSRR corporate jet." He smiled. "Even, if you just want to take a brief overnight vacation in Barbados."

It was more than Jane had ever anticipated. She stared at Briggs, then at her wine glass.

Briggs had a smile on his face as he picked up his scotch. "Mucho largesse, no?"

"Profitability has its rewards, doesn't it?"

"Yes, I must confess it does," he answered. "We're good for each other, Jane, which means we're superb for the company. I respect your thought process in taking a product to market. It's innovative and always viewed in a fresh light. And though I haven't discussed it with you, I was impressed with the report you sent me indicating that more of our R&D resources should be directed at the aging segment of the market. It makes a good deal of sense, especially with most of our competitors targeting the younger demographic almost exclusively." Briggs signaled the waiter to begin serving. "I believe we should get started on an analysis of your recommendations immediately. What I would like you to do, Jane, is to outline a preliminary overview of what and how, then huddle with our research and financial groups to put together some demographic and revenue profiles. I think we'll be ahead of the curve on this one."

"Consider it done, John," Jane said, in the back of her mind trying to figure where she would find the time.

Briggs nodded. "I have all the faith in the world in you."

∞

Following lunch, Briggs selected a cigar from a box offered by the steward. "I hope this doesn't offend you, Jane. It's Cuban and illegal, but, hey, we're worth it." He hesitated. "May I interest you in one?"

Jane shook her head. "No, thank you, John."

The steward snipped the end of the cigar and held the lighter flame in place. Briggs puffed, then nodded, dismissing him.

"So what do you think of my proposal, Jane?" Briggs asked as he touched his necktie.

The steward returned and placed a snifter of Courvoisier first in front of Jane, then Briggs.

"I'm grateful that you have this confidence in me, John," Jane answered. "I assure you, I won't let you down."

"Then we have a deal," Briggs said.

Jane nodded. "If the board agrees."

"Trust me, the board will agree with just about anything I say as long as we continue to show substantial profits."

Jane smiled. "I'm excited."

"Likewise," Briggs answered.

Jane felt Briggs' hand touch the front of her thigh. She shifted, moving her legs to the side.

"Working together, there's no limit to the amount of income we can generate for the company, and therefore, ourselves." The cigar was planted between Briggs' upper and lower teeth. "Know what I mean, Jane?"

This time Jane felt Briggs' hand rest on her thigh. "John, what are you doing?" She shifted away again.

"Feeling my oats? Communicating with a future executive vice president? You tell me, Jane, what am I doing?" He removed the cigar from his mouth and clasped it between two fingers of his free hand. "What am I doing, Jane?" he repeated.

"John, I don't know what you have in mind, but this is not something that I'm comfortable with." She glanced at Briggs, then unintentionally made eye contact with the wine steward standing in the corner of the room. He looked away.

"Regrettably, Jane," Briggs said, "this is a cutthroat business with many talented people for a few coveted positions." He reached out and placed his hand on her thigh once more.

"John, stop it," Jane said, this time pushing his hand away.

Briggs smirked and looked down. He sipped the Courvoisier, then placed the snifter on the table and faced Jane. The smirk faded. "I don't know what's come over me," he mumbled. Clearing his throat, he continued, "I do apologize,

Jane. Sometimes I think I'm overworked, and as a result, overtired, and then I have a drink or two and act outrageously." He looked her squarely in the eyes. "I do apologize, Jane, I should know better." He thought a minute, then said, "I think you're very attractive, but I've behaved boorishly, like a ditch-digger, with no breeding." He placed his cigar in the ashtray. "Will you forgive me?"

Jane forced a smile across her lips, attempting to hide the fact that she was shaken. "I understand, John. These things happen sometimes. No harm done."

"None intended," Briggs answered, signaling the steward for a refill of the cognac.

∞

As the Mercedes stopped in front of the DSRR building, Jane turned to Briggs. "John, I've already forgotten about the incident at lunch today. I hope it won't affect our relationship or have any negative impact on the new job."

Briggs shifted toward her. He lifted the cigar from his mouth. "What new job is that, Jane?"

CHAPTER 16

"You have got to be joking," Carrie exclaimed the following day, her eyes wide as she peered over the lunch table. "Tell me, Jane, please, I'm begging you, I'm friggin' begging you, tell me you're joking."

"I'm not, Carrie," Jane said, "that's the whole story."

"You mean to tell me that moron tried to feel you up in the Versailles Club? Just like that he put his hand on your leg?"

Jane nodded.

"God Almighty, not only is he an idiot, he's acting like a high school kid in the cafeteria. When is the last time some guy came on to you by putting his hand on your thigh, for God's sake, and under the damn lunch table no less. I'd slap him silly just for being such an amateur."

"Now I think he'll hold this whole thing against me. First, I had a promotion, then I rejected his advances, and then the promotion disappeared," Jane said.

"Did you ever stop to think that maybe the promotion was all made-up, that it was never going to happen in the first place?"

Jane stared at Carrie.

"Maybe it was all a line just to get you in the bedroom," Carrie continued. "Maybe he was offering you something that was never going to materialize—he was just using it as a point of leverage to get what he wanted."

Jane shook her head. "That's hard to believe. I mean, come on, Carrie, in this day and age, with Human Resources being so tied into every facet of the workplace, the president propositions the head of the marketing group by dangling a promotion in front of her if she sleeps with him. That's ridiculous."

"But that's what he did," Carrie answered.

"True."

"It's your word against his though, so you lose."

"I've already lost," Jane replied, "because I said no."

"You would have lost if you said yes. He's a lowlife. Best thing is to pretend nothing ever happened." She paused. "Did he discuss his artistic skills? From what I understand, that usually goes with the tour."

"Tour?"

"I've heard that when he's trying to score points, he talks about himself being the second coming of Willem de Kooning, then launches into his hand-painted necktie story. Once during the Christmas season, he sent a catalogue of his ties out to everyone here and kept a list of who made a purchase and who didn't." Carrie shook her head. "Everyone was afraid not to buy the stupid things."

"I never got a catalogue."

"All executives were spared." Carrie laughed. "Briggs is something else." She paused a moment. "And speaking of crazies, are you still seeing Twyla?"

Jane shook her head. "No, those sessions were getting too spooky."

"Couldn't be spookier than her discussing dark matter. Who the hell does she think she is, Vonda X from Galaxy 10?"

Jane thought a moment, then mentioned the hands across the windshield, the field, the farmhouse, and how she seemed to stay longer in each regression. "Actually, Twyla cut me off. She said it was getting too intense for her. She didn't understand why she couldn't bring me back when she wanted to."

"Well, for once she got it right. Paging Mensa."

"The thing is, the whole geography is starting to feel familiar. Before I belonged with the nuns and now I belong in that farmhouse. I need to be there."

"I love you, Jane, but you don't need a farmhouse and a meadow. What you need is an uber-passionate, fall-on-the-floor, runaway-train sexual encounter followed by a sack of Oreos and a half-gallon of ice cream that you don't have to share. Trust me on that one, baby."

Jane stared at Carrie and smiled.

"I think I'm giving you good advice. Staying away from Twyla is very, very smart. Very, very smart."

"I know," Jane said. "I agree."

It didn't matter anyway. She had another plan.

∞

That evening, Eric asked, "Where in Illinois did you live?"

"An outer suburb of Chicago—a place called St. Charles. Forty-five minutes or so from the city.

Eric smiled. "I know it well."

"How?" Jane asked.

"I did my residency at Richey Memorial in Elmhurst."

"That's amazing," Jane said. "I had my tonsils out in that hospital." She paused. "I don't remember the surgeon's name though. I was old for that type of operation. I was nineteen. It took me a long time to recover."

"At that age, it's more sophisticated surgery," Eric said.

"I didn't go back to college in Ohio because of it. I hurt for two months, and was incapacitated for three. I eventually finished up at the University of Illinois."

Eric nodded.

"And you completed medical school in Boston? Where was your undergraduate?"

"Right, med school in Boston. Undergraduate at Auburn," Eric said. He tapped his notepad with the end of his pen. "How are you doing otherwise, Jane?"

During the small talk, she had been considering the direction the evening's conversation should travel. Despite the loss of time in her last regression, she was so comfortable in the former life, she didn't want it intellectualized away.

Then there was the job offer from Briggs, which turned out to be a proposition as well—and, of course, Eric's sleek, beautiful wife was upsetting.

Which direction should she travel in? Certainly not the wife.

"How's Jimmy?"

Jane thought. "The same."

"Meaning?"

She sighed. "Meaning, Eric, how long can I delude myself? He's an alcoholic and I don't have much in common with him except the past." She paused. "I'm not happy."

"Because."

"Because I loved him once," Jane answered. "Now I don't even know him, or want to know him." She shook her head. "I thought I could try and make it work again, but it's not going to happen. And that's sad—all the time spent, all the false promise."

Eric nodded.

"I suppose I have to take some kind of action," Jane said. "But I don't know what." She looked at the psychiatrist. "Could we postpone this discussion for another time?"

"That'll be fine," Eric answered. He glanced at the clock on the wall. "How's the job?"

Calculating rapidly, Jane figured that this subject matter might be the safest to discuss, and perhaps, helpful, which was supposed to be the reason she was there in the first place. "I had an odd experience," she said.

"How so?"

Jane described her luncheon with Briggs, concluding with the president's contention that no new job existed.

Eric shook his head. "I'm frequently disappointed with the direction the business world has taken. It seems any type of offensive behavior can be justified as long as revenues aren't jeopardized." He glanced at his watch and clicked his pen shut. "Let's talk more about this in our next session."

Jane nodded.

"I think that meeting twice a week now is helping our progress."

"Agreed."

∞

Jane pulled into her driveway and clicked the remote to open the garage door. Ahead on the blacktop, in the headlights, a foreign object, small and lifelike, stood still. She stepped out of the car, leaving the engine running and the headlights on. In front of her was a squirrel's head that had been crushed with such force the remainder of the body was standing upright creating a tombstone to itself. Tiny streams of blood had trickled from the creature's head and dried, creating maroon circles on the blacktop.

Instead of being sickened by the sight, Jane knelt and studied the squirrel. Had it been oblivious as it crossed the driveway in a series of hesitant, intricate steps—a natural enchainment from *The Dying Swan*? Was its own death anticipated an instant before Jimmy kamikazied his car down the driveway? She paused. Did the squirrel in the last second of life, hearing the fury from afar, freeze, and summon the fire and steel forward?

Jane returned to the car, took a handkerchief from her purse, and walked back to the mangled creature. She lifted the squirrel, then placed it in the bushes beyond the blacktop, mentally marking the location so that she might return in the daylight and bury it.

Moments later, Jane eased the car into the garage and clicked the remote to close the door.

She recalled the arabesque position from *The Dying Swan* as one of the most beautiful, sensual poses in ballet. The dancer stood on one foot, arms outstretched, bending forward, with the other foot raised to form a ninety-degree angle, creating the longest and sleekest body line possible.

Jane had named DSRR's new lipstick *Arabesque* for its precision and sterile eroticism. She had fashioned an image for the advertising agency to recreate, one containing a ballerina with pale cheeks, dark eyes, crimson painted lips, and infinite beauty. The classic pose was frozen on stage in arabesque position surrounded by red roses thrown from male cast members in white ties.

She had crafted the vision for dreamers like herself—a brief escape, a staccato moment, before the ballerina pirouetted away, leaving only the bloodied head of a squirrel to accompany her into the night.

CHAPTER 17

Friday, after finishing for the day at DSRR, Jane took a cab to West Fourth Street and walked two blocks to "GET HIP-notized," a New Age store specializing in natural vitamins, organic food and alternate lifestyle publications. If Twyla wouldn't take her to the farm, she would devise her own method of transportation.

"I called earlier about the self-hypnosis kits," Jane said to the multi-pierced clerk behind the counter.

"Far aisle, down to the end, on the left. Let me know if you have any questions."

Jane walked to the back of the store and perused a section of self-hypnosis books covering hypnotic induction procedures.

She was only interested in achieving a depth of relaxation and comfort that would lead to the state she had attained with Twyla. She needed to continue the exploration. The pull was too strong; her need too great, even if she was unsure why.

Jane settled on a sealed package containing a book and recorded program by a Philadelphia PhD. The back-cover blurb explained that she could learn the procedures necessary for effective self-hypnosis.

Jane walked to the front of the store and placed the package on the counter.

"Ah, Robert Grassley," the young woman said. "He's good. I believe he's head of the psychology department at Cranford State, outside of Philadelphia."

"Terrific," Jane answered. She handed the clerk her credit card. "Do you have any books on regression therapy?"

"Regression therapy?" She gave Jane a quick glance. "We don't have anything on that. But hypnotism is real. I've seen it work."

"Firsthand?"

"Yep, every night before I go to sleep. I could tell you I used to weigh four hundred pounds, but that wouldn't be the truth. It's about simple stuff now. I think more positively—my life is easier." She handed Jane the receipt to sign. "You have any questions about hypnotism, feel free to give me a call. We're a resource for a lot of customers."

"Thanks," Jane said, sliding the receipt back across the counter. "I'll remember that."

∞

Outside, she was confronted by a homeless man, "Lady, you got a buck for a Vietnam vet?"

Jane gaped at the broken figure in stained fatigues standing in front of her, his outstretched grimy hand in her face.

"Just a buck, that's all I want. I don't want nothing more. I got arthritis and my friend died 'cause of Agent Orange, and I'm all messed up in the head, and the VA won't take me no more, but I don't want no more than a buck."

"Just a minute." Jane fumbled through her purse and locating a five-dollar bill, handed it to the man.

"That's five lady, I didn't ask for no fiver," he said, taking the money. "I ain't a charity case. I only asked for one, not five."

"I don't have a single bill," Jane answered. "Just keep the five."

"All right," the man said. "You got what you got. You get what you get. You get what you got and when you get it, you got it."

In spite of herself, Jane smiled.

The man eyed her, unsure, before offering a grin, his eyes momentarily tamed. Then his laughter started, stopped, paused, started, stopped, paused—a pattern uncomplicated in its simplicity, and comforting, like warm water sprinkling over her. She'd heard the cadence somewhere before. Jane touched his shoulder. "What's your name?"

"James. People call me Jimmy. And I promise I ain't going to drink this away," he said, holding up the five-dollar bill as he walked down the street. He stopped and turned. "But you, lady, I hate to tell you this, lady, but jes' like the rest of the world, you look wound up like you could use a drink. Know what I mean, huh?"

∞

Jimmy the Vietnam vet was right. Jane refilled a glass of wine and placed the bottle back in the refrigerator. She leaned against a line of kitchen cabinets. His laugh. Where had she heard it before?

Jane picked up the self-hypnosis kit and read the directions. Her first goal was to achieve deep and complete relaxation, but before that, Dr. Grassley suggested she decide upon a daily time when she would be able to practice the process. According to him, learning how to self-hypnotize was equivalent to mastering a musical instrument or discovering how to ride a bicycle—it took practice.

She glanced at her watch. It was early evening. She would never be able to self-hypnotize at work, or on the train, or anywhere outside the house. The only consistent free time frame in her day was when she slept. Jimmy was out every night, but she didn't want to risk the chance of him interfering, so instead of using their bedroom, she decided to lie on the rug in the narrow space between the bed and the wall of the guest room. Even if he went looking, he would never think to search there. And it was warm and quiet, and she knew the radiators in the room clinked, offering a gentle reminder of comfortable morning and evening sounds from her youth.

Jane also decided that after each session she would return to the master bedroom, so if Jimmy did turn up, nothing would seem out of place and she could maintain her secret.

Upstairs, she gathered a pillow, a down quilt, a flashlight, and earphones, then moved to the guest room and settled on the rug. She plumped the pillow beneath her head and pulling the quilt up to her neck, began the program.

Jane made a conscious decision to keep the cloud in the process. She wanted to see the fields and farm from afar, and then leisurely drift down to them as she had before.

She liked Robert Grassley's voice. It was calm and reassuring—interested—while at the same time progressing in a leisurely manner. He suggested that Jane recline in a comfortable position and attempt to relax. He recommended that she breathe deeply in and out, with each outward breath releasing more and more of the tension that was stored within her.

At first, she was unable to concentrate. She found herself on alert for the sound of the garage door opening, or a faraway cough, or footsteps in the hallway. But gradually she grew comfortable, first listening to the clinking radiators, and then focusing on Grassley. Her mind and body began to incrementally meld together into one life force, following the psychologist downward through the steps of hypnosis.

"One. Going deeper and deeper into relaxation, all the way to . . ."

Five seconds passed.

"Two. You are falling deeper and deeper still."

Grassley's voice became a monotone in the background. "Three. You are deeply relaxed."

Jane was nestled on the cloud. Grassley's voice was fading, becoming a distant reverberation drifting through the surrounding sky. From her position, she could see the vast country fields, and as she had learned to do, she clasped a piece of the cloud in her hand to use as a canopy, then rolled off into the bright blue sky surrounding her. She could hear her own breathing in her ears as she floated down, down, further down. By focusing her eyes, she could see the farmhouse bordering on the wide-open fields and rolling meadows. She knew it didn't matter if she landed next to the house or a mile away, she would find her way there. She felt such comfort and inner peace that her eyes brimmed with tears of joy that overflowed and rained down through the cornflower blue—shimmering diamonds sliding on satin. She was home, at last she was—

"Ah, ah, ah," Jane was panting as sweat slid off her forehead. One arm was around a man's neck while the other clutched his back. She could feel the waves of tension mounting around her breasts, and across her lower abdomen.

"I love you, Janey, I love you," the man said, his voice low and raspy.

The heated pace of her own breathing turned to gasps as she strained against him, pushed against him. She pulled him closer, tighter, running her fingers through his hair.

He pulled his head away. "Oh, God, Janey, oh God."

Uncontrollable waves raced through her, over and over, one on top of another—a power tide, grasping and releasing, then grasping once more. Her breath choked at the end of her throat and emerged as a protracted sigh while he shuddered, his head buried next to the side of her face.

Baby.

Their breathing rose and fell through the silence, first co-mingling, then drifting in different directions until her fingers slid through the perspiration on his neck, then again the dark hair on his head.

Baby. A baby in the air!

As her eyes wandered, she could see she was in the backseat of a car.

She couldn't see his face, but was unable to stop touching him.

"You're beautiful, Janey," he whispered, beginning to stir. "I love you."

"I love you too."

He didn't respond.

"I love you too," Jane repeated.

Nothing.

She sat up and flicked the flashlight's beams around the dark corners of the guest room.

She was alone. The program had automatically ended.

Where was he? She was filled with emptiness. Where was he? She glanced at her watch. It was only 9:30. She rose unsteadily to her feet.

Minutes later as Jane stood at the living room window stirring a cup of tea, she stared outside at the moon crater shadows—the street lights filtering through the trees.

What happened?

Who was he?

He was already in her blood.

And she felt like she'd had sex.

How did that happen?

Who was he?

She trembled.

She could still taste him.

She thought of a child.

Who was he? Where was he?

Jane stood motionless attempting to reconstruct the scene.

Where was he?

She walked into the kitchen and leaned against the counter, bewildered. But for the first time she could remember, the first time she could ever recall, Jane was not considering everything lost, but instead . . . what could be gained.

A brief smile crossed her lips.

CHAPTER 18

Jane hadn't seen much of Briggs in the days since their luncheon and was uncertain if that was good or bad. She couldn't imagine that she would suffer professional repercussions due to his failed overture, but she understood enough about corporate America to know there were no honest heroes in the ranks, that anything was possible. Brainchildren attired in Brooks Brothers' finery, with MBAs from Harvard, BMWs from the Hamptons, and CYA memos flying from their desks, thought nothing of lying to her face as a matter of course if they could get away with it. It was a daily occurrence and she had grown used to it, convinced that the liars were desperately insecure, and anxious that they would be devoured by their exorbitant life styles if they dared slow down, looked over their shoulders, or spoke the truth.

But Briggs was president, known to be immensely wealthy, and she had been unable to figure him out, other than his shadow reputation as a predator. She had never suspected him of having much in the way of character, and her only surprise was that he had shown a sexual interest in her. She still was uncertain if the job he had offered was genuine or manufactured for the occasion.

Jane sat behind her desk and stared at the notes spread in front of her. Her treatment for the *Arabesque* campaign was falling into place. The advertising agency creative gurus had seized her concept imagery almost exactly, and she was in the process of overseeing the final stages of copy and media analysis.

She had called Tom Turner at Barlow, Blake, and Turner, and told him that she had heard rumors that they were keeping track of her menstrual cycle at the ad agency, then using those guidelines to determine when and how to deal with her. Although Turner vehemently denied the allegation, she knew it was true. One of the drones at the agency told Carrie, Carrie told her, and she relayed the information back to Turner. She noticed she was now getting calls every day. In the past, communications had been light during her indisposed days, though it took Carrie's revelation to put the equation together.

She felt the *Arabesque* campaign was going to be a monster success. It had a classier sense to it, with a broader appeal, in direct contradiction to the party-girl spirit of *Scarlett!*. Jane felt strong and at the top of her game. She knew she was making a fortune for the company and was confident that the board cared about little else.

But then there was the hypnosis, the other side of the life she was leading. She paused. Who was he? His memory was haunting. Where was he?

"Jane, have you got a second?" Carrie stood in the doorway.

"I do," Jane answered. "Come in."

Carrie walked inside the office and closed the door behind her.

"Sit." Jane motioned to the chair in front of her desk.

Carrie sat down and crossed one leg over the other. "Did you know Briggs was bringing in The Grey Street Group to evaluate the marketing department?"

"What are you talking about, Carrie?"

"The Grey Street Group. You know who they are— hatchet men who come in, analyze everyone's position, and write an evaluation indicating overlapping jobs, then recommend that thirty percent of the workforce be eliminated for the sake of cost-efficiencies. They're a bunch of hacks whose mission is to do the dirty work for the big shots."

"I know them well and I know how they operate."

"How come you didn't know about this?" Carrie asked.

"That would appear to be the question," Jane answered. "How did you find out?"

"From Patty," she answered. "You know we're friends and she tells me the inside info on what Briggs is doing."

"And you're sure?"

Carrie nodded. "Unless Patty was lying, and she has no reason to. We're close."

Jane nodded, picked up the phone and pressed three buttons. "Patty, Jane McBride here. Is he in?" She sat motionless, the phone to her ear. "Sure. Would you ask John if I could stop up?" Jane covered the receiver with her hand. "He's in a meeting. Patty's checking." She waited. "Yes? Very good, I'll be there in twenty minutes."

She placed the phone in the cradle and sat back in the chair. "Not good," she said at last.

"I bet it has something to do with your lunch where he tried to get a little springboard action going, the moron," Carrie said.

"You haven't told anyone about that, correct?" Jane eyed Carrie.

"Of course not. I told you I wouldn't," Carrie answered.

"Because something like that getting around would give him ammunition and cause major problems for me. With his ego, I don't think Briggs could handle the rejection becoming public knowledge. And he would know who did the talking."

"I think he's trying to get back at you for refusing him. That's what's going on here." Carrie leaned forward. "You can take that to the bank, pal, right to the friggin' bank."

∞

"Come in, Jane," Briggs said, moving from behind his desk and pointing to the sofa. He strode across the office and closed the door. "I love Patty," he said, his voice a contrived whisper, "but sometimes I suspect she hears more than she should." He walked back across the room, sat behind the desk and clasped his hands behind his neck. "Sit, sit. So, what's on your mind, Miss Marketing Guru?"

Jane forced a smile of appreciation for the compliment. "A couple of things, John. First, we never talked about our luncheon last week. I wanted to confirm that we were both in the same place with the situation being resolved."

"I apologized then, and I apologize now, Jane. It was completely inappropriate on my part." He brought his hands down from behind his neck and fiddled with one of his cuff links while eying her.

"I know you mentioned a promotion," Jane said, "and we haven't talked since, so I—"

"Ah, yes, the promotion. I'm glad you brought it up, Jane." He stopped toying with his cuff link and interlaced his fingers in front of him on the desk. "We have a board meeting next week and I'm going to float the idea of your executive vice presidency. As I mentioned, with our profits on track, I'm certain I'll have no issues to contend with." He smiled and paused several seconds. "Is that it?"

"Just that I appreciate everything you're doing for me, John."

"Only because you're the gold standard, Jane." He cleared his throat. "So I guess we've solved the problems of the world in," Briggs glanced at his Piaget watch, "five minutes."

"Just one other question, John," Jane said. She detected the slightest of frowns creep across Briggs' forehead before quickly disappearing. "I've heard rumors that my department is going to be evaluated by The Grey Street Group. Is there any truth to that?"

Briggs brushed the air in front of him as if swatting at a mosquito. "Truth, yes, but relevance to you, no. I'd planned to mention it, but have been inundated with meetings. The internal memo will be out by the end of day." He stood and leaned against the front of his desk. "Pure formality, Jane. A new board directive insists that we evaluate our personnel system annually to assure efficiency. You know, basic overview parameters—they want to be certain there's no redundancy. This year it's your group, next year it will be someone else."

"I've never heard of Grey Street being associated with DSRR before, John. Is this a new initiative?"

"Indeed it is. We've got to be current, Jane, and if the board thinks The Grey Street Group is the future, who am I to argue?" He smiled. "But, again, I must reaffirm this has nothing to do with your group or its competence. The board simply needs to be certain the company is on the cutting edge of corporate thinking." He shrugged. "Just another step in that process."

Jane wanted to ask more questions, like how her group was selected from the entire division, but she could see that Briggs was reaching the edge of his charm quota. "I appreciate your time and your candor, John," she said, standing.

"As always, my pleasure, Jane," Briggs replied, leading her to the door. "You know what I think of you."

∞

"Cutting edge of corporate thinking, my Aunt Gina's big, fat, Italian bazoo."

"Bazoo?"

"Rear end," Carrie said from a chair in Jane's office. Her nostrils flared. "The guy has too much money, too much power, and too much time on his hands."

"I agree," Jane answered.

"So what are you going to do?"

"There's nothing to do," Jane answered, "except continue our jobs and wait to see how it all plays out. Maybe he's sincere."

"Maybe Coco Chanel played for the Los Angeles Lakers."

Jane shook her head. "I know."

"What about the executive vice president deal he was offering you?"

"Just like with The Grey Street Group, I'll have to wait and see what happens."

"Briggs is bad news—very, very, very bad news," Carrie stated.

Jane nodded. "No doubt," she said at last.

CHAPTER 19

Jane thumbed through a three-year-old issue of *National Geographic* as she sat in Eric Alford's waiting room Tuesday night. She was considering discussing her Friday night self-achieved hypnosis. Though she had mentioned regression therapy to Eric before, and he had dismissed the idea, her latest episode with a stranger in the car's backseat seemed so real that she was elated . . . but also concerned.

What was happening to her?

What if she slipped into a regression and never returned?

But that was impossible—she was alive, and only being hypnotized—something people had been doing for centuries. She would have to be in a coma, or dead, not to come back, and she was neither.

Jane brushed her concerns aside. She loved what she was doing, reliving her lives by traveling the hypnosis path. She knew that being a Sister of God in a former life had challenged her with purpose, renewing the religious vigor of her youth. The open farm fields appealed to her vision of how an ideal life should be spent, and the silver-haired man with rifle in hand, she conceded, could be the father figure she had never known.

Then there was the sex, the passionate sex with a stranger in the backseat of an unknown car.

Twyla claimed the purpose of regression therapy was to learn about oneself through the examination of past lives, and Jane was doing that. What she had not been prepared for was how real the past lives had become.

She thought about the sex again. She couldn't stop thinking about the sex. The passion in the backseat of the car seemed as genuine as the *National Geographic* in her hand, and not only had she reveled in it, for the first time in her life she understood lust.

But the sexual episode hadn't happened—how could she want more of what never occurred? It made no sense.

∞

"It makes perfect sense," Eric said after listening briefly to Jane's abridged, nonsexual version of the regression. "Hypnotism can surely be tricky because there are degrees of depth that can be achieved, along with varying amounts of time required to be considered 'under.' Thoughts and ideas can seem very real. The important thing is to recognize that you never lose contact with the hypnotist even if that hypnotist is yourself."

"When I was hypnotized by the . . . " Jane hesitated, then continued, "by the regression therapist, she said I was unreachable for two hours."

Eric smiled. "Jane, you were working with an unlicensed, uneducated individual who was claiming to be legitimate. The very nature of what she was professing to do raises an immediate red flag, not just in psychiatric circles, but I'm certain in a good portion of the educated community. With no disrespect intended for you, the notion of regression therapy is—how can I say it—far-fetched."

Jane clenched then unclenched her fingers on her lap. "You must think I'm a total fool."

"No, as a matter of fact, I think you're very bright and interesting. I admire you and your accomplishments."

Jane could see that he was serious. "Except?" she asked.

"No except. You're a human being like the next person down the line. Nobody's perfect. No one makes all the correct decisions." Eric thought for a minute. "But I am curious why someone with your education and capabilities would be involved in an unproven activity such as regression therapy."

Jane squirmed. How long had she been attracted to Eric? Whenever she allowed herself to feel that way, it embarrassed her to look at him. "I'm not sure," she said.

"Sometimes when we're having problems in our existing lives, we look for escape mechanisms," Eric said. "Perhaps it's as simple as that."

"It started off just as something unconventional to try, and now I'm addicted," Jane answered.

"I can understand that," Eric replied. "You're consistently in a state of semi-crisis with your husband, and the other significant part of your life, your job, is increasingly stressful." He hesitated. "Tell me though, what fascinates you about past-life regression?"

Jane considered for a moment. "I seem to belong back in those lives," she answered. "Maybe not all of them, but a couple—no, one specifically, has a familiarity that makes me want to get closer."

"How so?"

"I don't know, Eric. It feels right. Today I'm unhappy, uneasy, like I'm on pins and needles. Everything is a little bit off." Jane thought for a moment. "But with the regressions, it's a natural, comfortable fit. I don't know exactly. I just belong there."

Eric stared for several seconds. "Well, Jane, I think we should continue to work on today's life. After all, that's the one you live."

Jane nodded. "I know. This all sounds kind of ridiculous, doesn't it?"

"I believe you're under a lot of pressure, some self-imposed, some not. My feeling is that we should try and relieve some of it. The more we explore, the more solutions we'll come across." He tapped his pen against the pad in his hand. "What do you think?"

"You're right, of course. But what about this self-hypnosis I'm doing—this whole regression thing? Should I continue?"

"Do you want to?"

Jane again contemplated the past lives she had visited. "Yes."

Eric shifted in his chair. "Then there's no reason for you not to, Jane. The part of your self-hypnosis you refer to as regression, suggests you're dealing with repressed feelings and memories—but there's nothing wrong with that. It certainly won't be detrimental in any way, and may uncover some emotions that will help us in our sessions. And you'll still maintain the same kind of psychological protective devices during the self-hypnosis process that you have any other time." Eric considered his statement. "I guess what I'm saying is that you wouldn't do anything in self-hypnosis that you wouldn't ordinarily do."

"Would I lose contact by doing self-hypnosis?" Jane asked.

"With who?"

"Myself. Would I lose contact with myself?"

Eric smiled. "Nope. It's not that easy, as much as a lot of people would like to go that route. You may fall asleep. That happens occasionally."

"Could I ever, you know, not wake up?"

"Zero chance. I can assure you of that. Pulling out of a hypnotic state is never a problem, and I mean *never*. Again, you might fall asleep, but you'll wake up just like you always do."

"That's reassuring."

"Bottom line, Jane," Eric said, "if self-hypnosis is something that relaxes you, do it. It's completely safe. If it becomes uncomfortable, stop. You know best. Either way works."

Jane nodded. "Okay."

"Good." Eric studied her for several moments, then began slowly. "You know, you've been coming here twice a week for a while now. After that many sessions, I usually have a pretty good sense about what's going on with an individual, but I'm not so sure with you." He thought for a few seconds. "You seem to accept an abusive, alcoholic husband, yet in your professional life you're quite a different person—driven, on target, take charge." He leaned back in his chair. "I don't understand the dichotomy."

Jane didn't respond.

"Do you?"

"Eric, we've talked about this before," Jane answered. "Jimmy has been a big drinker as long as I've known him. I don't care."

Eric hesitated before answering, "Okay, if you say so. Then just give me an overview of what you're about from your own perspective, Jane. I need to know what I'm missing."

"Missing?" Jane answered. "I don't know that you're missing anything. I think I've been very candid with you."

"Okay. But I'm still uncertain about what goes on inside Jane McBride." He clicked the pen in his hand. "What do you think?"

Jane looked at Eric, then stared away, preoccupied with a strange, fleeting vision of a pastel backyard, a summer day, champagne, a lone candle. A distant smile touched her lips. It was a vision she vaguely recognized. She turned her attention back to the psychiatrist. "What do you want to do, Eric, excavate my heart?" she asked.

He leaned forward in his chair. "Yes. That's exactly what I want to do."

Jane nodded. "It's impossible."

"What would I find in your heart, Jane?"

Tears touched her eyes as she turned away. "You would

find air. Emptiness and air," she answered slowly.

"Nothing else?" Eric asked.

"Nothing else," Jane replied.

"Is that why Jimmy doesn't matter?"

"It's why nobody matters."

"Not even you?"

"That's right. Not even me."

"Then why are you here?" Eric asked.

Jane focused on the psychiatrist. "I don't know," she said at last, her voice low and guarded. "I don't know."

Chapter 20

Jane thought of a pale green, Royal Copenhagen porcelain candy dish. Six inches across, gold around the lip, numbered, initialed, and stamped on the bottom with the traditional Royal Copenhagen blue, it hung in the forefront of her mind—a green-cheese moon, alone, unencumbered, until it flipped in the air and shattered into pieces on a cement floor.

"What?" Jane stared at the preliminary copy.

"What do you think?" Carrie asked.

"Hold on, my mind was wandering." Jane was in Carrie's office, attempting to focus on the *Arabesque* copy written for the twenty-one to twenty-eight demographic. No matter how clever and convincing the Barlow, Blake, and Turner copywriters were, she knew that she'd be very lucky to capture significant market share in the first year.

Jane concentrated and reread the words. "Good, not great," she said to Carrie as she straightened up. "Have you got any input?"

"It needs something," Carrie said. "Our little ballet dancer can be beautiful and stand-offish, but we've got to generate a little sexual tension. You know, like no one can get close to her, but then she hooks up in the hallway with one of the producers."

"Now there's a concept," Jane said. "Why don't we try and see if we can incorporate that in the final creative?"

"Briggs would love it, the pervert." Carrie laughed. "Anyway, we've got to do something to jazz up the copy, otherwise we die on the vine."

"Yup," Jane answered. "Why don't you tweak it and then bring it by around noon. We can get a bite to eat if you're free."

"Okay. I think it's just a word change here and there to get the effect we want. We need to imply, not state."

"Strongly imply," Jane said. "See what you can do, Carrie, and don't be afraid to call the ad agency if you need some help. That's what we pay them all that money for. See you later"

As she neared her office, Jane noticed a young woman in a blue pinstripe suit sitting in the waiting area. She stood as Jane approached. "Ms. McBride?"

"Yes?" Jane answered.

"I'm Lauren Fritz." She held out her hand. "I'm with The Grey Street Group."

Jane returned the handshake, fully conscious of the business-school, conservative hairstyle and firm, practiced grip. "Yes, Lauren, what can I do for you?"

"I wonder if I could have a few words?"

Jane glanced at her watch. "Just a few, I have a meeting in ten minutes."

"That's fine," Lauren assured her.

"Okay then, come." Jane led the way into her office. "But I've got my stopwatch going." She sat behind her desk and gestured for the young woman to take a chair opposite her.

Jane had her figured out before she stood up in the waiting area—Lauren Fritz, the corporate clone whose studied, controlled bedside manner reeked of snake oil and appetite. Combined with a smile practiced to achieve the right combination of business acumen and overt friendliness, Jane sensed this Grey Street robot would only be able to claw her way to middle-management at best, despite her high-strung ambition. "What can I do for you, Lauren?"

"As John Briggs has told you," Lauren said, crossing one leg over the other, the steel in her eyes now unconcealed, "The Grey Street Group has been retained to evaluate the efficiencies of the DSRR marketing department." She launched the practiced smile again, then continued, "I wanted to introduce myself and at the same time make you aware of our strategic partnering efforts on your behalf."

"My behalf?" Jane frowned. "Tell me what you're going to accomplish for the company."

Lauren began a canned background on The Grey Street Group, segueing into the synergy concept that "she was certain would appear" once the process began. "Our hope," she continued, "is to discover ways to grow your business while implementing fewer resources. Of course, that—"

"Let's get to the point, Lauren," Jane said, glancing at her watch. "I believe your group works on a contingency basis, meaning you get a percentage of the total annual savings you bring to the company." She stared across her desk. "Is that pretty close?"

"No, no," Lauren insisted, holding up her hand, "there's much more to it than that. This is about streamlined growth, yes, but it's also about changing the dynamics, refreshing the existing paradigm."

Jane had figured correctly that Lauren would use the business-school buzz word "paradigm" within five minutes of their meeting, even though it was now almost extinct. "Gotcha," she said. "What do you want from me?"

"Our people will be working with your team to better understand the processes involved in the marketing department. I wanted to make sure you understood the Grey Street protocol."

"I do," Jane said. "But before you begin, I'd like your proposal on my desk—who's working with whom, specific goals to be achieved, and a time frame for completion. After

I look at it, I'll sit with you and we'll discuss any areas that I think need to be revised. Now, if you'll excuse me." Jane rose from her chair.

Lauren stood. "We've already gotten approval from John Briggs. I wasn't aware of the need for a formal proposal."

"If you're going to involve my people, Lauren, I have to know how much time you're going to take from their work. As you know, we're running a business here and time is a precious commodity."

"Understood," Lauren answered, regrouping, the practiced smile comfortably in place. "I'll be sure to have a time assessment flowchart available within twenty-four hours." She extended her hand just as Jane turned away.

"Good," Jane said over her shoulder. "It was nice to meet you."

∞

"That better?" Carrie asked.

Jane completed the review of the *Arabesque* copy and pushed it across the table, then picked up her iced tea. "Good," she said. "You tweaked it just enough. I like the tone better—there's a subtle undercurrent of sexuality."

"Do I get a raise?" Carrie asked while she pushed her empty spinach salad plate to the side.

"As soon as I get one," Jane answered.

"Any more feedback from Briggs?" Carrie asked.

"Nada. But the female cobra from Grey Street slithered by my office after I left you this morning.

"What did she want?"

"A courtesy call to build bridges she's intent on knocking down. She wanted to let me know she would be evaluating our department. At Grey Street, they're all alike. I've heard too many horror stories." Jane sipped her iced tea. "Are you having dessert?"

"Nope." Carrie touched her stomach. "Not today. Got to diet. When I look down, I can't see my toes, which is pretty damn depressing. Would you like to have sex with someone who can't see their toes?"

"Probably not," Jane replied, a smile crossing her face.

The waiter appeared at the table "Dessert, ladies?".

"Would you like to have sex with someone who can't see their toes?" Carrie asked.

The waiter shrugged, his face noncommittal.

"Very smart non-answer," Carrie said. "Very, very smart."

The waiter grinned. "Okay, so I see you here at Ruocchio's often enough. You're good customers." He thought for a second. "Would you be willing to request me as your waiter each time you're here? I like to have my regulars—it helps with job security." He pointed at his name badge.

"Thank you, James," Carrie said, nodding in Jane's direction. "If my boss agrees, we'll ask for you all the time."

Jane watched James abruptly twist his head at an awkward angle, reacting to the clatter of a plate being dropped on a tile floor.

Suddenly she was on the verge of a panic attack and didn't know why. Out of nowhere, fear was raging inside her, devouring anything rational in its path. Her heart pounded and she began to hyperventilate.

Carrie leaned in toward the center of the table, closer. "Jane, are you all right?

Jane's perspective was changing, distorting. She could see Carrie bending toward her from across the table, and watched as her lips enunciated words, but all she heard was garbled gibberish.

"Jane, are you all right?" Her voice burst through the underbrush, then spiraled away again. As if superimposed on ocean waves, Carrie's face began to lose shape, her eyes staring, then looking away, staring, looking away, rippling, rippling.

Jane stood, grabbed her purse and left the restaurant.

She dodged two taxis crossing the street, barely noticing their blaring horns, then rushed into the DSRR building, and waving to the security guard, charged the bank of elevators. She pressed the button, springing a door open and once inside, repeatedly hit the close button with her thumb until the doors slid together.

She stood alone in the corner, her arms spread, her hands touching the walls for balance as the elevator flew up to the fourth floor. The doors opened and Jane rushed past the receptionist. Once inside her office, she closed the door.

Was she losing her mind? She took several deep breaths.

What had happened back there?

Jane knew she was emotionally beaten up, and Eric had emphasized that she was under significant pressure between her job and her relationship with Jimmy. Yet her mind had never played tricks on her like that before. She'd heard Carrie's words, then she hadn't, and for no reason, her friend's face warped right in front of her.

Her mind was racing, but as she continued to deep breathe, Jane began to reel herself in. Just forget about it, she thought. Forget about it.

Eric had told her that extended stress could distort awareness.

What she was experiencing was probably that simple.

Jane calmed as rationality flooded back.

She picked up a mirror from her desk drawer along with a shade of *Scarlett!*. After examining her face, she retouched her lipstick, then tucked both back into the drawer.

Moments later, someone knocked.

"Come in."

"Are you all right?" Carrie asked. "What happened?"

"A lot of pressure, Carrie. I'm feeling a lot of it." Jane paused and walked to the window. She stared down at the street, then turned. "And something else—I hate to admit it, but I'm still doing this regression thing."

"I thought Twyla cut you off."

"I'm self-hypnotizing. And now I'm making love to someone I'm crazy about."

"Here in the office? Come on. There's no one around here hot enough to waste a calorie of energy on, much less a hundred. They're all friggin' centaurs."

"No, someone in the regression."

"Someone in the regression? Really?" Carrie studied Jane, then spoke cautiously. "Did you ever think this job isn't worth it?"

"Not until now."

"Jane, you are totally stressing out. That's what's going on here. We both know how bogus this regression thing is. What are you thinking? You're not screwing a guy in some past life." She eyed Jane. "Don't let Briggs or this phony from Grey Street get the best of you. You can eat that witch for lunch. And bringing her on board has got to be one of the reasons for all your anxiety."

Jane nodded.

"Look," Carrie interrupted, "if she gets too pushy, I'll slap her around myself. I don't care. What's a job anyway?"

"I appreciate your concern, but I know you're kidding."

"Of course, I'm kidding," Carrie said. "Sort of."

∞

At 3:15 in the morning, Jane suddenly sat up in bed, the sheets held to her neck. She'd almost forgotten what it was like to wear his ring and feel his fingertips pressed against hers.

Chapter 21

"Jane, how are you? I missed you Thursday night."

Jane glanced up from the Sunday newspaper spread on the counter in the Andover coffee shop. "Hi, Eric." She was surprised, then immediately dismayed with her attire—sweat clothes and Nike's.

"Looks like you've been exercising," Eric said.

"Yes, all the way from the car to the front door." She smiled. "I dress this way sometimes on Sunday—you know, to get the city out of my system."

"Mind if I join you for a minute?" he asked.

"No, please do," Jane answered, surprised. She folded the newspaper.

"Jen," Eric said, summoning the girl behind the counter, "a cup of coffee for me, please." He looked at Jane. "How about a refill?"

"I'm good."

"Why don't we adjourn to a booth?" Eric asked after picking up his coffee mug.

Jane nodded. "Fine." She lifted the newspaper and mug, then followed Eric to the corner of the restaurant.

"I apologize," he said, settling on one side of the table, "if this is not the most professional of circumstances. I hope you don't feel I'm intruding or crossing a boundary by being too informal."

"Not at all," Jane answered, sitting opposite him. "It's a small, friendly town. As a matter of fact, I saw you in here a couple of weeks ago with a woman I didn't recognize. You were buying a paper."

"The only person it might have been would be my niece." He smiled. "Tall, dark hair?"

"Yes, I think so," Jane said, pleased with the unanticipated information.

"Aubrey. She's in medical school in the city. She comes up to stay every once in a while to get away. She's from Mississippi, but has a boyfriend here." He sipped his coffee. "She's great company. It's difficult when she visits, then leaves."

"Oh."

Eric leaned back. "Jane, when you canceled Thursday night, I was disappointed because I thought we were making substantial progress." His expression was thoughtful. "I don't mean to make judgments, but sometimes when one gets close to a sensitive area, the tendency is to go in the other direction, to run away, if you will—sometimes forever." He hesitated. "Is that a possibility? I've just been wondering if there's any correlation between the progress I believe we're making and your cancellation."

"I wasn't feeling well." She hesitated. "Another thing too, I've been trying to self-hypnotize again and can't make it work. It's been like that for a while now."

Eric nodded. "That means you're not comfortable with it."

"It's safe, right?"

"Yes, of course. You'll only go as far as your mind will take you."

"So my mind is saying, 'Don't hypnotize.' Is that it?" Jane asked. It made no sense—she was so anxious to return.

"A good possibility, or sometimes the mind is not in a

receptive mode," Eric replied. "If you're interested, I could hypnotize you in my office, although we should have a reasonable justification for doing it."

Jane knew she wasn't ready for that. "I'd have to think about it," she said.

"That'll be fine," Eric said, picking up his cup and finishing the coffee. "I won't keep you, Jane. I was going to call, but I thought as long as I ran into you here, I might as well touch base." He began to rise.

"Could I just say one thing, Eric?"

"Of course." He slid back into the booth.

"I think I figured out why I've stayed with Jimmy all these years." Jane looked at the psychiatrist, then at her hands in front of her on the Formica.

Eric nodded.

She paused. "I feel sorry for him."

"How so?"

"I'm not sure. I just think he's had a tough life, and I cared about him once, so now I feel sorry for him. We've been together a long time and I'm not totally devoid of compassion."

"Feeling sorry for someone is surely not love, although it can be a part of it," Eric answered. "I think the question you might want to consider is whether feeling sorry for Jimmy is reason enough to continue your present relationship with him." Eric stared at Jane. "Food for thought anyway."

Jane nodded. "I can do that."

"All we have is time, Jane," he said, rising again, picking up his mug. "I'll see you Tuesday night."

∞

Sunday afternoon, and as usual, Jimmy wasn't home. It occurred to Jane that self-hypnosis didn't have to be attempted only at night. She had chosen that time because of her work schedule, but on weekends the empty hours engulfed her.

She climbed the stairs and walked to the guest room. The pillow, quilt and earphones were just as she had left them.

Jane studied the rays of sun slipping in through the windows—light beams capturing the motes of dust, tiny tropical fish held prisoner in tanks, bubbles in champagne, aliens being pulled to the Mother Ship—all the same. Everyone, everything, in its own vacuum, bursting with its own agenda. Occasionally, the circles intersected, but did it matter?

She recalled being in the backseat of the car just days before, and her fingers running along the back of the man on top of her. She had felt the madness of passion. She could not pull him far enough inside her, or tire of the taste of his perspiration. She wanted to hold him, enfold him, consume him.

She had been in someone else's body, yet the physical sensations seemed to remain.

She had to find him again.

Jane lay back, started the instructions, and listened to Robert Grassley's relaxed monotone.

Suddenly, she was on an oiled slide, sweeping through a black passage before being fired from a circus canon into the cornflower blue. She soared for miles then skidded to a stop atop the white cloud. Digging with her hands straight through to the bottom, she stared down at the vast, rural countryside. Far to the east, was a blotch of dark city towers, a grove of diseased trees perched on the horizon.

The breeze pushed her hair across her forehead and Jane recognized the first hint of calm and joy infiltrating her. She seized a piece of the cloud and casually rolled off into the sky, and with closed eyes, willed herself to go wherever the wind might lead.

Her eyes blinked open and she was in a simple cotton dress, barefoot, and sitting on the steps of the farmhouse. She glanced up at the sky, then at the trees. I'm here now, she thought. I'm here now.

In the background she heard the sound of a motorcycle echoing away in the distance. Somehow she knew the rider was the same man who had made love to her in the backseat of the car. She had just missed him!

The porch was gray with knotholes peeking upward, exposing the ground beneath. Jane held her breath and listened.

Nothing.

I'm here now, she thought. I'm here now. My name is Jane McBride and I'm here now, but I'm not totally in control. She was on a tour, looking through eyes from a skull that was not her own, touching with hands belonging to someone else, walking with foreign legs.

How did she get here? She was Jane McBride. Why was she here?

Rising to her feet, she moved to the screen door and looked inside. Gray shadows hung in the corners of the room. She tapped on the door and heard the sound echo through the house.

No response.

Jane twisted the knob and pulled the door open, causing the rusted springs to screech as she stepped inside. Her eyes gradually adjusted to the dimness and she could make out two chairs, a sofa, and a fireplace, with a corridor leading from each end of the room. The country smell was everywhere—wind-soft freshness, cedar mixed with pine. A gentle breeze toyed with the chintz curtains, lifting them forward, relaxing them back. She saw a framed photograph sitting on the fireplace mantle.

"Hello."

No response.

She walked cautiously to the picture and looked at a soldier in uniform, his arm around the tiny waist of a pretty woman in a suit with accented shoulders. Both were laughing amidst a celebration in the center of a crowded city street.

She moved to the far end of the room, then peeked into the kitchen. She heard the faint hum of the refrigerator. On the counter was a loaf of bread, the trademark Sunbeam girl with blonde hair piled on her head, gazing back at her from the wrapper. Against the wall, opposite the refrigerator and beneath a window, was a wooden table with two chairs, one facing the other. Another chair stood in the corner. The appliances were timeworn— she hadn't seen a non-defrosting refrigerator in years—and pine cabinets with black enameled hardware sat above a gray linoleum floor.

"Anyone here?" she called.

Jane studied the kitchen so that she would be able to mentally retrace the interior, then moved back across the living room and entered a corridor with a room at each end—a bathroom situated between the two.

All three doors were open.

The bedroom at the back of the house contained a double bed, with a chenille spread, a bedside table, and a chest of drawers. None of the furniture matched. The bathroom was tiny and pink with a combination shower-tub, toilet and sink. Several steps down the hallway, she peeked into the front bedroom. Like the rest of the house, the room was patchwork. A single bed, its head against the wall, was covered with a handmade quilt. On the far wall was a framed black-and-white poster of a tree, and over the head of the bed was a familiar wooden crucifix, the Holy Savior grimacing in pain. Next to the door was a dresser with a small mirror over it.

Jane moved to the bureau, ran her fingers across the grainy wood, then raised her eyes to the mirror.

She stared in disbelief.

She was in her own body, but her face was years younger! Long strands of auburn hair touched her shoulders and ran down her back.

She had forgotten she was once so attractive.

And she knew she should be frightened with what was happening, but instead, she was fascinated, and grateful—grateful that she was trapped in the wonderful snapshot of time.

Then concern roared back.

What was happening to her?

How was she even in the farmhouse?

Slowly looking past herself, she saw the tortured face of Jesus Christ gazing at her from the cross on the wall. His agony made her uncomfortable. She had seen it somewhere before. She understood the suffering.

Jane retreated from the bedroom and walked back outside to the front porch. Instead of sitting on the steps, she moved to the rocking chair. Rocking slowly, easily, was familiar. She had done it before.

She was still scared.

A cawing crow winged past an overhead telephone line.

The motorcycle she had heard—where was it headed? Jane tucked her legs up under her. She thought she recognized the scent of lilacs next to the porch. And she knew she had lived there. The last bedroom had been hers. The other belonged to Russ and Marie. That was right, Russ and Marie. How did she know that?

Who were they?

It didn't matter. She was content to be rocking backward and forward.

"You are going to return to your normal consciousness."

Jane continued to rock.

"You are ready to resume your daily activity. You are now ready to exit this state of hypnosis."

The rocker was beginning to disintegrate beneath her.

"One," Grassley said. "Begin to think about returning to your normal consciousness."

Jane could sense the front porch fading.

"Two. Prepare to return to your normal self. When I say three, you will have returned, fully refreshed and comfortable. Three."

Jane opened her eyes.

"You are awake and refreshed."

Grassley had brought her back.

"You are awake and refreshed," he repeated.

Jane was still relaxed.

She was beginning to understand the triumph of illuminating her own dark matter.

∞

Hours later, she slipped into her sheepskin coat, and, bracing herself against the cold, stood on the back deck of the house watching the silent parade of jets' lights, miles away, as they vectored across the black sky toward La Guardia Airport.

Dust motes in a sunbeam—bubbles in champagne. No difference. She was certain.

CHAPTER 22

"Oh Sacred Leader, it's Monday morning." Carrie's head peeked around the door to the office entrance. "It's time to go meet all the wonderful people from Barlow, Blake, and Turner. As you prefer, they are all quaking in their boots at the prospect of disapproval from you."

"Good," Jane said, standing. "Quaking expedites creativity."

"Anything you say," Carrie responded. "How was your weekend?"

"Interesting. I should tell you about it when we have some time."

"Good," Carrie said, following Jane down the hallway. "I had nothing to do. Howard was working the entire two days for a change. You don't think he's trying to avoid me, do you?"

"Some folks are just workaholics," Jane answered.

"Or workaholics to escape from their wives," Carrie added, opening the door to the conference room.

Four men and three women were standing in the room, coffee cups in their hands. When Jane entered, the group hushed and moved to their chairs scattered around the teak conference table. Carrie closed the door.

Gene Dyson, the ad agency's creative director, was already at the table, his wheelchair parked and locked in place. Everyone was dressed in a suit, except for Gene who wore Harley-Davidson attire—boots, leather, and tinted glasses. Jane let the sophomoric behavior pass for two reasons—he was a brilliant creative mind, and he had stepped on a land mine during some generic jungle patrol in Vietnam and lost both legs, one above the knee.

"Good morning, everyone," Jane said, placing her notes in a stack in front of her at the head of the table. "Everyone had a good weekend, I hope."

There was a flurry of nods and mumbled assents.

"Good," Jane answered. "I would like—"

The conference room door opened and Lauren Fritz entered, notebook in hand. "Excuse me everyone, I was meeting with John Briggs and we lost track of the time."

"Lauren, please close the door behind you," Jane said. "This is Lauren Fritz," she added, addressing the table, "who will be sitting in on the meeting this morning. Lauren is with The Grey Street Group. They're currently working on some projects here at DSRR."

Len Stein, the agency account supervisor, turned to Jane. "I trust that the agency's confidentiality agreement applies to everyone in the room."

"No worries," Jane replied, watching the pulse rate in Len's neck. He wasn't nearly as calm as he appeared. "That's not a problem, is it, Lauren?"

"Absolutely not," Lauren answered, settling into a chair at the back of the room as she opened a notebook. "Everything is proprietary."

Jane nodded. "As you know," she said to the assembled group, "today is D-Day. I'm here to look at all final creative, final copy, and final media recommendations for *Arabesque* in preparation for our first-quarter launch. All the stages I've reviewed seem to be on target and in accordance with my instructions." Jane paused and looked around the table.

"Thank you for your diligence and cooperation." She thought for a second. "So, again, to be clear, today I want to see the primary, secondary, and tertiary creative waves, along with a psychological and statistical rationale for each. I'll expect to see recommendations for line extensions combined with well-reasoned time frames. I'll also want to look at the finalized package design on screen one more time from all angles." She turned to Gene Dyson. "That shouldn't be a problem, should it, Gene?"

"Any angle you want to see, Jane, we can do."

Jane nodded. "I never had a doubt." She looked around the table. "We still have the opportunity to make minor changes, but that's all. In other words, after today, we should be ready to rock and roll." She paused. "Any questions?"

No one moved.

"Very good," Jane said, "then I'm going to turn this meeting over to you, Len." She nodded to the account supervisor and took a seat off to the side of the table.

"Thank you, Jane," Len said, rising from his chair. After lifting several sheets of paper from the table in front of him, he continued, "I'll pass out the meeting agenda so that we can keep a timely schedule. Also, if anyone has to make a phone call, you'll know when breaks are scheduled. Unless we run into problems, I expect to be completed by noon. If we have a stumbling block or two, with Jane's permission," he nodded at Jane, "we'll order in lunch and continue until everyone is satisfied with the specifics and overviews of the campaign." He glanced around the room. "Sound fair?" He waited. No one moved. "Good. Well, what I'm going to do is give a brief, conceptual outline for the *Arabesque* introduction, then following Jane's approval, we'll let Gene go through his creative strategies."

Jane sat with the back of her chair resting against the paneled wall. She was out of the spotlight which meant she could relax, even mentally doze while listening with one ear. She knew every aspect of the forty-million-dollar launch campaign backward and forward. She had authorized each step of *Arabesque* as it had been initiated and completed. This was a dress rehearsal before the product went to market. She listened to Len speak as he used a presentation remote to display his graphics and bullet points on the screen in front of the room.

Jane saw Lauren Fritz taking notes, while the two agency account executives faked the same process. If they didn't know what was going on by now, they never would.

Jane smiled to herself. She had been a young account executive once. Briefly.

With the overhead lights dimmed, she could see shadows in the far corner of the room. There was Lauren on one side, and far away in the distant corner . . . the shadows.

"And you're in agreement with that, I presume, Jane?" Len asked.

"Specifics?" Jane responded. Her radar had picked up most of what he had asked.

"*Arabesque* premium fulfillment will be handled by two shops, McCready out of Princeton and Synergy Associates out of Des Moines. It was my understanding, Jane, that you were on board," Len said.

"Was and am," Jane answered, "but as I've discussed with you previously, Len, I'd like to see the agency branch out and look for new vendors. I think we could realize better efficiencies with other fulfillment houses, or at the very least, we should test the waters." Jane's undertone was obvious to everyone in the room: Barlow, Blake, and Turner owned both fulfillment houses being employed, and the *Arabesque* business would be highly profitable for them, even marked down.

"Agreed," Len answered, turning back to his audience. "Once the fulfillment mechanisms are in place . . ."

Jane's eyes moved to the shadows in the room's corner again. How comfortable it would be to be sitting on the porch, far away from the stress and ulcer game of advertising.

And he would be there; the man on the motorcycle would be waiting for her.

"I have a question," Lauren said from her chair in the rear of the room. "What would happen if we consolidated all the fulfillment business within one company?"

Jane immediately stood. "That's a valid point, Lauren, but we've already evaluated and resolved the fulfillment issues." She cleared her throat. "In the interest of time, Lauren, if you have questions, perhaps it might make sense to discuss them with me after the meeting."

"Of course." Lauren nodded, her smile in place.

"Good," Jane said, "please continue, Len."

He nodded.

The shadows; there was something soothing about the darkness away from the spotlight. Jane could feel a sadness returning, the deep desire to return to the farm with the wide-open fields.

And further down, somewhere deeper than her longing, was an ache that she never remembered feeling before. She wanted to see him, to be with him—the man with her in the backseat of the car, the one she somehow knew rode a motorcycle.

Who was he?

Where was he?

She glanced around the room. Everyone was watching Len.

She thought of the pale green candy dish again, and knew it had been on a steel mesh table. She watched it flip in the air and turn side over side downward until it fractured into pieces on the cement floor.

Jane stood and walked toward the far corner of the conference room.

Len Stein paused briefly, seeing her movement with his peripheral vision, then continued.

As Jane drew closer to the shadows, she realized the twilight represented the truth.

Truth? Yes, she could very faintly smell the lilacs at the end of the farm porch. She remembered rocking in the chair, the fields extending far in the distance.

"Any questions, Jane?" Len asked.

Jane shook her head. "None. I'll interrupt if I have anything. You know me, I'm not shy."

"Yes, for sure, I know that," Len replied, a slight smile crossing his face as the group chuckled on cue. "But that's the way we work best," he continued, seeing the opening for scoring additional points, "complete candor and honesty. That's why we appreciate you, Jane."

Jane nodded as she leaned against the wall.

"Anyway," Len continued, "that sums it up from my perspective, so now I'm going to turn the creative over to Gene." He slid the remote to him.

The lilac scent was like an aphrodisiac, and the more Jane pushed herself into the wall of the conference room, the stronger the fragrance became. She leaned harder.

Would he be there?

If she walked into the fields, would she find the boy, the man? She needed to feel the overpowering love, the overwhelming physical commitment.

"What do you think?" Carrie whispered. She had left the conference table and was standing next to Jane in the back of the room, her notepad in hand.

"No surprises, so far," Jane answered. She was annoyed that her thoughts had been interrupted.

"I like the statistical analysis of the market," Carrie said. "If *Arabesque* goes after LoBelle's market share and we're only moderately successful, we could actually see two percent growth in one year."

"Going after the weakest link is always good marketing strategy," Jane whispered. "But I don't think LoBelle's is sitting on their hands either. My sources tell me they have three new brands being introduced in the next nine months."

"No kidding," Carrie whispered. "I didn't know that."

"Carrie, do you smell lilacs?"

"What lilacs?" Carrie asked.

"You don't smell anything?" Jane asked.

"Only my own perfume," Carrie answered, "which means I put on too much." She thought for a second. "But I'm not a good one to ask, Jane, I'm the only woman alive with a worse sense of smell than a man's. If I was a lioness, my cubs would be eaten by the first predator that came calling while I was still shopping."

"Kind of like the marketing business," Jane answered, "you miss the cues and wake up without a job."

"Wrong," Carrie whispered. "You miss the cues and you wake up dead."

Chapter 23

"I'm getting a beer, but I'll see if they got a Coke for you, Janey," he called over his shoulder as he climbed the cement steps to the concession stand.

Jane watched him disappear into the crowd, a head of dark hair, a pin-striped polo shirt and long legs clad in jeans. She called out for him to turn around so she could see his face, but her voice was lost in the noise of the crowd.

Okay. I am Jane McBride, she thought, just twenty years younger. I know that now. This is just a regression. I'm in sync with my past life. This is just an episode from that life. There is no reason to be alarmed.

She glanced around and observed she was sitting in the midst of a crowd in a small stadium. Everyone around her was staring at a football game in progress on the field below. The sky glittered in the afternoon and the warmth of the sun reached into the corners of her psyche leaving her at peace.

She knew she looked good, with shoulder-length shiny auburn hair, and a thin gold bracelet on her left wrist.

And she was in love.

She paused.

The sun was unexpectedly very bright. It was difficult to breathe. With the weight on her chest she could barely inhale. It was scary how heavy it felt.

The crystal sky was cracking. She couldn't breathe. She struggled to inhale!

It was a heart attack, she knew it!

Jane realized a man was on top of her. "No, no, no!" she screamed as her shoulders were pressed backward. "No, no, stop it!" She thrashed her arms and legs, violently pushing, shoving. "Stop it! Stop it!"

"God, Jane," Jimmy slurred, "relax, we won't do it, for God's sake."

Jane continued to battle until she realized she was in her own bedroom. She stared at Jimmy, and with her fright retreating, was instantly wild with rage. "Get away from me!" she screamed, pushing him back. "Do you understand? Get away!"

"You're dreaming, Jane, you were having a bad dream."

"Get away! Do you understand English? Leave me alone!"

Jimmy moved to his side of the bed. "You told me we were having sex more than once a year," he said, "but I guess this proves it isn't true at—"

"Stay away from me, do you hear? You don't remember a damn thing." Jane sat straight up in bed. She was trembling. "I don't want you to touch me. Do you hear me, Jimmy? I never want you to touch me again!"

"Hey," Jimmy said, sobering up due to Jane's intensity, "if you want to get out of the bedroom, get out of the bedroom."

Jane reached over and slapped the back of his head as hard as she could.

Jimmy swung around and grabbed both of her wrists. Pushing her backward on the bed, he rolled on top of her. "I can do anything I want now, Jane," he whispered. "I'm your husband, and you're my wife, and I can do anything I want, and there's not a damn thing you can do to stop me."

Jane struggled, shaking her head from side to side. "Let

me go!" Her voice was a guttural rasp straining with the effort to free herself. She could feel her wrists being squeezed so tightly that her fingers began to tingle. "Get off me," she spit out, "get off me, get off me!"

Jimmy released her and she covered her face with her hands.

He moved to the side of the bed and stood. "Even when you were young, you were a self-centered, unforgiving bitch, Jane, and it's my fault for putting up with it. I know that now." He strode across the bedroom, then swept the back of his arm across the top of her bureau sending several perfume bottles and a framed picture of her mother clattering to the floor. "Go to hell, Jane," he said and left the bedroom.

She lay unmoving, hearing the sound of the garage door opening, then seconds later, closing, as Jimmy drove from the house.

∞

Jane dozed, then reawakened. Her cheeks were parched from the salt of her tears or from the sun at the football game.

She had been dreaming when Jimmy interrupted her, but remembered now. She had come home after what turned out to be an all-day *Arabesque* meeting with the ad agency, and exhausted, had eaten, then gone directly to bed. She hadn't attempted to hypnotize herself. She had only been trying to get a full night's sleep.

Yet her dream had seemed like a regression—a continuation.

No, she had been dreaming when Jimmy crawled on top of her.

Jane smelled the pooled perfumes that wafted up from the floor.

Was it a lilac scent? Yes. No. Maybe.

Her eyes closed.

Minutes later, rolling over in bed, she heard a baby whimpering a soft, preoccupied cry of need. Sitting up, Jane quickly moved down the hallway to the guest bedroom. She switched on the light, but saw nothing unusual.

The night surrounding her was vacant, still.

As she moved back down the hall, a sound drifted toward her again, but now she recognized the lonesome whistle of a distant train echoing from miles away. She could visualize the headlight spearing the night, moving forward on a track leading away from all she understood, to new crossings, fresh towns and different lives. If she was aboard, she could look back at the lights of Andover, or just sit, hugging herself with the realization that she had truly disappeared.

Jane concentrated on returning to sleep, but after ten minutes, rose again and crossed to the bathroom. She was restless, but always avoided the use of sleeping pills because she thought she might have inherited her father's addictive tendencies. She took two aspirin and swallowed them with water.

As she stood in the bathroom with the medicine cabinet door ajar, she could see that she was ensnared in a crossfire between the cabinet mirror and the mirror on the opposite wall. Her image ricocheted back and forth, growing smaller and smaller until she was indiscernible.

With her own eyes, Jane watched herself disappear.

CHAPTER 24

"And it just occurred to me that symbolically the vertical stripes on his polo shirt were bars, keeping me from him."

"So what is your subconscious telling you?" Eric asked.

"That I can't get to him, and he can't get to me," she answered.

"Who is he?" Eric asked.

"I don't know."

Eric made a notation on his notepad. "And you awoke and Jimmy was smothering you?"

"Yes," Jane answered.

"And this was a dream, not self-hypnosis?" Eric asked.

"I think so," Jane responded.

"I don't understand. Did you hypnotize yourself first?"

"Not that I recall," Jane answered.

"Well, surely you would have remembered if you had. Wouldn't you agree?"

Jane nodded. "Yes. I didn't hypnotize myself. It was a dream." She stared at the psychiatrist. "But it felt like a regression."

Eric tapped his pen against his notepad. "You know, Jane,

we've covered some important ground, discovering clues, identifying feelings, and I think the self-hypnosis has been helpful. But you keep equating hypnosis with the concept of regression therapy, something that doesn't exist, at least in the professional community. I wonder," he said, tapping his pen against the notepad again, "I wonder if it wouldn't make sense to forgo the hypnosis for a while and refocus on current events and conscious memories."

"Why?" Jane asked. The suggestion was upsetting. The self-hypnosis was too important.

"Gut instinct," Eric answered. "I have the feeling the hypnosis is leading us in directions we don't need to travel. I think there's a certain amount of confusion associated with it for you, and at least for the short term, we might work on what we know consciously."

"So you're suggesting there's something wrong with it?" Jane asked.

"Nope," Eric replied. "I just think we can gain more ground away from it for the time being."

"Are you saying, don't do it?"

"I'm suggesting other options for a while," Eric answered. "That's all."

"Okay, you're the expert."

"It makes sense." Eric said. He glanced at his watch. "We're about out of time. Thanksgiving is Thursday, so I won't see you for a week. Next Tuesday's good?"

Jane nodded.

Eric rose. "Any plans for the holiday?"

Jane stood. "You know my circumstances, Eric. I doubt if there'll be much of a family celebration."

Eric nodded. "I know." He walked with her across the office. "But it's not going to be that way forever, Jane." He smiled as he opened the door. "Believe me."

∞

On her way home, Jane stopped at one of the chain drugstores near the Whitman Mall for a *Scarlett!* retail check. She periodically evaluated different stores, not only to make certain the DSRR products were displayed properly, but also to see what the competition was doing. She had her contacts in the industry, but nothing was better than a personal visual audit.

At the first drugstore, she was pleased with the shelf space allotted for *Scarlett!* and the inventory on hand. All eighteen shades were present and available. "How's *Scarlett!* moving?" she asked the platinum, painted cougar behind the counter.

"Love it!" the woman answered, using her pinkie to touch the corner of her pursed lips. "Young working girls adore it. It's long wearing and intense. Plus the shades work with the color of their cars."

Jane smiled. "Interesting. I hadn't considered some of that. I'm Jane McBride, vice president of marketing for DSRR. We make *Scarlett!*" She held out her business card.

"I'm Terry," the siren replied, taking the card.

"Question, Terry." Jane said. "Do you ever get any requests for a lilac fragrance of any kind?"

"Lilac?" Terry pursed her lips and touched her mouth with her pinkie again. "No, I don't. Never had a request for anything like that. It sounds heavy, like a perfumed sachet you'd find in your grandma's underwear drawer." Terry paused. "Know what I mean? Women today like light fragrances."

"Do you think you could sell it as a new perfume?" Jane asked.

"Anything can be sold," Terry responded, "assuming it has an appealing package, a decent scent, a competitive price, and people know about it. It's all about the advertising."

"Right," Jane answered. "You're right, Terry. Thank you."

Jane walked away from the department with a new campaign for a light lilac perfume percolating in the back of her mind—something to do with combining a country life experience with the adventure of being a contemporary woman. She made a mental note to speak with the DSRR chemists over the next week.

Jane made a second store audit and was pleased to see that an end-cap had a complete inventory of *Scarlett!* She knew that high-volume stores did not offer products an opportunity for a long life unless they moved quickly, and DSRR revenue projections were not met unless the stores gave products a long life. It was pretzel logic she dealt with on a daily basis.

She went inside the mall and visited a gourmet coffee shop, ordered a skinny latte, then with the coffee in hand, joined the stream of people on their way to the parking lots.

As she passed a photography studio, Jane was struck by a series of black-and-white posters titled: *Face In The Crowd*. She stopped and looked first at a twelve-by-eighteen-inch picture entitled: "Telling It Like It Is: Jimmy Walker, Mayor of New York City, 1925." A huge crowd of men and women watched a man in tan suit and skimmer, arms extended, finger pointed, speaking from behind a lectern. All eyes were directed on the mayor except for a single pair, far in the background, staring at the photographer, and Jane. She moved to the next poster: "Home Run Denied, Jimmy Piersall, Fenway Park, 1955." Throngs of men and women in the stands were focused on a ball landing in a leaping outfielder's glove. But in the upper right corner of the photograph, a pair of eyes as attentive as those of a caged animal, watched the photographer, and Jane. "Grand Ole Opry, Little Jimmy Dickens, 1965," a third photograph offered the back of a four-foot, eleven-inch country-western singer in denim and custom beaver Stetson standing in front of a huge audience. As he strummed his guitar, every eye in the auditorium reached out to him. Except . . . except one faraway woman, arms folded, pointedly staring away from the musician, her indignant eyes turned toward the photographer, and Jane.

Jane took several steps backward from the photographs, and transformed the crowds of individual faces into swarming, buzzing bee colonies.

She was afraid. She didn't know why. She steadied herself against the wall.

"You okay, lady?" A gaunt senior citizen in a mall security uniform stood next to her.

Come, sweetheart, tell me,
Now is the time.
You tell me your dream,
I'll tell you mine.

"Who's that singing over the sound system?" Jane asked, nodding at one of the mall's speakers located overhead.

The guard concentrated. "Sounds like the Mills Brothers to me, but that was before your time, I suspect."

Jane looked at him, then nodded.

"You okay, lady?" the guard asked again after several moments.

"I'm fine, I'm fine." As she moved down the long mall corridor, she saw a larger-than-life cardboard lingerie model posted in a clothing store window. The model's eyes greeted her as she approached and followed her as she passed.

A chef, his moustache sprinkled with flour, kneading pizza dough in the window of an Italian restaurant, scrutinized Jane as she walked by.

As she left the mall, the ancient security guard who had been trailing behind her called, "Goodnight now."

After she unlocked her car in the parking lot and slid inside, Jane could see his silhouette still watching her from the doorway.

CHAPTER 25

Jane sat with her back to the door looking out the ceiling-high windows. As she tapped her knee with her glasses, she was considering all the Jimmys in the photograph collection she had seen at the mall the night before, not to mention Jimmy the cook at Flanagan's, or Jimmy, the homeless man, or even James, the waiter. It was very odd and more than a little disturbing.

She forced herself to focus on her work. The *Arabesque* campaign was officially launched internally—the advertising agency and her communications group were now in high-gear production mode, working with the manufacturing division—assuring that the product would hit the streets in the first quarter. Her gut feeling was that *Arabesque* would be a smash, neatly complementing the *Scarlett!* sales instead of cannibalizing them. *Arabesque* would have its own niche, and might even represent the opposite side of a woman's personality. Jane could already envision a second media blitz: *Arabesque* for the workplace, *Scarlett!* for night passion.

She would let the copywriters play with it some more.

There was a light knock on her door. Jane swung around

in her chair.

"Jane, Mr. Briggs wants to meet with you in five minutes," one of the assistants said. "He's in his office."

"Why didn't he just call me?" Jane asked.

"I'm not sure."

Jane nodded. "Okay." She glanced at her schedule. "I'm supposed to meet with Tom Turner to kick around some creative ideas for a new product I'm considering." She looked at her watch. "That's scheduled for ten this morning, right here. If I'm going to be tied up any longer, I'll call down to Carrie."

Jane picked up her *Arabesque* file and walked to the elevator. She stepped inside, pressed the button and moments later stepped out on the tenth floor.

"Hi, Jane," the receptionist said. "Patty said to go right on down to Mr. Briggs' office."

"Thanks," Jane answered.

"He's waiting for you." Patty nodded as Jane walked by.

"Please, come in, Jane," Briggs said after she lightly knocked on the outside of the open door.

Jane walked into an office that offered spectacular views west and south; a crystal palace. Briggs was seated behind his desk. Lauren sat on the leather sofa.

"Hi, Jane," Lauren said, her smile perfect.

"Lauren." She sat down in the chair next to the sofa.

Briggs stood and walked to the door, pointing to his ear, then Patty, before pushing it shut.

Jane glanced at her watch. Tom Turner was due in forty-five minutes.

"Jane," Briggs said, as he sat behind the desk again, "You know me and I believe it's critical to address issues of concern immediately." He paused. "Frankly, I'm troubled with your meeting protocol."

Jane was taken aback. No one had ever criticized any aspect of her work. "I'll be happy to discuss it with you, John," she said, revealing nothing. She glanced at Lauren then back at Briggs. "But certainly, any conversation would be private."

"Normally, I would agree, Jane," Briggs replied, "but the contract with The Grey Street Group and DSRR states that Lauren is responsible for evaluating all levels of personnel, and she has brought some inconsistencies to my attention."

"Inconsistencies?" She glanced at a composed Lauren. "What type of inconsistencies, John? Tell me more."

"Well, for example, Jane, at your latest group meeting with Barlow, Blake, and Turner, you publicly rebuked Lauren for arriving after the start of the session—something out of her control as she was previously meeting with me."

"Nonsense," Jane replied. "I asked Lauren to close the door once she had entered the conference room, after which I introduced her to the agency personnel." She could feel her face becoming warm. "John, I'm very uncomfortable—"

"And as I understand it," Briggs interrupted, "when Lauren asked a perfectly sensible question, you cut her off, quite rudely, I'm told."

Jane kept her voice low and even. "John, our advertising agency relationship is not fee-based, so Barlow, Blake, and Turner lives or dies on the number of hours they can bill. Lauren's question involved an area that had previously been discussed and settled between the agency and DSRR. Retreading old information would be neither beneficial nor cost efficient. I also told Lauren she could ask me any questions when I was not involved in a meeting." Jane made an effort to control her mounting fury. "John, I insist—"

"And apparently," Briggs interrupted again, "while the creative part of the presentation was in progress, instead of monitoring the information, you spent the time standing in the back of the conference room whispering with your associate. What's her name? Carrie, is it?"

Jane stood. "Just to be very clear, John, I'm not going to continue this meeting under these circumstances. End of story."

Briggs fiddled with his cuff link. "Jane, I believe that—"

"That's fine, John," Lauren said, standing. "I've got other areas to observe today." She glanced at Jane. "I hope this doesn't offend you, Jane. I'm only interested in what's best for the company."

Jane stared directly at Briggs, ignoring Lauren.

"I'll touch base later, John, if that's convenient for you."

"Yes, fine," Briggs answered.

Lauren crossed the room, then opened the door and walked out, closing it behind her.

"It is unacceptable to me, John, to be publicly reprimanded at any time, and certainly not in front of a vendor."

"Jane, Jane," Briggs said, "no one was reprimanding you—least of all me. I'm an open-door kind of guy and I had issues of minor concern to be addressed."

"Not publicly," Jane said.

"With whomever is involved," Briggs responded.

"John, this is a lack of professionalism that I've never encountered before in any aspect of my career. I don't have to defend myself or the job I'm doing. The results speak for themselves. And frankly, John, I'm very disappointed with you. I expected more."

"You're being far too sensitive, Jane. I wasn't trying to embarrass you."

"Let me make sure I understand this, John. Lauren Fritz is here as a team leader for The Grey Street Group, whose role is to uncover and eliminate redundancies within the marketing department. Is that about right?"

"It's exactly right," Briggs answered.

"Then there was no reason for her to take part in the *Arabesque* meeting. She's not responsible for any marketing or advertising decisions."

"Lauren has free rein. I've given it to her."

"Not to interrupt my meetings," Jane insisted. She took a step forward, her body language obvious. "John, I have the ultimate responsibility to make sure that down the road DSRR products move off the shelves. Within that framework,

I will not, repeat, will not have Lauren involved in the marketing business meetings. Her job is to analyze company infrastructure, not to participate in corporate strategy."

Jane could measure the tension in Briggs' eyes. He ran both palms across his mahogany desk, as if smoothing away wrinkles, then raised his eyes to meet Jane's. "I'm afraid, Jane, that remains my decision, not yours."

Jane stared at Briggs. "Since when, John, have you started overruling my judgment when it's related to the marketing department?"

"I've always had the power, Jane. I've just never had reason to employ it."

"Why would you want to, John? Profits are sky high and a remarkable and dedicated marketing group is in place."

Briggs shifted in his chair and straightened the knot of his necktie, then studied the end of his Mont Blanc pen. "As president, I have certain responsibilities, Jane."

Jane studied Briggs. Everything he had said in the past few minutes was bogus, including his policy of being an "open-door kind of guy." That was as phony as his implanted hairline. John Briggs, the midnight marauder, who partook of oral sex in the backseat of his limousine from naive twenty-year-olds, and who thrived in a self-created illusion of respectability and managerial know-how, always took full credit for profits while quickly assigning blame for any losses. He was her least likely candidate to be an honest, folksy "open-door kind of guy."

But he had never interfered with her before.

Jane continued to stare, then began to focus on the gray areas of their conversation, the spaces between the spaces between the lines—hostility cloaked as corporate concern. "Your involvement with the marketing department has nothing to do with business, does it, John?"

"I beg your pardon?"

"John, you're still upset about our luncheon, aren't you?"

"I have no idea what you're talking about, Jane." His words were clipped.

"This is about me rejecting your overture. That's what we're talking about here, isn't it, John?"

Briggs vigorously shook his head. "Ridiculous, Jane. That is an uncalled-for accusation to say the very least."

Jane knew she was delving into dangerous waters, cornering Briggs, yet she continued. "John, any updates on my promotion? I've been holding off asking you about it, but maybe now is a good time."

His response was instantaneous and practiced. "The board has instructed me to keep all positions at status quo for the time being, Jane. They're hesitant to make any personnel restructuring with Wall Street predicting a mid-year downturn in the economy." He forced a smile. "But certainly your name will remain at the top of the list."

"A downturn in the market is when I would want my strongest people in power positions," Jane answered. "That's just Business 101, John. Any sales or marketing management officer would understand that. I'm very surprised that you don't."

"I just salute when they give the orders, Jane. I can only do so much." He glanced at his watch. "Is there anything else we have to discuss?"

"It was your meeting, John."

"Well, I'm glad we cleared the air," Briggs said, standing. "As I said, I just like to make sure I understand what's going on with my troops." He began moving across his office to the door. "Thanksgiving tomorrow. Any plans?"

Jane followed Briggs. "Nothing special."

Briggs opened the door and turned to her. "You may want to take off early today, Jane. I think I'm going to give everyone a break and close the offices at three. It's a small thank you for being such a loyal group of workers."

"Appreciate it, John, but I'll have to see how the afternoon plays out. In my operating arena, profits come before socializing." She stepped outside the office.

"Oh, one last thing, Jane," Briggs said, checking to make

certain Patty was not at her desk. "I do have to insist that Lauren continue to work closely with you over the next two weeks. You're probably unaware that she does have a marketing background—before Grey Street she was a manager at L & M."

"A very minor player," Jane responded.

"Not a DSRR, but reputable nonetheless," Briggs said. "Enjoy your holiday."

Jane stared at Briggs. "Enjoy yours."

CHAPTER 26

Thanksgiving morning, Jane slept until nine. Despite the desire to roll over and block out the sun, she rose, showered and dressed in jeans and a sweater. Jimmy hadn't been home in days and she figured he had moved in with Katy. She didn't miss his presence, but remained curious.

After finishing breakfast of a pear and yogurt, Jane lit the burner beneath the tea kettle, waited for the water to boil, then poured it into a mug and headed for the living room

Seated and facing the TV, it occurred to her that no matter what she might have considered in the past, she had to divorce Jimmy. It was now painfully clear, and by asking tangential questions, Eric had led the way.

But despite the years of dysfunction, the end was sad, and, she thought, a personal failure.

Jane picked up the remote and clicked on the TV. The Macy's Thanksgiving Day Parade marched into view with a green-and-white uniformed high school band from Farmingdale, New York striding across the screen. She could see the red fingers of the "Dalers" pressing on trumpet valves with clouds of condensation puffing from their noses. In the background, steam rose from manhole covers, sending smoke signals to her, telling her that she was already bored, and more important, that today especially she didn't belong in the TV family atmosphere.

"Yes, the Farmingdale High School band conducted fund-raisers for one year to be able to make the trip to this amazing parade," the female commentator sporting mink earmuffs said. "That's a lot of bake sales and car washes. And aren't they a good-looking group of youngsters."

"Indeed they are," her male counterpart added. "Their parents should be very proud of these kids, who represent what America is all ab—"

Jane pressed the mute button. Moments later, the high school band was followed by the silent march of the Rockettes, wooden soldiers clad in red and white, topped with plumed black helmets. The formation suddenly turned their painted faces to the screen.

Halfway through their precision performance, the camera panned the crowd, bundled and smiling on the family day—the official kick-off to Christmas. Jane was about to click off the television, when the camera scanned the tiered seating in front of the department store. She spotted Jimmy and Katy sitting with a blanket wrapped around their shoulders—cozy, warm, and smiling, offering national infidelity.

Jane waited for another forty-five minutes to confirm the sighting of her husband on the town with her neighbor, but either the camera angles changed or the two had departed.

Or they had never been there. That was the problem. She was beginning to question everything that went on around her.

The doorbell rang. Jane looked at her watch, then walked to the hallway and opened the front door.

An elderly African-American man in an overcoat stood on the porch. "Jane McBride?" he asked.

"Yes," Jane answered.

"I'm sorry to have to do this on such a nice holiday

morning," he said, handing her an envelope, "but you have been served."

Jane took the envelope and opened it. Jimmy had struck first—he was seeking the divorce. The papers were dated two weeks before.

The elderly man watched her expression and tipped his cap. "So sorry, ma'am, to have to do this today. They give us old guys the dirty work. I had to go to a topless joint yesterday. No place for a religious man." He turned and walked down the steps toward his car parked in the driveway.

Jane closed the door and went back to the living room. Irreconcilable differences were cited as the reason for the marriage dissolution. She tossed the papers on the coffee table. Somehow Jimmy initiating the divorce made her the guilty party.

She slumped down in the chair.

Here she was, alone in her fortress in Connecticut, knowing practically none of her neighbors—she had never made the effort—with her job now appearing to be in jeopardy and her soon-to-be ex hunkered down in some Manhattan hotel with a bottle of champagne, a case of Guinness, and a woman with an artificial chest.

Jane was crossing a frozen lake with the fault lines appearing in every direction—fractures that might break open in weeks, or days or minutes.

She walked down the hall to her office and dialed Carrie's home number.

After two rings, a resonant male voice answered, "Good morning."

That had to be Howard, Jane thought. "Good morning, is Carrie there?"

"Of course, who's calling?"

"Jane McBride."

"Oh, hi, Jane," Howard replied. "Sure, let me get her for you."

Moments later, Carrie picked up. "Hey, are you all right?"

"Of course, Carrie. I just called to wish you a Happy Thanksgiving." Her voice was trembling despite her attempt to control it.

"What's happened, Jane?" Carrie asked. "Is everything all right?" She waited. "Was something going on at work that I missed? We didn't get much of a chance to talk yesterday."

"No, no, nothing," Jane answered. She was having trouble controlling herself.

"It's Briggs, isn't it? He's up to no good again, I bet."

Jane didn't reply.

"What did he do, Jane, try and hook up with you again and then when you said no, try to fire you? That sounds like the sleazebag!"

Jane took a deep breath. "Carrie, I didn't mean to interrupt your holiday. I wanted to wish you a Happy Thanksgiving. That's all."

"Why don't you come down?" Carrie asked. "We're having Howard's family for dinner, which at the least, is very, very, very grim. His mother puts a load on and does impressions of famous actors. Trust me, it's terrifying."

"Thanks, Carrie, but I can't."

"Are you sure, Jane? With that crew around here, you would be doing me a personal favor."

In spite of herself, Jane had to smile. The quiver in her voice slipped away. "Maybe next year, Carrie, but I have dinner plans for today. You're very nice to offer though."

"Are you sure you're sure?" Carrie asked.

"Yes, I am," Jane answered.

"Tell me, did Briggs hit on you again?"

"No," Jane said, "but we can talk on Monday."

Carrie hesitated. "Jane, I want you to feel you can call me anytime. Life is short, no?"

"It is indeed."

"If you change your mind, you don't even have to call, just show up here," Carrie said.

"Thank you. If my plans change, I will."

"Then if not today, I'll see you Monday," Carrie replied, "assuming they don't commit me first after spending four days with Howard."

"I'll see you Monday, Carrie. And thanks," Jane said.

"Anytime, pal, anytime."

∞

Jane decided to pick up a local newspaper and then head for the diner near the mall. She didn't want to be part of a restaurant scene loaded with families, and figured she'd sit and read in a booth by herself, enjoy some soup and empathize with the harried waitress who had to work on Thanksgiving.

It was a plan—a blueprint for the afternoon—and it didn't work. The coffee shop was out of newspapers and about to close when she arrived. The diner was jammed, with cars waiting for parking spots and people lined up outside the door.

So the decision was a simple one. Despite Eric's recommendation not to self-hypnotize, she needed to be in love again, at least for the afternoon.

Who was he? Where was he?

She had to discover him once more. She had to see him, touch him.

Her heart was unexpectedly breaking.

∞

At home, Jane poured a glass of wine and lifted it to herself in an ironic salute to the holiday. She took two sips, then poured the remainder down the sink drain.

Moments later, settling in the guest room, she pulled the quilt up to her chin and started the program. Robert Grassley's voice immediately summoned her inward.

Jane was unexpectedly fired skyward—rocketed through a kaleidoscope of blue and violet, the shades and shapes wildly mutating before her eyes. With her arms at her waist, and her hair driven backward in auburn streaks, she was breathless . . . and suddenly . . . in his arms. Her head rested against his shoulder, her fingers locked behind his neck.

Come, sweetheart, tell me,
Now is the time.
You tell me your dream,
I'll tell you mine.

They were dancing barefoot. She could feel the weight of his ring encircling her middle finger.

Baby in the air! Baby, Jimmy, in the air!

"What, Janey?"

"Nothing."

"I don't understand why you cry sometimes."

"I know. Sometimes I can figure it out, sometimes I can't."

She knew what she had to do.

"I love you, you know," he said.

"Almost as much as I love you."

Being fully clothed and dancing with bare feet was more intimate than the sex. But she knew what she had to do. Slowly lifting her head from his shoulder, hesitantly, she looked up into his eyes.

"What, Janey?"

"Nothing," she answered, resting her head back on his shoulder, a smile crossing her lips.

She knew him.

Darkest Hour

CHAPTER 27

"I'm so glad you were able to join me tonight. I mean, I'm not happy Howard has the flu, but I'm glad you could take his place." Carrie examined the plastic stemmed glass she was holding. "How much was the champagne, $12.75 a glass? That's $4.25 a swallow and I'll bet the bottle had a screw-off top, for God's sake!"

Jane sipped her champagne. "Well, the play is supposed to be good."

"I hear very visual, very, very visual," Carrie answered, "but designed for morons. Nothing is cerebral anymore."

"And the romance is gone," Jane said.

"So, what's with Briggs?" Carrie asked. "I didn't see him today."

Jane detailed her discussion the week before, including the fact that Briggs appeared to be enamored with Lauren Fritz.

"Why? "Carrie asked. "For sex on the conference table?"

Jane shrugged. "I'll bet that's part of it, or will be part of it. He wants Lauren to spend more time with me, becoming familiar with what I do. Sounds like he wants me to train her to do my job."

"You know, Jane, as absurd as it is, like I've said before, I think Briggs is still all worked up about being sexually rejected, like some overindulged schoolboy who got his hand slapped. But I got to tell you, even he wouldn't be stupid enough to replace you with a lightweight like Lauren."

"I wouldn't think so, but nothing is sacred. You know that," Jane answered.

"But it would make no sense," Carrie responded. "He'd be cutting off his own nose. You're making him look smart which is very, very difficult to do. Not to mention that Lauren has no credible track record."

"True," Jane answered.

"No, he wouldn't consider firing you for a thousand different reasons, the first being that you'd sue him for sexual harassment and he'd be so broke he'd lose that Connecticut mansion." Carrie fired back the remaining champagne.

"I've heard of people being let go before for no reason other than 'creative differences,'" Jane said.

"Nah, that's Hollywood," Carrie answered, brushing Jane's remark aside. "You're fine. We're in a society of Human Resources, political correctness, and lawyers looking to sue deep-pocket Fortune 500 companies like DSRR. You've got nothing to worry about."

Jane nodded, encouraged with Carrie's optimism. She thought a few seconds. "Picture this: You're on an old-fashioned porch rocker next to a lilac bush as the twilight falls. Your feet are bare and you're in a pastel cotton dress, and for once, the world is simple." She looked at Carrie. "What do you think?"

"That depends. Am I sitting on some young stud's lap and is he breathing in my ear?" She grinned. "No, seriously, what are you talking about?"

"I'm thinking of a new product line using the scent of lilac. The fragrance of flowers tends to be on the heavy side, but this will be light, with a sophisticated country approach."

"Isn't that an oxymoron?"

"Almost a third of *Scarlett!* sales are in the rural C and D counties," Jane answered, "but I think this would perform better in urban markets. Every city woman thinks she's a country girl at heart."

"As long as there's a Marriott in Hooterville."

The ushers began to close the doors inside the theater as the overhead lights started to blink, signaling the beginning of the performance.

"Can we do it?" Carrie asked.

"As long as I'm running the marketing department," Jane answered. She placed her empty glass on the bar and began to walk across the lobby.

"Then we can," Carrie said. "Can't we?"

"I think so. Start thinking of product names."

Jane knew she wanted to be on that porch. What would it be like to return to the farm with the open fields and the man she loved, and stay?

She sifted through her thoughts. Was it even possible? What would happen to her body? Could she keep her mind?

Above the stage she could almost see him reaching out, urging her to be with him, to remain with him.

Jane paused. Her thinking was growing psychotic. She glanced through the cast of characters in the *Playbill*. Her eyes halted on the name Annie Evans. She'd attended college with a girl who had the same name—a friend and a multi-talented theater major, who had moved to Manhattan to pursue an acting career. As the lights dimmed, she wondered if it was her old classmate.

∞

Later, as they as they moved through the lobby, Carrie voiced her opinion for passersby, "Very colorful, but pure crapola. Very, very show-biz, plastic, high-energy crapola."

She pushed her way into the crowd. "See you in the morning, hon."

Jane wasn't done. She wrote a note and asked an usher to deliver it backstage.

Twenty minutes later, Annie walked into the lobby and stopped ten yards from her. "And here you are," she said, tears in her eyes. She walked over and wrapped her arms around Jane. "And here you are at last. We must be the only two St. Charles girls in New York City."

∞

It had been more than twenty years.

"Twenty-two, I think," Annie said.

The two sat at a window table in a wine bar. Jane smiled. "After college, I think we said goodbye in a restaurant parking lot back home. You'd won a scholarship and the Broadway stage was only a year or two away."

"Nothing is ever as it first appears, huh?" Annie shook her head. "This is the biggest part I've had in more than a year and it's in the chorus." She sighed. "And it hasn't been announced yet, but the show is closing next month so I'll be auditioning again."

"That's not good." Jane thought a moment. "Where do you live?"

"On the Upper West Side. I've had the same studio for years. It's nice."

Jane knew studio meant one room. After all the years, Annie was still living in a box. "Having familiarity with a place can be comforting, I think."

Annie nodded. "You're kind, Jane. You always were. I read such great things about what you're doing at DSRR."

Jane hesitated. "I'm sorry I never called."

"I'm sorry I didn't call either." Annie answered. "I don't know why. I think I wanted to wait until I became a star and could return to my old life as a conquering hero."

"What happened with Kenny?"

Annie looked away. "He got tired of waiting for me to commit. He married someone else."

"I'm sorry, Annie."

"Me too. I think he's a school principal now and has a house full of kids."

Jane nodded. "I'd heard that." She'd also heard variations of Annie's story from female actors who auditioned for commercials. It was all the same—the years eventually began to attack, the body and mind sagged, the significant work never developed. Yet despite acting careers on life support, they continued to invest in new vocal arrangements, jazz and tap-dance lessons, all the while waltzing through fewer and fewer available auditions. They were so dedicated to the acting craft they never realized that age thirty, the bewitching hour, the moment to jettison the wasted sweat equity and still have time to begin a normal life, was long gone.

Annie glanced at her watch. "I should go, Jane. It's been wonderful to see you again."

"Here's a thought. Let's have lunch and in the meantime, I'll see if I might be able to arrange some broadcast work for you. If DSRR products aren't the right opportunity, I could arrange auditions with our ad agency." She slid a business card across the table. "That has my direct number on it. Call me"

Annie took the card and studied it, then stood. "I can't thank you enough, Jane."

She didn't have to. Jane doubted Annie would ever telephone. The reunion had been forced and self-conscious; two careers, one highly successful, one dismal and poverty-stricken. Their shared history couldn't bridge the space between them. Jane watched Annie walk out the door, turn left, and disappear into the dark.

Should she reach out again—or instead, out of respect for an old friend—simply let the humiliated, the dedicated but defeated, rest in peace?

She knew the answer.

They were light years apart in the same city.

Distance kills.

∞

Jane waited by the track entrance in Grand Central for the train to Andover.

The old building had been restored, with decades of grime removed, allowing the original stars to twinkle down at her from the ceiling.

Jane stared up at Cassiopeia, the Lady in the Chair, and Cygnus, the Swan, and Ursa Major, the Great Bear. And when she tilted her head to the east, the stars spelled Jimmy, and to the west, Jimmy. And to the north and south, Jimmy.

Baby Jimmy, looking for her.

She had no children. But that evening in Grand Central, unlike the *Faces In The Crowd* series of photographs in the mall, the name Jimmy was not threatening; just sad. Bitterly sad and icy as the stars resting in the endless heavens beyond the ceiling.

She lowered her eyes.

Jimmy was in the stars.

Jane glanced at her watch and then walked down the stairs to the tracks.

On the platform, waiting for the train, she realized she was planning. She knew she had to stay for now, but soon, yes, soon . . .

Soon.

CHAPTER 28

Tuesday afternoon, Jane finished a meeting at the ad agency and walked to the library on Forty-Second Street.

After searching, she found only one acknowledgment that past-life regression even existed, and that was in a generic text on memory-related topics. She located the book and discovered that the entire past-life regression segment was covered in a half a page, and was nothing more than a scathing denouncement, claiming the theory to be "unproven hokum of the highest order."

Jane glanced at the back cover of the book, at the bearded author of the text, Whitfield Howell, PhD. According to his biography, he was a professor emeritus and world-renowned memory expert.

First Eric, and now Whitfield Howell dismissed her experiences.

∞

Back at her office, Jane saw Lauren waiting for her.

"Jane," Lauren said, rising, "a minute of your time, please."

"I've only got a minute," Jane answered, turning, "I've got an afternoon that's already backed up."

"I was in conference with John most of yesterday, and to make a long story short, he wants me to shadow you for the next two weeks." She stood six inches from Jane, a clear invasion. "He needs me to learn as much as possible about your job."

"Why is that, Lauren? My understanding was that you're analyzing the entire marketing department, not just me."

"Look, I don't like this any more than you do, but John's the client. He makes the rules and I have to do what he says."

Jane heard the beginning of good-cop, bad-cop. She would have anticipated something more sophisticated. "Have a seat out here, Lauren," she answered. "I'm going to speak to John and get this matter straightened out."

Jane walked into her office and closed the door. She picked up her telephone and pressed the digits for Briggs' office. "Is he in, Patty?" She paused. "Sure, of course, I'll hold."

Several seconds later, Briggs picked up the telephone. "Yes, Jane."

"John, I'm down here with Lauren Fritz. She claims you want her to shadow my workday for the next two weeks."

"Not me personally, Jane," Briggs answered. "The board is insisting."

Good-cop, good-cop, bad-cop. Moving on up the ladder.

"Why would the board suddenly make that decision, John?"

"It appears to be sudden, but conceptually, it's been discussed for the past year. You're so valuable to the company, Jane, that should anything happen to you, we would be in desperate trouble."

"Wouldn't it have made sense for you and me to discuss this?" Jane asked.

"I believe that's what we're doing right now, Jane," Briggs responded.

Jane decided to plunge into sacred territory. "I'd like to

speak to a board member, not to question the judgment, but to make my case against such a distraction as Lauren following me around for two weeks. It's not good for the company to have me so tied up."

"Ah, were it possible," Briggs answered. "But it's not something that I could allow. As the president, I'm sure you can understand that I can't have employees badgering board members. They would throw me out on my ear."

"John, I don't have time to train someone to do my job. A good deal of it's instinct anyway."

"Make time, Jane," Briggs responded. "It's now part of your responsibility."

Jane paused, her face burning. "Thank you, John," she answered abruptly.

"You're quite welcome, Jane," Briggs responded. "Keep me posted on how you progress."

"If I forget, I'm sure Lauren won't," Jane answered.

CHAPTER 29

When to de-toupee—an intriguing question. If a man wore a hairpiece, when in the relationship did the woman acknowledge that she knew it was a rug? Did she ask, and if so, when? After the first date? Second? Fifth? And if he lied, did she refrain from running her hands through his hair, afraid that she might accidentally lift it from his head? Or worse yet, what if the toupee or hair weave was so realistic that she didn't realize it was phony and yanked it from his scalp during a moment of passion?

When did honesty kick in for the couple? When were the personal safety barriers lowered, allowing the genuine relationship to begin?

Was her lack of candor with Eric as obvious to him as some of the nasty-looking hairpieces that she saw strolling down the Manhattan streets? Was he seeing through her, aware she wasn't being completely honest? Could she be candid with him about her most recent regression? He had asked her to refrain and she hadn't.

Yet she didn't believe Eric would ever criticize. Instead he would want to explore the reasons for her actions.

∞

"So what's new?" Eric asked, sitting opposite her in his office that evening.

"Nothing," Jane answered.

"Nothing?"

"Not really." After several minutes of small talk, Jane began to detail the politics transpiring at DSRR, ending with her thought that Briggs was preparing to push her aside.

"And that was the end of your conversation with Briggs?" Eric asked.

"Yes, he just said to stay in contact with him regarding Lauren," Jane answered.

"Look you've tried to level with him and he's tap dancing," Eric replied. "I agree with your analysis. It looks like he has his own agenda."

"So what do I do?" Jane asked. "I don't want to spend my time babysitting the female wonder. And I sure don't want her to learn how I do business—the way I think, and the way I bring a product to market."

"Let me put on my business hat for a minute," Eric said. "Don't give her any depth. It's a game, Jane. Outsmart both of them while the process is advancing and don't take any of it personally."

"It's hard not to take it personally," she responded. "Especially with Ms. MBA, the barracuda, prepared to destroy anything that stands in her way."

"Ah, but you're smarter than she is, Jane. And I'm certain you're more intelligent than Briggs as well. That doesn't mean they're not formidable foes, but you can outthink them." He considered his statement. "It's war, but it's also a psychological chess match."

Jane nodded. "I suppose that's true." She thought a moment. "I have to give a speech at the Waldorf-Astoria for

NCA in a week. That should give me a chance to shine."

"NCA?"

"National Cosmetics Association."

"In the main ballroom?" Eric asked.

Jane nodded.

"That will be a wonderful opportunity to show your leadership skills." Eric tapped the back of his hand with his pen. "Look, you're a woman, a giant in your field, and the bottom line you create for your company is substantial. You're going to be center stage, nationally recognized, and any executive would be foolish to take on a power player like you. He might win, but at what cost? Briggs strikes me as a survivor, Jane. Survivors rarely take on battles they know in advance they can't win."

"But that's what he's doing," Jane protested.

"That's what we *think* he's doing," Eric said. "We're not sure. My suggestion is to stick to your guns. Don't waver, but always be ready to discuss the situation rationally. And, of course, document, document, document."

Jane sighed. "Okay."

"What else?" Eric asked.

"I hypnotized myself again."

"When?"

"Thanksgiving."

"Why?"

"I was lonely."

"Did the self-hypnosis make you feel less lonely?" Eric asked.

"Yes and no." She continued to stare at him.

"I don't understand," Eric said.

"When I hypnotize myself, I'm in another life," Jane answered.

"I don't understand," Eric repeated.

"I'm in another person's body. I mean, my own body, but I'm twenty years younger."

Eric tapped the pad with his pen. "I'm surely having

trouble following this," he said. "Hypnotism doesn't place you in another person's body or make you a younger version of yourself."

"Yes, it does."

Eric eyed her carefully. "Then tell me about it, Jane."

Cautiously, she disclosed the dancing scene and the ring on her middle finger.

"Do you know who you were dancing with?" Eric asked.

"No," Jane lied.

"Do you remember the music?"

"The song was 'You Tell Me Your Dream, I'll Tell You Mine,'" Jane replied.

"I don't know it."

"The Mills Brothers, I think."

"And you don't recall who you were dancing with?" Eric asked again.

"No, I don't," Jane answered.

"You didn't look at him? Was it Jimmy?"

"My head was on his shoulder. I couldn't see who he was," Jane said.

"What else do you recall?" Eric asked.

"Nothing."

Eric watched her closely. "Well, I guess the starting point is for us to try and determine what your subconscious is attempting to tell you."

"Eric, with respect, this feels much more real than anything on a subconscious level."

"Jane, you're here. It's now. We don't time-travel or move from one body to another." He paused. "It's important for you to listen to what you're saying."

"I hear what I'm saying, Eric," Jane answered. "You're just not accepting it."

"I'm surely listening, Jane," Eric replied.

"I know how peculiar this all sounds, Eric, but what I'm explaining is very real."

He studied her, then glanced at his watch. "You know, I

mentioned hypnotizing you once before. Why don't we try it here on Thursday night? It might help me to see what you are experiencing."

Jane only considered the suggestion because the rational side of her was troubled with the past-life scenario. "How would we do that?" she asked.

"I'll rearrange the appointments so you'll be the last of the night and we'll have more time."

Jane thought about the suggestion.

"And," Eric said, "if you're uncomfortable with a one-on-one scenario for the hypnosis, I'll arrange to have another colleague present." He thought a second. "Or maybe Dr. Greenman would be available."

As much as she didn't like exposing herself further, Eric's suggestion made sense, especially because her life seemed so unstable. "Okay," she answered. "I guess we could do that."

"Colleague or Dr. Greenman?" Eric asked.

"Dr. Greenman would be fine."

"I'll see if she's available," Eric said, rising and placing his notepad on his desk. He crossed to the office door. "If she's not, I'll make the other arrangements."

Jane followed him to the door.

Eric turned toward her and placed his hand on her shoulder. "I think this will be good for you, Jane."

"Okay," she answered. "I'll give it a try."

Eric lifted his hand. "I'll see you Thursday night. I'll call you to confirm the time."

"Thank you," Jane said.

She walked across the waiting room and out the door to her car.

The entire drive home, she could feel his fingers resting on her shoulder.

Chapter 30

As she pulled into the driveway, Jane saw Jimmy's car parked in front of one of the garage doors.

He was leaning against the counter, sipping from a delicatessen coffee cup when she entered the kitchen.

"What brings you here?" Jane asked, wishing she had changed the door locks.

"I missed you, Jane," Jimmy said.

Jane placed her purse on the kitchen counter, turned on the stove burner beneath the tea kettle, then walked across the floor to retrieve a mug from the overhead cabinet. "Let's see, you tell me what a cold, unforgiving bitch I am, file for divorce so that I have the papers served to me on Thanksgiving, and you miss me?" Taking the mug from the cabinet, she turned to Jimmy. "That doesn't make any sense."

Jimmy stared at his paper coffee cup.

Jane took a teabag from a counter canister and placed it in the mug. "So what are you doing here, Jimmy?"

"The water should be almost ready. I heated it for you."

"Thank you. Why are you here?"

"I came by to tell you I stopped the divorce proceedings."

Jane hadn't even consulted an attorney, figuring she would allow Jimmy to do the lion's share of the work as he had initiated the action. "Why?" she asked.

"Because I don't want a divorce."

"Katy getting boring?"

"I don't love Katy," Jimmy said.

"I saw the two of you on TV in the stands of the Macy's Thanksgiving Day Parade. Two lovebirds wrapped under a blanket, televised nationally."

"It was a mistake," Jimmy said.

"I thought Katy was married," Jane said. "But then I thought you were, too."

"I don't love Katy," Jimmy repeated.

"And therefore, what?" Jane asked. She walked to the tea kettle and poured the boiling water into the mug.

"I stopped drinking, Jane," Jimmy said.

"For how long?"

"Four days," Jimmy answered.

"So, let's see, is this the hundred and twentieth or the hundred and twenty-first time you've stopped since I've known you?"

"I'm serious this time," Jimmy insisted.

"I never saw an attempt from you that wasn't serious," Jane answered. "At least temporarily."

"Just watch," Jimmy said.

"I have no intention of watching," Jane answered, lifting the teabag from the mug and placing it in the sink. "You watch. I have a job."

"I don't understand you, Jane," Jimmy said.

"And according to what you've told me before, you never did," Jane replied. She turned and faced her husband. "Look, Jimmy, we haven't gotten along for years. We went our separate ways long before you began divorce proceedings. What makes you think a simple retraction of legal paperwork is going to change our relationship now?"

"Because I stopped drinking."

"Please," Jane answered, annoyed. She sipped from her mug of tea.

"Well, I have, Jane," Jimmy said. "And I'm not going to start again. I'm beginning to get an idea of the damage I've caused between the two of us because of me being out of control." He hesitated. "I'm going to change, Jane. This time I'm going to make it work."

She didn't want him to make it work. She didn't want him in her kitchen, her house, or her life. She viewed Jimmy as a broken-down alcoholic and pitied him. And the last thing in the world she wanted to do was share a bed with him again. Her love for him had disintegrated. She sipped the tea again. "Jimmy, there's nothing to make work," she said at last. "Nothing. I don't know how to say it any other way."

"Come on, Jane, I'm sorry about the divorce papers. Katy split up with her husband and she was pushing me. I should have just forgotten about it. I didn't know how to say no."

Jimmy was below her pity. He was a blind street-corner beggar, peeking around the sides of his sunglasses to see how much spare change he had hustled. In real time, he was a marginal insurance salesman who had chewed up his knee on the college football field and never made it to the NFL glory he dreamed of—a broken warrior who'd had no life plan beyond professional sports.

"Jimmy, with the divorce going forward, we're going to have to discuss living arrangements."

"I just told you, Jane, I've stopped the proceedings."

"Then I'll start them again." It was as if she were addressing a childish staff person at DSRR who couldn't handle a straightforward conversation. "It's over, Jimmy. I want out. I'm done."

"I don't know how you can be this way," Jimmy answered. "We go back so many years together. We can't just say goodbye to all that." He placed his coffee cup on the counter. "Come on, Jane. We met when we were still practically kids." His face reddened. "That has to mean something. We just can't walk away from it, especially after all these years."

Jane looked at Jimmy and sipped her tea. "We had some good times, but it's time for a change. For me, anyway."

"Jesus Christ, Jane, what do you want me to do, beg?" His face was contorted, wounded, confused.

"You already have," Jane snapped. "Look, Jimmy, there haven't been good times, or respect, or love for many years, if ever." She placed the mug on the counter. "You drank me away, and one way or the other, I have to move forward." She paused. "I'll help you financially if you need it, and I'll split our assets down the middle of—"

"You know what I remember about you, Jane?" Jimmy interrupted.

Jane stared.

"Clean," he said. "You were always so clean. You always smelled good and looked so clean. And your clothes always fit because you were slender. A guy like me, big and bulky, always had to wear lumberjack crap. But you were always so clean. I think I could've washed for a week and never been like you."

"Jimmy, I'll have my attorney contact yours. I want to get this started and behind me as soon as possible."

"Going somewhere?" he asked.

"You never know."

"I don't want to go back to Katy's," Jimmy said. "I've got all my clothes in the car."

"You can stay here until we work out the details, Jimmy," Jane said, "as long as you leave me alone."

Jimmy studied her. "You know, I've been complaining that I don't know you now. But I'm thinking I never knew you. It's not that you changed, or I changed. You were never what I thought you were."

"Okay, I'll bite. What was that?"

"Kind, compassionate, loving."

"Jimmy, you're talking yourself into victim status and not only is what you're saying not true, it's not becoming."

Jimmy finished his coffee, placed the cup on the counter and nodded, at last resigned. "Do you want me to get this whole divorce thing going again, or do you want to?"

"Either, or," Jane said.

"Okay," Jimmy replied slowly. "I'll call my lawyer. I guess I'll take the guest room until we get everything worked out."

"If it's all the same, Jimmy," Jane answered, "I'll stay in the guest room. You need the bigger bed."

He nodded, then with his voice barely above a whisper, said, "Isn't it funny, Jane, that after all this time together, this is the way it ends?"

Jane didn't respond. She knew it was the last time he could reach for her and maintain any dignity. She had left no wiggle room.

Jimmy stared at her. After a moment, he said, "I'll get my stuff," and walked out of the kitchen into the garage.

∞

As she stood in the bathroom, Jane was aware she had been cruel, or at least, she could have been kinder. There had been a handful of tender moments with Jimmy in the past, and she could have dwelt on those with him for a minute or two, but her patience was gone. She was committed to her decision to end the marriage and didn't want any last-minute emotion blocking the way.

She brushed her teeth, swallowed two aspirin, and walked into the guest room, locking the door behind her.

She switched off the light, sat on the edge of the bed, and massaged the bottom of her foot. Jimmy was the only man she had ever slept with, though not even he knew that. He had always been rough, and for years she thought that was normal. But then she had seen movies of great desire, and read books about burning love affairs, and heard secretaries giggle about how good their boyfriends were in bed, until she realized that her life was devoid of passion. The two of them might as well have been animals performing behind bars at a local zoo.

Jane lay back on the bed and stared at the ceiling. Jimmy was grieving due to the end of the marriage, and she realized she was grieving that it had ever begun.

So much had passed her by. So much wasted time.

She closed her eyes and began to count backward.

So much wasted time.

Chapter 31

The reflection of a red light blinked with metronomic regularity on the curtain next to the window.

She was on her back and didn't move. The arm of a man was resting across her bare breasts. He lay on his stomach, his breathing rhythmic, his head turned away.

She recognized the scent of him.

They were in a tiny room barely big enough for a bed, a chest of drawers and a desk. She shifted slightly, causing the springs below the mattress to groan. To her left was an open door to a closet where several articles of clothing hung, and next to that, a closed door which she assumed was a bathroom.

She carefully slid from beneath his arm.

He sighed.

Once on the floor, she tiptoed toward the closed door.

"Where're you going, Janey?" he mumbled.

"Bathroom," she whispered.

"Don't lock yourself out again. I'm too tired to hear you knock."

"I'll be careful," she answered, not knowing what he was talking about.

Jane opened the second door and found another closet.

The bathroom must be down the hall, she thought. She glanced at her watch and saw it was 12:45 a.m.

She slipped into a robe lying over the desk chair, then after quietly opening the room door, she glanced around and picked up a heavy textbook from the floor to use as a wedge. Once outside, Jane moved down a narrow corridor past three closed doors. At the end was the bathroom.

She switched on the light and locked the door behind her. The ancient toilet had an overhead water tank with a chain extending downward. Next to it was a cracked white porcelain sink with an empty glass sitting next to the faucet.

She glanced in the mirror and discovered she was young again. But no, she had to remember that she was the older Jane McBride appearing in her younger body. And she was positive she had never been in this bathroom before, yet some remote part of her knew that was untrue.

She moved closer to the mirror. Had she been this beautiful once?

Jane guessed she was about twenty-three or twenty-four, the same age as when she stared at herself in the mirror at Russ and Marie's house. Why wasn't she panicked with what was happening to her? Why would she think she had been in the bathroom before?

No answers.

Once finished, she switched off the light and walked out into the hallway. The building was now more familiar and she was positive the man in the bedroom was the same one she'd been with before, in the back of his car, at the stadium, and dancing barefoot.

She stood outside the door.

She really wasn't afraid, and all at once, she knew why. She was loved. The sense of being wanted was unlike anything she had ever before experienced. It infiltrated her, filling every corner, coloring every breath she took.

Jane crept back into the bedroom and slipped into a pair of jeans and a sweater she found in the closet. She located a pair of sandals under the window. After picking up a ring of keys from the desk, she stepped into the hallway and tried several of them in the lock before she found the right one. She locked the door and walked down a flight of stairs to the street.

Once outside, Jane looked back at the building. It had three floors, the bottom level a hardware store. Across the street, a blinking red neon sign spelled out Jack Reed's Tavern, the same flashing red she recognized from the upstairs room.

Jane looked up and down the street, but saw no one.

She glanced at her watch again: 1:00 a.m. She crossed the street and entered the tavern.

The television over the bar was broadcasting a western and two men sat down at the far end talking to the bartender. All three looked at her as she walked in.

The bartender walked toward her. "Hi, Jane, where's Ricky?"

"Sleeping," she said. Ricky, that's what he calls himself, she thought.

The bartender recognized her. Jane wanted to learn more, but now figured she was in a game of charades—receive the clue, figure out the answer. If she asked too many questions, they'd start to wonder about her. She had to acquire information without betraying her lack of knowledge.

You want a Coke?" the bartender asked. "Or maybe something stronger."

"Refill when you get a chance, Jack," one of the men at the bar called.

"Be right there," the bartender responded over his shoulder.

"What do you recommend?" Jane asked.

"Recommend? If you're drinking, you always have the same thing, a screwdriver."

"Good point," Jane responded. "That'll be fine."

Jack took a bottle of vodka from behind the bar, mixed the drink, and placed it in front of her. "On the house," he said. "Someone as beautiful as you shouldn't have to pay for anything. Ever." He winked, then walked toward the other end of the bar and began refilling a beer glass.

Jane sipped the drink and attempted to memorize every detail of the tavern.

When she had crossed the street and entered the bar, it had been like being shoved into an Edward Hopper painting of light and shade, of hushed nighthawks, who would evaporate at the first sign of light in the east.

She stared at the vodka in the orange juice. It reminded her of a tropical sun.

She watched the three men huddled, their heads close together, probably discussing baseball, their wives, or how it would feel to be twenty all over again.

Jane was lucky.

She knew.

∞

Jane sat up, fully dressed, her feet still on the floor of the spare bedroom.

What happened?

There had been a power failure and the red numerals on the electric clock were blinking.

She had visited her former life, but this time without any attempt to regress! With no premeditated intention, she had been placed back in her younger body next to her boyfriend. With no hypnosis, she had been kicked back to her youth, just as when she had been at the football game!

Or was it a dream, again . . . a dream?

No, it had been too authentic—Ricky, her nakedness, the building—all too real.

Jane switched on the light and glanced at her watch. It was 1:30 in the morning. She had traveled backward and then returned with no hypnosis!

She left the bedroom and walked down to the kitchen, removed a container of orange juice from the refrigerator and filled a glass.

She stared at it.

Despite what Eric told her, she knew she had time-traveled without plan or intent.

It had just happened.

Chapter 32

It was reassuring that Eric wanted to hypnotize her. Jane was growing increasingly fearful that she was trespassing into a restricted and murky zone, and having Eric controlling her travel was comforting.

"So here we are, Jane," Eric said Thursday evening as she entered his office. Barbara Greenman was seated to the right of his desk.

"Hi, Jane," Barbara said. "This is new stuff for me. It should be interesting."

"How's the tennis game?" Jane asked.

"No backhand, no forehand, no drop shot, and I can't rush the net," Barbara answered. "But I get a lot of cardiovascular work chasing the ball."

"I could use a little more exercise myself," Eric admitted.

"Come on down then, Eric. We're just a bunch of old ladies unsuccessfully trying to stay fit. If nothing else, it could amuse you."

Eric chuckled to himself. "You would outplay me. I haven't been on a tennis court in years." He turned to Jane. "Dr. Greenman was kind enough to observe this hypnotism session, Jane. And I think it puts us both at ease to have a third person in the room."

Jane nodded. "That's fine, Eric."

"How do you feel?" he asked.

"Okay."

Eric turned to Barbara. "As a means of stress relief, Jane has developed some self-hypnosis skills. It seems to be paying off because she feels so relaxed that she enters another life—a sense of regression, I suppose, and she's quite comfortable there. I thought we would see if Jane could enter that state tonight and perhaps we can zero in on some subconscious thoughts and issues."

"It sounds interesting, Eric," Barbara responded. "I'm glad you called me." She directed her attention to Jane. "And it sounds like something I'd enjoy trying. I'd like to learn something here and maybe achieve the same stress relief you're experiencing. I could use it."

Jane knew the two were working her.

"I'm going to have you lie on the couch, then lead you through several steps of relaxation, Jane," Eric said. "We have all the time we need. The idea is for you to be completely relaxed so that we may approach different memories and concerns. It's safe—there are no negatives.

"Okay," Jane answered, "that sounds reasonable."

"Good," Eric said. "Now what I'm going to ask you to do, Jane, is lie on this sofa, facing away. I'll be in this chair next to you. Dr. Greenman will remain where she is and will not interact. This is strictly between you and me." He paused. "Any questions?"

Jane shook her head. "None."

"Let's begin the process."

Jane moved to the sofa, lay down on her back and positioned herself, one ankle across the other until she was comfortable, then closed her eyes.

"We're ready to begin," Eric said, his voice calm and soothing. "What we're going to do first, Jane, is start the relaxation process which we will slowly deepen before moving into suggestion application—a period when your subconscious mind is more susceptible to sending and receiving information." Eric cleared his throat. "I want you to think about unwinding the coil of thick wire that is wound around you. I want you to think of it unraveling, first from your feet, then moving up your body, leaving you more relaxed as you are set free of the stress and pressure of daily life. We'll begin by focusing on your toes . . . "

Jane easily responded to Eric's suggestions and was able to recognize entry into the deepening phase.

She was floating in the pure blue sky again, resting on a soft cloud, a cloud that Eric didn't know existed.

"Where are you, Jane?" he asked.

"I'm floating," she answered.

And as she drifted overhead, she looked down for the rolling meadows and the farmhouse, or the building across the street from Jack Reed's Tavern, or Ricky signaling her to join him, but she saw none of them—just the cornflower blue, above and below.

She vaguely heard Eric's voice in the background.

After several minutes of unsuccessful exploration, Jane decided to take a piece of the cloud and use it as a canopy to float downward. She was confident that the breeze would define her course, directing her to where she wanted to be.

She tugged, but the cloud wouldn't tear, infuriating her. She tried again, without success—something that had never happened before.

Jane was unconsciously searching through her pockets for a knife or scissors when she heard familiar laughter that had left her life long ago . . . laughter imprinted so clearly in her memory she would recognize it even if ten thousand years had passed. She stopped fumbling with her pockets and glanced around. Fifteen feet away, a toddler—a boy—sat on a separate cloud, staring at her, pointing. He resembled her; he was a part of her.

His laughter gurgled out of him. Joy was scribbled across his face as he smiled and clapped.

She knew he wanted to be held in her arms, his head resting against her neck. And at night, he needed to be tucked into his bed, covered with his blanket and clutching his soft rabbit as the bright calico birds suspended from the ceiling looked down on him.

She was frozen.

His laughter began to fade and his face trembled as tears began to fill his eyes.

"Jimmy," Jane called, her eyes reflecting the little boy's panic. "Jimmy, come to Mama."

"Mama," he called, tears running down his cheeks. His arms were outstretched, waiting to be picked up. "Mama."

Jane moved to the back edge of the cloud, then raced forward, attempting to leap over to him, but she couldn't jump. Her feet were locked.

His fingers wiggled on his outstretched hands.

"Hold on, Jimmy, hold on. I'm coming."

His cloud began to rise as his voice grew fainter.

"Wait for me, Jimmy, I'm coming." She tried to jump again, but now her entire body was weighted down.

"Ma-a-a—" The thin wail was dissipating into the distance; a rumble of thunder from a buried storm.

And as brightly as he had shone, he was as quickly gone.

Jane sank to her knees, awash with a deep penetrating sorrow. Her insides were torn into a million fragments, black tears drizzling downward through the cornflower blue.

She heard Eric's voice faintly in the background, but she ignored it.

"When I say one, Jane, you will consider returning to the waking state. One."

She heard him. She understood him.

"Now, when I say two, Jane, you find yourself becoming increasingly alert."

A long pause.

"Two."

"When I say three, you will awaken alert with no ill effects. You will feel rejuvenated and refreshed."

Jane waited.

"Three."

She opened her eyes.

Eric moved to the side of the sofa and bent down, staring at her. "How are you, Jane?" He paused. "You can sit up now."

She didn't move on the sofa.

Eric waited several moments before crossing to his desk. "Whenever you feel like sitting up, you may," he said.

Jane moved her fingers and uncrossed her ankles, then pushed herself up. She knew she had been crying.

"What are you thinking?" Eric asked as he moved his desk chair so he could sit across from her.

Jane didn't reply.

"Can we talk about your experience?" Eric asked.

Jane looked from Eric to Barbara. "I don't know what to talk about."

"We had a lot of smooth sailing, then you became very emotional, much of which was incoherent."

Jane thought about Eric's statement. "So what does that mean?" she asked.

Eric shrugged. "I don't know. You weren't responding to me during part of the session and when you did, I couldn't always understand it."

"How long was I hypnotized?" Jane asked.

"About forty-five minutes."

"So that's not so bad," she answered, remembering Twyla's criticism for taking up the better part of an afternoon.

"It's neither good nor bad, it's just a hypnotic experience." Eric looked closely at Jane. "How do you feel?"

"Very sad." Jane answered.

"It sounded like you were trying to communicate with someone. You were upset," Eric said. "Any idea what that was about?"

"No." How deep was bottomless pain? And would she ever survive if she reached for it, confronted it, and attempted to dethrone it?

Eric looked at Barbara. "Do you have any sense of what Jane was saying?"

"You sounded distressed," Barbara said, "as if you were living through a bad experience of some sort."

"I guess you're both right," Jane answered. She stood. "I think I've had enough for the night."

"That'll be fine, Jane, but wouldn't it make sense to analyze what we do know while it's still fresh in our minds?" Eric asked.

Jane peered past the two doctors. "It would make sense," she said, "but you know what, Eric, I just can't. I'm not feeling well. Maybe tomorrow."

"Do you have any idea why you were so upset?" Eric asked.

"No," Jane repeated. "I appreciate your help, Barbara—and of course, yours as well, Eric." She picked up her purse from the floor. "Goodnight."

"Please call me, Jane," Eric said, walking with her to the door of the waiting room. "Whatever it is, we can solve the problem." His hand touched her shoulder again. "We'll figure this out."

CHAPTER 33

Carrie sat across from Jane's desk at seven o'clock Monday morning. "So, based on everything I've researched, that's it."

"Only one lilac scent exists and that's private label?"

Carrie nodded. "It's sold to bodegas and low-end mass merchandisers in the metropolitan area—no national distribution, of course. Wholesale per unit is three dollars. Retail is around six."

"So it's garbage."

"Yes."

"What's the trade name for the perfume?"

"Lilac Twilight. Clear medicinal bottle, two ounces, with a violet label."

Jane sighed. "No wonder it's got problems, I even have trouble pronouncing it." She tapped her fingers on the desk. "So, we buy the line, discontinue it, create our own lilac fragrance, do the marketing research for an engaging name and package, organize the advertising campaign, and boom, we're off and running with no lawsuits."

"If you believe the country wants a lilac perfume," Carrie said.

"What do you think?" Jane asked.

"I think that we should test the market using focus groups. Have the DSRR chemists come up with a few variations on the lilac theme, then along with a couple of other scents, put the question to American women."

"Amen," Jane said. "I wonder if we could have something ready for evaluation within thirty days."

"We've done it before," Carrie answered.

"Any brand names jump out at you?" Jane asked.

"Not really. For some reason, I'm drawing a blank. I think once we address the target market question, the name will fall into place."

"I agree," Jane added, "but I still want a sophisticated country softness. I don't know what that means yet, but we'll figure it out."

"Focus groups never lie," Carrie said. "All we have to do is listen. Ignoring their input is the only way we can get into trouble."

"Who made you so smart?" Jane asked. She smiled. "I'm glad we work together, Carrie."

Carrie returned the smile. "I'm—"

"I resent this." Lauren Fritz stood at the entrance to Jane's office.

The two women stared at her.

"May I help you, Lauren?" Jane asked.

"This is exactly the type of behavior The Grey Street Group attempts to identify and disband: power cells, small cliques thriving undercover within an organization, attempting to dismantle the corporate infrastructure."

Jane stood and leaned forward, the tips of her fingers resting on the top of the desk. "Lauren, I think it's important for you to recognize that you're a vendor working at the pleasure of DSRR, who is your employer. Analysis on redundancy is fine, and it's what you're paid for, provided it's open-ended and accurate. Widespread accusations, especially to executives is unacceptable."

Lauren's face was a mask of indignation. "I resent very much, Jane, you holding early morning meetings specifically so that I won't be present." She appraised the two women. "And I can see that is what's happening here."

"Who died and made you Queen of the Nile?" Carrie asked, turning in her seat to directly confront Lauren.

"You have spent an enormous amount of time with me over the past week, Lauren," Jane said. "You have been briefed on every meaningful bit of marketing business we are involved in. But just so you get it, the creative process takes quiet time, down time. If I decide to talk with my associate in the morning without you present, that's my prerogative. End of story." She sat and turned her attention back to Carrie who had swiveled back to face the desk.

Lauren remained erect in the doorway. "John is going to be very disappointed that you're discussing a potential new product without having me present."

"How about listening outside the door, Laurel?" Carrie asked, deliberately misstating Lauren's name as she turned to face her again. "Is Eavesdropping 101 a mandatory course for graduation from Ivy League business schools these days?"

Lauren ignored the remark. "Jane, if you plan to include me in marketing functions today, which I strongly advise, please let me know. I'll be in conference with John for the next forty-five minutes." She turned and walked away.

Jane was shaken by the raw assumption of power that Lauren was exhibiting. It spoke volumes about how she was being perceived by Briggs.

"We just have to play it smart, Carrie," Jane said. "I have to stand my ground and not let her get under my skin."

"She's under mine," Carrie said.

"Let's compartmentalize and go about business as usual," Jane said, "with Lauren's presence a necessary evil, at least for the time being."

"She's a hot steaming mess."

Jane shook her head. "You're funny sometimes."

"Then how come you're not laughing?" Carrie asked.

Chapter 34

Briggs stared at Jane from behind his desk. He was adorned in an Armani, navy double-breasted suit. His pale blue shirt with white collar was accentuated with a painted yellow silk power necktie.

With Briggs' European luxury attire murmuring success, Jane knew he could easily pass as the general manager of Georges Cinq, or a hotshot executive on Wall Street.

His office door was closed.

Jane was seated opposite him.

The two continued to stare at each other.

It occurred to Jane that Briggs must have a tanning bed at home. He always appeared as though he had just returned from the Caribbean. She tilted her head toward the president.

"You're dead meat, you know," Briggs said quietly.

"Excuse me?" Jane was startled.

"Not literally. Figuratively, I suppose, is the correct word."

Jane still didn't understand. "I must have heard you incorrectly."

"I don't think so, Jane," Briggs responded. "I said you're dead meat. And you have two choices, you can be a good girl and go with the flow, or you can fight me and lose everything."

She didn't know how to proceed. "I—"

Briggs held up his hand. "Enough, Jane. The charade is over, the gloves are off, the war is completed . . . and I've won."

"What war?" She could feel her heart thumping. "John, I have no idea what you're talking about."

Briggs tapped the manicured nail of one forefinger against a Roman coin cuff link. "Nor do you have to understand, it just is." He forced a grin. "Oh, relax, Jane. If you cooperate, you'll come out of this just fine."

Jane stared at Briggs. "I still have no idea what you're talking about."

"A shift in corporate strategy; a new paradigm; younger people to rally the troops. We're getting stale in our marketing ideas and efforts, Jane. It's time for a change from the current dinosaur thinking."

Jane shook her head. "Profits are at a record high this year, up twenty-eight percent, and due almost exclusively to increased market share. What are you talking about?"

"You heard me," Briggs answered, his face breaking into his sound-bite smile. He was enjoying himself.

"So why would you want to fix a machine that isn't broken?" Jane asked.

"Because the machine is capable of more," Briggs snapped.

"Precisely," Jane replied. "And the machine is producing more. Each year the company is more profitable than the year before."

"Ah, but not fast enough." Briggs shrugged.

"Give me a break, John. This is ridiculous," Jane said.

"Call it what you will, Jane. I'm only responding to the recent directives of the board."

Jane could feel the blood rushing to her face. She sat back, crossed her legs, and rested her elbow on the arm of the couch. "What's going on, John?" she asked, her voice now a cold, efficient, penetrating sword.

"Jane, corporate life is nothing if it doesn't embrace

modification. Fortunately, or unfortunately, it's the nature of the beast. Nothing stays the same no matter how much we may want it to. Change is a way of life."

"Get to the point, John," Jane said. It was obvious that whatever was going to happen had already been decided.

"Ah, the point." Briggs beamed. "Yes, the point." He leaned forward on his desk. "Effective January 1, you're out as vice president of marketing."

"You're not serious."

"Quite so," Briggs said. "With the board's approval, I have named Lauren Fritz to be your replacement." He gazed at Jane for a prolonged moment. "You look shocked, Jane, but you shouldn't be—these types of purges happen daily across America."

"What business logic would ever justify you ousting me as VP of marketing?" Jane asked.

"I'm paid for my knowledge of how to implement and run a people machine that maintains a leadership position in the marketplace," Briggs replied. "And that is what I intend to do."

"What do you think is happening here, John? What about the fact that when I was hired, fifty-eight percent of the company's products were either losing money or just breaking even, and now we're up twenty-eight percent across the board. What about the dollars, John?"

"Change is neither good nor bad, Jane, and if—"

"Let me make sure I understand what's happening here," Jane interrupted, her voice still controlled. "We're having a record year, and every one of our competitors is struggling—Klayborn's down eleven percent for the third quarter; LoBelle's is off eight percent and Hudson-Schenck is up one point." Jane leaned forward, her hands gripping her knees. "And you have the stunning audacity to tell me you're going to replace me? Are you kidding me, John?"

"It's not just about profits, Ja—"

"Not about profits?" Jane interrupted. "Since when has DSRR been about anything *but* profits?"

"Sometimes a personality change is just in order," Briggs stated calmly.

"Oh, please," Jane said, shaking her head. "You would have Fidel Castro as vice president of public relations if it meant more dollars in the coffer." She shook her head. "I'm not buying any of this, John, and I'll be damned if I'm going to be railroaded out of a job that I have more than excelled at because you arbitrarily feel like making a change."

"Alas," Briggs said, "the decision has already been made, Jane." He shrugged. "It's out of my control now."

"And you're going to tell me you fought to retain me as marketing VP every step of the way."

"Of course. Unfortunately," Briggs said, raising an eyebrow, "I was unsuccessful."

"John, it's a brave, new world we live in, a different corporate culture from the good-old-boy network that you grew up with. The days are gone when you just decide you want to make a change, then go ahead and do it."

"Please, please, please, Jane." Briggs held up his hand. "No one is talking about letting you go from the company. You will maintain a commensurate salary and most important, your dignity. We're just talking about a new position."

Jane hesitated. "What new position, John? The one we discussed at lunch?"

"Not exactly." Briggs tilted his head. "But here's where the fun comes in. With the board's approval, I've created a new opportunity for you."

Jane eyed the president.

"And I think you're going to enjoy it. It will be beneficial to the company, and you as well."

"What's the position, John?" Jane asked.

"Vice president of field research," Briggs replied. "A very necessary and important job." He hesitated a moment. "We want you to go out and analyze what the competitors are doing. Naturally, we would expect you to travel eighty percent of the time. You can understand that would be a mandatory requirement for this type of position."

"So you want me to resign, John. This offer has been designed specifically for that purpose."

"I beg to disagree," Briggs responded. "I like to move people around to enhance the vitality of the organization. That's all I'm doing."

"No one is capable of eighty percent travel for an extended period of time. You know that. And what would ever possess you to think that Lauren Fritz is capable of assuming my position? She's an untrained neophyte. Why would you ever, ever take such a risk?

"I happen to believe that Lauren has a brilliant mind. She has already given—"

"Give me a break, John." Her anger was mounting, borders eroding. "It's not Lauren's mind that gets you off in the backseat of your limo, is it?"

Briggs stared at her, his face flushed. "I certainly—"

"Am I the first one in years, outside of your wife, to say no to you?" Jane interrupted. She could feel herself trembling.

"Oh, please," Briggs said, his voice ratcheting up. "Don't start this nonsense again. Do you think this is about a middle-aged woman refusing sex? You're flattering yourself, Jane. You would be lucky to have me take you to bed."

Jane glared at the president, her ears burning. "Likewise."

Briggs shook his head, now back in control. "For someone as bright as you, Jane, it's hard to believe that you don't understand everything is about power, control, and money. And that's why I approached you—for control. We have a physical relationship, you get emotionally involved, and I end up controlling your mind."

"You have always been in charge, John," she said.

"Then figure it out, Jane." Briggs leaned forward so that his arms stretched across the top of his desk. "You're too good at what you do. The reality is that you've made too many positive advances at DSRR and the board is beginning to look to you instead of me for the future. I'm hearing the footsteps, especially because having a woman president is becoming a status symbol." He threw his hands out to his sides in a "What-are-you-gonna-do?" gesture. "It's just business, Jane, and I intend to remain on the throne. Kings have guillotines, and someone has to be beheaded."

"This has been a remarkable conversation, John," Jane said. "I intend to proceed from this office to Human Resources, after which I'll be speaking with my attorney."

"And lo and behold, I suspect if you were able to gain access to your personnel file through some expensive legal maneuvering over an extended period of time, you would find several complete and not totally positive evaluations of your performance, all signed off on by you."

Jane stared at Briggs. "You know no boundaries, do you, John?"

"I know of none because there are none, Jane. At the end of the day, my job is to keep my job."

"Even at the expense of the company," Jane said.

"*Especially* at the expense of the company, Jane. It's a wonderful lifestyle." Briggs stood and stretched. "So, I think that about wraps up our little meeting. Please let me know your decision concerning your new position." He paused. "Oh, yes, you can forget about your silly, little lilac perfume idea. From this point forward, everything must be cleared through Lauren."

Jane stood and walked to the door. "I'd like my new job description on paper, with the actual title, salary, bonus, and benefits indicated."

"And you shall have it, Jane, though I don't believe there is any provision for a bonus." He walked to the office door and stood next to her. "I trust you'll have a good day despite our unpleasant conference this afternoon." Briggs hesitated. "And needless to say, I expect you to represent DSRR in the best possible light when you give your speech at the Waldorf luncheon tomorrow."

Jane stood at the door facing the president. She was

reeling, struggling not to show her emotions.

Briggs opened the door. "Again, please don't take any of this personally, Jane. It's just business as usual." He held his hand with the forefinger pointed at her and his thumb straight up, simulating a revolver. "And you're looking a little haggard, so don't forget your vitamin C. Whatever your body doesn't absorb, you just pee away." He pretended to pull the trigger—at the same time winking. Turning away from Jane, he headed back to his desk.

CHAPTER 35

Jane rested in the brocade chair, wondering if the dust motes suspended in the sunlight would continue to float, or disintegrate as the dark approached.

The first stage of an arctic cold front had arrived. Strangers paraded past the window, their breath, vapor clouds. Could the dust motes escape through the glass and turn to ice crystals once outside?

And what about the baby on the cloud? Baby Jimmy. She knew him, but didn't recognize him. He was with her, but she couldn't see him, and saying his name aloud produced both joy and self-loathing.

Who was the baby on the cloud? She had no children. Why was the baby calling her mama?

And what about the pale-green candy dish locked in her memory?

Jane grieved. She had never been carefree, but she had once been young. She longed for the man named Ricky instead of her misspent youth with Jimmy. She wanted to be with him, in love, the way she always felt when he was near.

It had been almost a week since they had been together,

and on that occasion, instead of staying in bed, she had left to explore the surrounding area, ending up in Jack Reed's Tavern.

It had been a mistake. She should have stayed and savored their time together.

Jane had attempted regressions following the hypnosis session with Eric and Barbara, but each had been a fruitless effort, almost as if her mind was toying with itself, mocking its own desperation.

Or maybe she had been unable to regress because Jimmy was still in the house, and in the evening she could hear him fumbling around downstairs after returning from his AA meeting. His noise made it difficult to concentrate, and she feared that one day soon he would crash into the spare bedroom to offer his progress report in an attempt to win her back.

Jane rang the hand bell resting on the table beside her.

She now understood she was alone. It had always been that way. She'd had an unavailable mother, an unavailable father, then an unavailable husband, and now a job made unavailable by an unavailable boss.

Clarity reigned despite the confusion.

"Yes, madam, what may I get for you?" the waiter asked.

"Carrie, what are you going to have?"

"It's after five, I'm pissed off, and I feel like getting drunk," Carrie announced. She looked at the waiter. "Martini, two olives—the big kind. Up." She reconsidered. "No, make it one olive—the small kind—I don't want to displace too much alcohol. And have another one handy. I drink fast."

"Of course," the waiter said. "And you, madam?"

"The same," Jane answered.

"And I have to tell you something, Jane," Carrie said, her tone of voice dismissing the waiter, "I don't understand all this crap with Briggs. I can't believe he can pull something like this off."

"You underestimate him, Carrie. It's done. Everyone is

fearful for their jobs—no one will go up against him."

"What did your lawyer say?"

"I haven't called him yet," Jane answered.

"You've got to do that right away. Fast."

"Does it smell like lilacs in here?" Jane asked. She paused. "I can smell them."

"Lilacs? No. I can't smell anything except that cheap cologne the waiter is wearing. Where the hell does he think he's working, some strip joint in Omaha? We're in one of New York City's finest hotels, for crying out loud."

"I'd like to be on that porch near the lilac bush. The one I told you about," Jane said.

"Ladies," the waiter interrupted, "two martinis, straight up, as you requested." He picked a stemmed glass from his tray, placing Carrie's on the table first.

"Two things," Carrie said to the waiter. "First, be back in exactly ten minutes with a refill, and second, put a little vodka behind your ears."

The waiter placed Jane's drink in front of her and turned back to Carrie. "I do not understand, madam."

"Of course you don't. See you in ten." She looked away.

"Now that I'm a lame duck, I'm wondering if I should still give the speech tomorrow," Jane said.

"No choice, you have to," Carrie answered after taking a gulp of her drink. "Everyone is going to see how terrific you are, even though most people already know it. You don't get a lot of chances to speak at an industry conference at the Waldorf Astoria." Carrie sipped her drink. "I'm counting on you, Jane. The speech is going to launch you into a new job, and you're going to take me with you. Lauren Fritz isn't going to let me stick around either. You know that."

"You're right," Jane answered, nodding. "Lauren isn't going to let you stay, and I do have to give that speech."

"Damn tootin'," Carrie answered. "When is the last time you had a martini?"

"This is the first time," Jane admitted.

#8 12-30-2015 4:13PM
Item(s) checked out to p108021968.

TITLE: The last of us [PlayStation 3]
BARCODE: 31736005656311
DUE DATE: 01-06-16

TITLE: The Hobbit [electronic resource]
BARCODE: 31736005336229
DUE DATE: 01-06-16

TITLE: Kingdom hearts [electronic resour
BARCODE: 31736005093937
DUE DATE: 01-06-16

TITLE: After and before.
BARCODE: 31736006056024
DUE DATE: 01-13-16

Farmingdale Public Library
516-249-9090

Farmingdale Public Library
516-249-9090

DUE DATE: 01-13-16
BARCODE: 31723009029034
TITLE: After and before.

DUE DATE: 01-06-16
BARCODE: 31723005069637
TITLE: Kingdom hearts [electronic resour

DUE DATE: 01-06-16
BARCODE: 31723005339236
TITLE: The Hobbit [electronic resource]

DUE DATE: 01-06-16
BARCODE: 31723005959311
TITLE: The last of us [Translation 2]

Item(s) checked out to p10807159.
12-30-2015 4:13PM

#8 12-30-2015 4:13PM
Item(s) checked out to p108021968.

TITLE: The last of us [PlayStation 3]
BARCODE: 31736005656311
DUE DATE: 01-06-16

TITLE: The Hobbit [electronic resource]
BARCODE: 31736005336229
DUE DATE: 01-06-16

TITLE: Kingdom hearts [electronic resour
BARCODE: 31736005093937
DUE DATE: 01-06-16

TITLE: After and before.
BARCODE: 31736006056024
DUE DATE: 01-13-16

Farmingdale Public Library
516-249-9090

"Well, go slow, Jane, these suckers can knock you on your rear end and you may end up in bed with the train conductor." Carrie thought about her remark, darkly amused. "Of course, that's not necessarily all bad." She grinned and knocked back the remainder of the martini. "Know what I mean?" She winked and raised her hand to summon the waiter. "Garçon!"

∞

Jane sat in her flannel pajamas on the end of the bed in the guest bedroom. She wondered how she was ever going to summon the strength to march up to the lectern and deliver an impassioned thirty-minute speech hailing the successes of DSRR to hundreds of executives and their branding and marketing teams. She had written the words and had practiced the delivery, but she remained apprehensive.

She wished she could have seen Eric, but it was Monday and she was scheduled for Tuesday.

Jane could hear Jimmy knocking around in the kitchen below and then his footsteps on the stairs. She turned out the overhead light. To her relief, his footsteps entered the master bedroom, the door clicking behind him.

If she was honest, Jane knew that Jimmy, with his limited world vision, never had much of a chance, and now with the restricted interaction between them, he seemed barely able to manage his daily duties—a bear sorting through the garbage, searching for survival.

And what about regression and Ricky? If he wasn't so real, she would have dismissed the whole process long ago.

Baby in the air.

On a cloud or in the air? The fingers in the mouth, the sweet little eyes searching for her.

Baby Jimmy.

Jane set the alarm clock for 5:00 a.m., reviewed the key talking points of her speech, then lay back and prayed for victory.

Chapter 36

An industry sales leader once told her that to prepare for a major presentation in front of powerful decision-makers, he would spend an hour beforehand telling himself how good he was while at the same time concentrating on being wise, sharp and proactive.

He said it worked. He didn't always get them to purchase, but as a rule, potential customers were left with the favorable impression that he was excited about his message and interested in their business—meaning they would allow him to pitch again—which was new life, manna from heaven, in a torturous occupation.

Jane stepped off the train in Grand Central and ascended the stairs.

On the walk uptown to the office, she considered her options and decided she had only one: strength. She wouldn't give Briggs the satisfaction of seeing her dispirited. She wouldn't allow him the knockout punch, but instead would play the game, appear unconcerned, and at lunch give a brilliant speech that would leave the audience of high-powered management teams standing and applauding.

When she entered her office, on her desk was a memo addressed to all company personnel, stating that Jane was considering moving into a new role as vice president of competitive field research, and that her current position would be assumed, beginning January 1, by Lauren Fritz. The memo went on to detail Lauren's background, with the final paragraph stating that the board of directors was grateful for Jane's significant contributions to the company and they looked forward to the development of field research. An attached organizational chart showed that Jane would be reporting to Lauren.

While she was reading, Jane noticed that the normal stream of people walking past her office had tapered to practically none. After several minutes, two associates, Adam Jons, research and development, and Philip Dean, the finance hotshot, independently stopped to express their concerns about her position change.

Following those two, nothing.

"Leper," Carrie said minutes later, sticking her head in the door. "You're radioactive because of your job, and everyone thinks that if they come too close it will happen to them too." She stepped inside Jane's office and closed the door. "Don't worry, I'm leper number two. Nobody is listening to me anymore either. Bring out the cadaver dogs; we're dead and buried."

"Did you get home all right?" Jane asked.

"Yes, and I didn't know who I felt like meeting," Carrie replied, "Howard or the train conductor. Howard was still at work, but it didn't matter anyway because within five minutes, no one would have been able to wake me with a pitchfork."

Jane nodded. She was fighting to maintain her strength, her inner focus, to not revert back to her mother's fearful, weak mentality. She had plenty of money, certainly enough to conduct a job search for a year or two, and more than solid credentials. She could take her time, and if Briggs persisted in bad-mouthing her, she would sue him.

That was simple enough.

But it wasn't easy.

"Do you want to walk over with me to the Waldorf?" she asked. "I'd like to get the lay of the land."

"I'm so there," Carrie answered. "Let me get my coat and we'll go." She turned and opened the door.

∞

The grand ballroom of the Waldorf Astoria was impressive in its size. She would be sitting on the dais with several NCA officers. As the waiters were setting up the room, Jane walked up to the lectern. She looked out at what would be a vast audience and took a deep breath. The spotlight would spear her when she spoke, focusing on every word, leaving no room for escape.

"Are you ready for this?" Carrie asked. "Today you're the star. Today you wow them, and the two of us move forward to a better life with a superior company, leaving Briggs' to fall on his face." She rubbed her hands together. "Know what I mean?" Carrie looked closely at Jane. "Hey, pal, you've got to lighten up. This is going to be a big moment for you. Just remember you're hot stuff." She put her arm around Jane's shoulder for a few moments.

Jane nodded. "You're a good friend, Carrie. I haven't said it often enough, but I'm so glad you're part of my life."

"Same with me," Carrie answered. "Friends to the end."

∞

The moments leading to the speech were closing in. Jane chatted amiably with the man sitting next to her on the dais, the whole time, her inner eye watching, measuring, and wondering if she could give the speech effectively. What if she tripped on the way to the lectern? What if she lost her voice?

All at once, the waiters were clearing plates.

"And so it is my pleasure to speak of a woman . . ."

How did that happen so quickly? The waiters were just picking up the plates a few seconds before.

"Her vision for *Scarlett!* was a smash and took the industry by storm . . ."

Jane swallowed and attempted to relax.

"And we understand that there is a new product in the pipeline scheduled to launch in the first quarter of next year. If it's anything like her long line of previous successes, competition beware."

Jane swallowed again, as she slid her seat backward.

"Ladies and gentleman, it's my pleasure to introduce DSRR's vice president of marketing, one of the decade's huge success stories, Ms. Jane McBride."

The applause was instantaneous and thunderous.

Jane walked to the lectern and lightly placed a hand on each side of her written speech. She couldn't see five feet in front of her because of the blinding spotlight pinning her in place—a moth, wings spread, pinned to an entomologists' exhibition board.

"Thank you. Thank you all very much," she said, a smile forced across her lips. "You're very kind."

As the clapping began to diminish, Jane added, "And thank you for your support of *Scarlett!*"

The applause increased momentarily, then abruptly stopped.

"It's been quite a year, and quite a decade," Jane began. She could hear her own voice from the monitor on the side of the podium. "We've all come a long way, and if I could, I'd like to talk about the advances in the cosmetics industry, and what has been happening within DSRR's walls. And, I'm going to let you in on a few secrets—a couple of products that we almost took to market, but at the last minute had the foresight to call off." Jane ran her hand across her brow, feigning sweat—corny, but effective because it caused a ripple of laughter. She shrugged. "Hey, nobody's perfect." Another ripple of laughter.

As Jane spoke, she broke into a rhythm that was comfortable for her, and based on the audience's spontaneous reactions, pleasurable for them. They listened attentively as she focused on emphasis points, and laughed appreciatively, even at her weakest attempts at humor.

Gradually, she realized she owned them, and she knew Briggs was watching it happen. He would be in the audience, hungering for her failure, all the while praising her to associates and explaining, "I'm so sorry about Jane having to change positions."

Then almost imperceptibly, as she proceeded, Jane grew certain she was going to be hailed as a star—no one in the industry would have anything but rave notices. Briggs had grossly miscalculated her worth and power, and she would insist on payback.

As she paused for emphasis, staring out into the pitch black in front of her, Jane noticed dust motes captured in the spotlight. She looked down at her speech, then up again. The dust motes remained, still floating in front of her.

"So if the cosmetics industry is to continue with its goal of being part of the cutting edge of technology, we have several key factors to consider."

She didn't look up again. The dust motes would be closer.

"With financial margins lowering, one area we have to look at is cost reduction if we are to survive. Rather than have the mandatory cost of insurance built into any product's research and development, let's attack on the home front. Consider this: a woman cuts her finger on a mildly defective lipstick tube and wins a multi-million-dollar judgment. In another part of the country, a different woman develops a minor rash allegedly due to a reaction with a perfume and wins three quarters of a million dollars." Jane paused and stared out at the audience. "Are we crazy to put up with this, or what? Let's cut the tort lawyers off at the knees by legally counterattacking." She was building. "As an industry, let's hire some top-notch public relations firms to make Americans aware that the majority of these lawyers are not remotely interested in their clients, but only in frivolous lawsuits aimed at companies with deep pockets, companies that will help them increase their own personal wealth. That's the only reason they're suing in the first place."

The audience erupted with applause.

Jane looked into the blackness. The motes were gone. She smiled.

Suddenly she recognized the scent of lilacs, clean, clear, at the edge of the porch. And somewhere near the outer fringes was a baby she thought she remembered.

All at once, she could feel the wind blowing through her hair. Her arms were around Ricky. She struggled to hold back the tears of happiness.

Jane paused to regroup. "And second, let's talk about the politicians."

"Let's not," a man's voice rang out from the blackness, causing a groundswell of laughter.

"And that's the problem," Jane said, "We have to ask, are they working in our best interests?"

The wind was fiercer. She was on the back of his Indian motorcycle.

"Hell, no!" the voice bellowed back to more laughter.

Jane's visual images began to break up, flickering like the frames of a black-and-white silent movie as Ricky banked around a curve.

She tried to concentrate. "We have to ask . . ."

The ballroom images were fading and she was locked to him, her hair streaming behind her."

"We have to ask . . ."

The ballroom, the spotlight, the audience were disappearing as she watched Ricky's right hand twist the Indian's throttle, increasing the speed as the two leaned out of another turn.

"We have . . ."

Ricky reached back and patted her leg. "You happy, Janey?" he called, his words flying past her.

She nodded and tightened her arms around his waist as the countryside streamed by in long, flowing yards of dazzling color.

The ballroom had disappeared, the dust motes were gone, and she had never been happier in her life.

CHAPTER 37

Jane heard rustling around her and wasn't sure whether to open her eyes.

She listened closely.

A cough. Rubber soles squeaking. Further away—metallic clanking.

"Connie, don't forget two-twenty-one," a voice called.

She summoned the black fog to return, but it was receding, leaving her exposed and ugly. Her eyelids fluttered and opened to a fluorescent glare.

"How are you feeling today, Mrs. McBride?" a nurse asked.

Jane didn't answer. She was hooked up to an IV. The skin on the inside of her left arm was raw and stretched with tape.

"The doctor will be in to see you soon," the nurse said.

Jane closed her eyes, willing the blackness to return so she could begin her journey back to Ricky.

"You ought to try and stay awake now," the nurse added. "You've had a lot of sleep."

Jane ignored the advice and kept her eyes closed. The precious darkness was reappearing and she slipped into it, searching for an Indian motorcycle with a rider in a brown leather jacket.

She listened for an engine in the distance.

Instead, she lingered in half-light, half exposed.

∞

"Jane."

Another voice.

"Jane."

She opened her eyes. Eric was sitting next to her bed. Her hand was in his.

She stared at the psychiatrist. "What happened? Why am I here?"

"You fainted near the end of your speech yesterday. Fortunately, one of the men on the dais saw you begin to falter and caught you before you touched the floor." He hesitated. "Dr. Greenman called me."

Jane stared at Eric's fingers wrapped around her own.

"I'm sorry," he said, pulling his hand away. "That's beyond unprofessional."

Jane gazed at her fingers, then at Eric. "Am I all right?" she asked.

"Preliminary blood work is all negative. Dr. Greenman has scheduled you for a couple of tests tomorrow morning. If those are negative, you can go home."

Jane surveyed the hospital room. After a moment, she asked, "Why did you let go of my hand?"

He hesitated.

Jane raised her fingers toward him.

He didn't move.

"Please," Jane said.

Eric reached over and held her hand within his. "You're going to be fine," he said.

"I know," Jane answered.

"I promise."

Jane nodded again. She closed her eyes.

∞

"Hey, getting out of the city is a beautiful thing," Carrie said as the car left the hospital parking lot. "Which way? The arrow says 95 North. That's got to be the direction to Connect-eye-cut."

"That's right," Jane answered. "But you didn't have to drive me home, Carrie. I could have taken a cab."

"To Andover? Nobody's that rich, Jane. Not even you! Plus it's below freezing right now and those city cabs can't even close their damn windows!"

Jane paused, ignoring the comment. "You haven't answered my question yet. How badly did I embarrass myself at the Waldorf?"

"Forget embarrassment. I think the incident enhanced your reputation. You're the center of the industry buzz; a rock star. Everyone thinks you're a trouper who's been working too hard, and now you've put Briggs on the bubble. If he lets you go, he's the bad guy, deserting you in your hour of need. Not to mention how he is able to justify releasing someone who has done so much for our company in such a short period of time." Carrie glanced over at Jane. "I think he was planning to unload you in the dead of night, between product launches, when no one was paying attention. Now that you're industry news, he'll have trouble sneaking it through—it will make him look like the buffoon he is."

Jane was silent.

"And, by the way, your speech was sensational. Everyone was leaning forward to hear every word. Briggs had to be dying."

"Briggs will just say that I've taken a less demanding position."

"A demotion? How can he justify that? He can't."

Jane shook her head. "He'll try though. He'll spin it for his own benefit. And we know he's very good at that."

"If he's a fool, he can try," Carrie said, "but I think you've catapulted yourself right into the driver's seat." She glanced over at Jane. "Trust me, he's got a major-league problem."

∞

Jane sat in her home office. How was she in love with someone she had discovered in a past-life regression? How was she able to retreat there? Both questions should have been enough to terrify her, and did, sort of—but her feelings for Ricky were so powerful, they overshadowed the fear.

Everything was a mystery.

And baby Jimmy . . .

The phone rang six times, then silence.

She could still visualize the colors sliding past her as she rode on the back of the Indian, her arms around Ricky.

The phone rang again.

She picked up the receiver. "Hello."

"Jane? Barbara Greenman. How are you feeling?"

"How am I feeling?" Jane asked. "How should I feel?" She knew her voice had an edge to it. "I'm sorry, Barbara. I'm just overwhelmed."

"Understood," the doctor answered. "But you should begin to feel better because all your tests were negative."

"That's good news. What's going on?"

"Well, physiologically, you're in good shape."

"Why did I faint?" Jane asked.

"Anybodys guess," Barbara responded. "If I had to venture an opinion, I would suggest that you're under a lot of hindrance stress. You know, a lot of negative, political pressure in the workplace, and maybe at home."

"I don't mean to question you, Barb, and I appreciate your care and concern, but I think everybody has that. Isn't stress like a virus, another generic word used when there's no specific diagnosis?"

"To a degree," Barbara answered, "but it's still real."

Jane thought a moment. "Thank you."

"Make an appointment in a couple of weeks. We'll do the blood work again to see if there are any changes. And relax if you can. I would recommend you continue to see Dr. Alford."

"Yes, I intend to."

∞

Jane dozed on the couch until she heard Jimmy's footsteps tramping through the kitchen. He flipped the switch to the living room and stopped in his tracks.

"I fell asleep down here." Jane said.

"I was worried about you being in the hospital when your office called." He ran his hands on the front of his pants as if drying them. "When I called, the nurse told me you were being released."

Jane didn't speak.

"Are you all right?" Jimmy asked.

Jane nodded. "I think."

Jimmy sat on the edge of a chair. "I'm glad." He stared at Jane. "I'm doing pretty good, too. It's not easy to stop drinking."

Jane stared. She sensed a quiet desperation oozing from him, an individual attempting to survive in a no-man's-land he had never successfully navigated before. She could smell the unease, the discomfort, the fear.

"But I'm going to do it. For you, I'm going to do it." He ran his tongue around his lips. "I'm doing it for you, Jane."

Jane studied the floor. Poor Jimmy attempting to jump off the carousel. She looked up. "Don't worry about me. Do it for yourself," she whispered. "Please do it for yourself, Jimmy."

CHAPTER 38

Jane suspected she was on the brink—unable to effectively distinguish between two realities—floating from one to the other, committed to neither. Based on what had happened during her speech, she could no longer presume any control over her regressions—they would take her when and where they pleased—which was terrifying as it meant anything could happen to her vacated body once her mind slipped away.

And it was a waiting game. She couldn't bring herself to move. She hadn't consulted a lawyer about her job. She had done no additional work on *Arabesque*, nor had she been in her office since her speech at the Waldorf. She had canceled her Thursday evening appointment with Eric and slept in her clothes the night before.

Carrie had begged her to come to the office immediately so she could attack Briggs at his most vulnerable moment, and while her name was still white-hot in the industry. She was sure Jane could make demands of Briggs, and because of the public relations exposure, he would cave. Don't give him time to regroup, she insisted over the telephone during three phone calls, nail him now!

"Jane."

She looked up. Eric stood in front of her. "Eric. We meet again."

"I came to pick up a sandwich at the coffee shop and saw you sitting over here in the park." He stared down at her. "Do you mind if I join you?"

"No," Jane answered, sliding over on the bench.

"I'm worried about you," Eric said, sitting down. "Also, you canceled our appointment Thursday night, and right now—especially now, I think you need to continue what we started."

"I don't think less of you for holding my hand, Eric. I thought it was a very kind thing for you to do." She smiled.

"The problem," Eric said after several seconds, "is that you're a patient, and that type of intimacy is unethical."

"Do you like me?" Jane asked. She surprised herself.

Eric chuckled. "Yes, I like you."

"As a patient," Jane said.

"As a patient, and a person," Eric responded.

"So what's the problem?"

"Right now, there is no problem, but I sense that a little farther down the road there might be." Eric crossed his leg over his knee and grabbed his ankle. "It's difficult to explain, Jane."

"You look good in jeans. I bet I look a little grubby."

"You look fine," Eric said.

Jane's eyes filled. "I'm not, though."

Eric leaned toward her. "Tell me."

"We're all on treadmills, Eric. Isn't it obvious?"

Eric shifted. "Tell me what you mean."

"Can I tell you where I've been going and why I want to stay?" she asked.

"Please," he replied. "I would like that."

She stared at Eric, then tentatively asked, "Where do I begin?"

"Where would you like to begin?"

"I'm not sure."

"Wherever you like."

Jane nodded. Slowly, she began detailing the regressions except for the little boy, Jimmy, calling for her from the clouds.

After an uninterrupted forty-five minutes, she finished. "That's it."

Eric smiled briefly.

She hesitated. "Am I crazy?"

Eric shook his head. "Surely not. The subconscious is delivering an unfinished message—a series of powerful symbols that we have to interpret."

"I think it's all real."

"I know you believe that, Jane," Eric said. "Let's leave it there for the time being."

"So you're going to continue being my doctor?"

"As long as I can keep the professional role from becoming a personal one."

"You can do that," Jane answered.

"I can try to do that." He studied her. "Now what about your job? Do you feel you're able to tackle it, considering the emotional issues you're struggling with?"

"I can deal with the job. As a matter of fact, I need to go back."

"Only if you're up to it," Eric said. "I'm thinking you might benefit from some additional rest, some additional time off.

"I can handle work," Jane answered. "I'm okay."

Eric nodded. "Then it's important that you have a plan, Jane. You must have a strategy."

Jane nodded. She had to take some kind of control of what was left of her life, or at least make the token effort. "Today's Sunday. I'll go to the office tomorrow."

"If you'd like to structure a plan on how to deal with your president, it's certainly something we could work on. Remember, Jane, it's all a game, but the repercussions for not participating can leave you a bystander. You don't want that."

"I can handle Briggs," Jane answered. "I know what he's about."

Eric continued to stare at her. "Any history of seizures or mental illness in your family?" Eric asked. "I know we've discussed this before, but I'm just rechecking."

Jane shook her head.

"Do you hear voices?"

"I just heard yours," she answered, smiling.

"Have you ever taken illegal drugs of any kind?"

Jane laughed aloud. "If you're thinking something like that, you don't know me at all, Eric."

"Just checking," he replied. "Barb said you're not on any medication, correct?"

"Correct, unless you count calcium."

"No, that doesn't count." He hesitated. "And you're sure you feel well enough to return to work? There's no need to rush back."

"I'm sure." She stood. "The sun is still out, but I'm getting cold. Funny weather, warm one minute, freezing the next. I hear there's snow on the horizon."

"So I hear," Eric said, standing. "Where are you parked?"

"Across the street," Jane answered, pointing toward the coffee shop.

"Me too. I'll walk with you."

The two crossed from the park in silence.

"Last question, Jane," Eric said as they approached the two cars. "You don't know any of the people you've come into contact with in your regressions, correct?"

"None, except for one," Jane answered.

"And who's that?" Eric asked, surprised.

"The man," Jane answered. "I know the man I was dancing with."

"I thought you didn't."

"I couldn't tell you."

"Okay then," Eric said. "Who is he?"

"And I thought you were such a hotshot doctor," Jane said. "You don't know who Ricky is?"

"Nope," Eric said. "I have no idea."

Jane stopped and looked up at the psychiatrist, then giggled nervously like a seventh-grade teenybopper staring at her favorite music idol. "He's you, Eric. Ricky is you."

CHAPTER 39

Briggs strode to the lectern in the corporate auditorium Monday morning and slid prepared notes from the inside breast pocket of his suit jacket. He turned up his photo-op smile. "Good morning, everyone. I appreciate you spending a few minutes of your busy day with your president." He paused for emphasis. "So before I begin, first let me thank you for doing an extraordinary job keeping our company the fastest growing cosmetics division in America. We're a team, and you've shown what teamwork can accomplish. You should be proud of yourselves."

A murmur rustled through the auditorium.

Briggs paused again, and then put his solemn boardroom face into play to match his deep blue mourning necktie. "I know many of you are concerned about the status of our current marketing vice president, Jane McBride. Please, let me put your minds at ease. She's resting comfortably and, I am told, feeling much better. We all know the stress that accompanies the workplace environment, and Jane, with her dedication to this company, has probably worked too hard for too long a period of time. Perhaps, in a way, we're all guilty of that.

"For the past two years, maybe three, I have been concerned that Jane has been putting too much effort into her position, and then, alas," Briggs said, lifting his hands into the air simulating his helplessness, "her speech at the conference last week verified my concern. I have deep regrets that I didn't recognize the symptoms and intervene earlier." Briggs paused for another moment. "I believe that several days before her speech, Jane had begun to realize that she needed a rest, and therefore, reduced responsibilities." He lifted up a piece of paper for the audience to see. "I have her request here, and I must tell you because of her talent it was very difficult to honor. Being the trouper that she was, she felt she would be letting the company down by taking a less stressful position, but I assured her that my personal mantra is that faith, family, and health take priority over anything in our corporate lives. I think Jane understands that now."

Briggs resumed his smile. "As you know, Lauren Fritz of The Grey Street Group will assume Jane's position, which will greatly benefit us. She brings a wealth of experience and know-how to the job and is ready to hit the ground running on January second. Please make her feel welcome." He looked around. "Lauren, where are you sitting? Stand up, please."

Seated in the front row, Lauren stood, then turned to face the audience behind her and waved a friendly hello. Nodding, she said, "Thank you, John," and sat down.

"She's a brilliant marketer," Briggs said, "and because you know I've been instrumental in the process of bringing *Scarlett!* to market, and through my oversight the *Arabesque* campaign is due to start no later than end of the first quarter, I think it's fair to surmise you are all in good hands until Lauren gets up to speed. You're a wonderful group and I thank you from the bottom of my heart for your work ethic and your commitment to the company." Briggs looked across the auditorium. "Any questions." He glanced around once more. "All right, then—"

"Mr. Briggs?" A woman's voice from the back of the auditorium rang out.

Briggs looked in that direction, squinting to see. "Yes?"

"I wonder if you could read us Jane McBride's letter? You know the one you were holding up before?"

"I beg your pardon? That's an odd question." He shaded his eyes using the flat of his hand, looking out into the audience. "And you are?"

"Carrie Dreyfus," the woman called out.

"Carrie, that wouldn't be fair to Jane," Briggs said, lowering his hand from his eyes.

"I wouldn't mind," another female voice echoed from the rear of the auditorium.

Briggs shaded his eyes again. "Who's that speaking?" he inquired.

"Jane McBride," Jane said, rising.

"Jane, I didn't know you were back," Briggs said, rebounding quickly. "I'm delighted to see you. Please, following this gathering, let's meet in my office."

"I'll be glad to, John," Jane answered, "but again, you have my permission to read the letter. I'd love to hear what I wrote."

"Thank you, Jane," Briggs said, "but in the interest of time, and because these are Human Resources issues, I wouldn't feel comfortable making your confidential letters public without legal authorization." Briggs smiled. "Anything else?" It was a rhetorical question. "My thanks to you all, and Jane, I'm looking forward to talking with you." He clicked off the microphone and headed across the stage to the doorway, Lauren following in lockstep.

∞

"He is so full of it, talking about some bogus letter." Carrie said.

Jane sat at the desk in her office. "Should I go up and see

him?"

"Of course you should go up and see him. You have to do that!" Carrie responded.

"The funny thing is I'm not staying here anyway," Jane replied, then remembering Eric's words, continued, "but I guess I should go up and negotiate with him. He's got to pay me some hush money."

"See if you can get some for me too, will you?" Carrie asked. "I'm next in line to be let go."

"Are you sorry?" Jane asked.

"Nah, I can always do lap dances," Carrie said.

"Meet me at noon for lunch at Ruocchio's," Jane responded, standing. "I'll tell you what Briggs offers. I'll see if I can negotiate a buy-out package for you."

"You're the best," Carrie said, rising and heading for the door. "The very, very, very best."

∞

Carrie was seated at their usual table when Jane entered the restaurant.

"So?" she inquired expectantly.

"One week's pay for every year I've been at DSRR, which means a little over two months' salary. He'll up it to two weeks per year if I sign a legal agreement stating I won't sue the company or him."

"You've got to be kidding," Carrie said. "Two or three months pay for what you've done for this organization. That's criminal."

"You get the same deal," Jane said. "No more, no less."

"Is he going to force me out?" Carrie asked.

"Don't know. But knowing how Briggs operates, I wouldn't be surprised."

"John Briggs. What a guy!" Carrie said softly.

"I don't think he has to do anything beyond what's in the

employment policy manual," Jane said. We'll see. I'm going to talk to my attorney.

Carrie nodded and signaled James, the waiter, who crossed to the table. "Martini. Straight up," she said. "Hold the olives, hold the onions, hold the lemon peel, hold the vermouth, and hold me."

"Excuse me?" James inquired.

"Sorry, sexual harassment. Make it fast though. Bring one for my friend too." She looked at Jane. "Your corporate credit card still works, doesn't it?"

"As far as I know," Jane answered. She nodded her approval to the waiter, who crossed the dining room and disappeared into the crowd at the bar.

"Well, as long as we're temporarily equals, how about we fire down a couple of martinis apiece, then grab a couple of spinach salads, followed by a splash of post-luncheon port. Then I'll go up and tell Briggs what I really think of him."

"I don't think that's a good idea," Jane said.

"I know, but it would sure feel good."

∞

At 3:15 in the morning, Jane suddenly sat up in bed, the sheets held to her neck. She'd almost forgotten what it was like to wear his ring and feel his fingertips pressed against hers.

CHAPTER 40

The next evening, Christmas lights were draped across houses and trees—red, green, and blue pinpoints—forced bulbs, artificial in the winter. The effects of the one martini had worn off—Carrie drank three—it was four o'clock, and darkness was descending. As Jane approached her home, the twilight recast the driveway into iron, and the roof's textured architectural shingles had transformed to slate. Outside the car, the freezing air caused winter wood to creak with every breath of wind.

Jimmy now scheduled his insurance appointments up until he went to his AA meetings, so Jane knew she would be alone.

She walked into the kitchen and switched on an overhead light, then lit the burner beneath the kettle. Sifting through the mail Jimmy had left on the counter, she saw nothing of interest.

Jane poured the hot water into a mug and dunked the teabag. She had to remember to call her attorney in the morning.

After climbing the stairs, she kicked off her shoes in the hallway. It was early. She could take a bath, heat up a frozen meal, and be in the spare bedroom by seven-thirty or eight. Despite what she told Eric, she was still not sure about going into DSRR for the remainder of the month, but was leaning toward doing it—to make things tougher for Briggs and to keep her corporate profile elevated for any headhunters that might be interested.

Yes, it made sense to return.

With her remaining time, she was going to take full command of her job. She planned to continue the work on *Arabesque* with the ad agency and take full credit for it by announcing her accomplishments in the trade publications. The lilac perfume idea had been canceled, but with a little more thought, she could take it to the next company she landed with and become an overnight hero.

∞

The call she had long dreaded arrived in the dead of night. Jane's heart was racing as she picked up the phone at 2:15 a.m. After quickly dressing, she drove to the hospital.

∞

Jimmy's car had spun off the road and flipped, leaving him hanging upside down, limbs dangling from the seatbelt that held his torso in place.

When they were first married, he always told her that as long as he wore his seatbelt he would be safe.

And finally, he was. He never had to worry about dying again.

∞

Jimmy's face appeared particularly content, as if he was about ready to launch into his latest Irish tale about the Catholic priest listening to the farmer's daughter's confession.

"I'm sorry, Mrs. McBride," the ER doctor said, sliding a lukewarm paper cup of coffee into her hand. "His blood alcohol was way high, three times the legal limit, and as I understand it, he hit an icy patch." He paused. "Would you like me to call a friend or a family member for you?"

"Thank you, no," Jane answered. As she left the hospital, she dropped the cup of coffee into a trash barrel and then crossed to her car.

∞

Once home, Jane walked into the master bedroom, opened Jimmy's closet and ran her hands across his suits and jackets. He had his own particular scent that was a combination of Irish Spring and Barbados Bay Rum. She parted the suits and in the back of the closet noticed a white pair of shoes she didn't recall Jimmy wearing, or even owning. She reached back, pulled them out and stared at his old battered college football cleats.

Jimmy was dead, but his dream lived on.

As she stood, unmoving, concentrating, the essence of him surrounded her so completely he could have been behind her, his hands resting on her shoulders.

She sat on the floor in front of the closet and stared at each suit, each pair of shoes, each necktie, over and over again, memorizing and forgetting him, until she began to cry softly for herself, for her deceased husband, for days long gone, and for a life she deplored.

Jane covered her face with her hands.

She felt an arm around her shoulders.

Lilacs filled the air.

"I'm so happy you're here," she whispered.

"I'll always be here for you, Janey."

"He's gone. He's dead."

"Yes, that's true," Ricky said.

"What am I going to do?" she asked. Her body was trembling.

"Survive with me. That's the first step," Ricky answered. "That's what we do in life. We survive."

Minutes passed, her tears ended and her breathing normalized. She rose and sat in the rocking chair.

Ricky stayed on the steps and watched her.

"I understand," she answered at last. "I get it."

CHAPTER 41

Jane stared out the train window at the passing frozen urban decay.

Carrie had left a message on her home phone the night before, telling her it was urgent. Jane hadn't responded.

She knew Jimmy's blood was sprinkled somewhere in the snow, a red-and-white collage of holiday cheer.

She should have been grieving for the loss of her husband, or at the very least for another human being, but all she felt was relief.

Jimmy was gone. She had made arrangements to have him cremated and the ashes stored at the funeral home.

And his death seemed to legitimize Ricky even more. She needed to find him and be with him, or at least drive in that direction until she ran out of road.

∞

Jane stepped off the train in Grand Central, and once upstairs in the terminal, she paused to glance at the ceiling.

The constellations had regrouped in the heavens and revealed an outline of the baby's face. It was there—clear, engaging. Jane looked down, then up once more. The stars had realigned and the child had disappeared.

She realized she was traveling too far from shore. No one believed what she knew to be true. And Ricky's world was so compelling that if she were to discover—as she was sure Eric assumed—it was all her imagination, she would be crushed, a result of overwhelming disappointment.

Suddenly Jane was desperate. She needed confirmation that the regressions were genuine, that she could learn how to travel to and from her interactive life with Ricky, both safely and at her discretion.

Twyla. Not Eric. Twyla! Twyla! Twyla!

Medical science now understood that the human brain had infinite capabilities and was, at least according to Twyla, a microscopic complex of cells and dark matter loaded with questions and answers. It was possible people like Twyla, as unorthodox as they might appear, were the unidentified scientific pioneers, moving forward toward new frontiers of truth, leaving mainstream medicine behind.

Of course. And it gave her the hope that she desperately needed.

Jane blew off the office and headed downtown.

"Thank you," she said to the driver as she handed him a twenty-dollar bill, then opened the cab door and stepped onto West Eleventh Street.

Twyla's entrance was a block away. As she neared the building, an elderly man in baggy gold corduroys was leaving and held the door for her.

Jane climbed the stairs to the first landing, and as usual, saw the door ajar. She was about to press the doorbell, when she overheard Twyla speaking on the phone.

"So that's my conclusion, honey, never, never cut your hair while you're going with a man. Let that wait until he's married you." Twyla paused, listening, and then laughed. "Yup, for some reason men like long hair, but of course, they don't have to take care of it." She paused again. "Yes, yes . . ." She listened. "Not so good. No. No, I don't know why it's so slow."

Jane lifted her hand to ring the bell.

"I guess people are beginning to catch on to me."

Jane halted her hand in mid-air.

"Look, Lois, you know and I know that this whole business is a fraud. I've made some good money from it, especially when it was a hot item a few years ago. But now it's old hat—the classifieds aren't drawing more than two or three leads a week, barely enough to pay for the ads themselves, and the people with the real money aren't interested anymore."

Jane let her hand drift to her side.

"I know," Twyla continued, "and I'll always welcome new ideas, honey. The beauty of regression is that you can make it up as you go along, and nobody can ever prove whether it's bogus or not. That's a tough act to recreate." She paused. "Yeah, I know. If you think of anything, let me know. I've got to pay the rent and things are on the lean side these days." She listened for few seconds. "All right, honey, I will. You're right, maybe Florida would be another opportunity. See ya, hon."

Jane leaned against the wall. Her face was flushed. She pressed the doorbell.

"Who's there?" Twyla called.

"Jane McBride."

"One minute please."

Seconds later, the door swung open. "Jane," Twyla said, a surprised look crossing her face. "What are you doing here?"

"I needed to see you."

Twyla frowned. "I assume you haven't been waiting long."

"Long enough to know I shouldn't ever cut my hair before I get married," Jane answered in a low voice.

"Oh, you heard me talking with my sister, Lois, and heard the part about regression therapy too." She opened the door wider and gestured toward the center of the apartment. "Come in." She turned and walked toward the living room.

Jane followed. "Lois claims to be the world's leading realist," Twyla said over her shoulder, "and has constantly told me that regression therapy is nonsense. I agree with her just to appease her and keep family harmony. Know what I mean?"

"Not really," Jane answered.

"Sit, sit, honey. Do you have a minute? How about a Coke, or tea, or something?" Twyla asked.

Jane sat down in a chair next to the coffee table. "I just want a little information."

Twyla settled opposite her. "Okay, I can do that."

"How real is past-life regression?" Jane asked.

Twyla shrugged. "As real as you want it to be. It changes from individual to individual."

"It's very real for me," Jane said.

"Good," Twyla answered, "then you'll benefit the most."

"Are you sure it works?"

"Of course it works."

"And you believe it?"

"Of course, I believe it, Jane." She glanced at her watch. "I have—"

"I'm physically involved with someone I met during a past-life regression," Jane interrupted.

"Excuse me?"

"Now, when I regress, I'm younger, and I'm in love with a younger version of someone I currently know, and we're physically involved."

"Ah, yes, the lifelike beauty of regression. A dream—"

"It's not a dream. It's real. I'm physically involved with a man I met during a regression."

"That's impossible," Twyla stated.

"It's not impossible," Jane countered, "it's true."

"All right," Twyla said, "if you say so." She glanced at her watch. "It's good to see you, Jane, but I've got my boyfriend stopping over and I have to get ready."

"Have you ever heard of a situation like mine before?" Jane persisted. "You know, where people are physically together during a regression."

"No," Twyla said, "because it's not interactive. You watch and listen to the people and places you visit, but you can't engage them."

"But I did," Jane said.

"All right, fine," Twyla said, standing. "If you want to call it interacting, that's fine. I've really—"

"You brought me there," Jane said, her voice rising, "from here to there and there to here, and it's entirely real to me, and I need to be able to control the times I go back and forth because sometimes now it just happens." She abruptly halted and stared at Twyla.

"Jane, I think we've gotten way off base here. Regression is merely a process, a mental exercise achieved through hypnotism. That's all."

"You led me there, Twyla," Jane said as she stood, her voice more insistent. "Now I need you to teach me how to regress, and return, but only when I choose to. Right now it just happens arbitrarily and I have no control." Jane stopped.

Twyla eyed her, saying nothing.

"Help me, please, you have to help me!"

"That would be beyond me, Jane," Twyla said quietly. "What you're imagining is not making any sense."

"I'm not imagining," Jane said, her voice shrill as she stepped closer to Twyla. "I need you to figure out how to give me the control back."

"There is nothing to figure out," Twyla answered flatly, continuing to observe Jane carefully. "What I do is for a client's recreation and is not about life or death, or transubstantiation, or magic, or time travel," she said. "I don't know where you got all these ideas, Jane. Regression therapy is just a business. It's a business I do to make a living. That's it! It's no more than that."

"So what are you telling me?"

"Just that. I can't be more clear. It's a business. People come and pay money; people go. I guarantee nothing and they satisfy their curiosity. You're making it much more than it is."

"Then how in the name of God am I involved with someone I met in a regression? How did all that happen? How come I go back there and ride his motorcycle with him and make love with him?"

"I don't know, Jane. I don't mean to alarm you, but I've never heard of anything even close to that."

"But it *is* happening," Jane insisted, her voice rising again.

Twyla bent over and using her finger, rubbed away a smudge on the toe of her lizard boot. "You know, honey, the mind can play tricks on you or anyone. That's probably what's going on with you."

"They aren't tricks," Jane insisted, tears filling her eyes. "Please Twyla, I need your help."

"I have nothing to give, honey. I just am what I am, a Dolly Parton look-alike who's found a way to make a living. I've never heard of anything like what you're telling me." She lowered her tone. "You might want to consider seeing a psychiatrist."

"I *am* seeing a psychiatrist," Jane exploded. "I'm seeing one now and sleeping with him when he was in his medical residency. And sometimes I'm with him and sometimes I'm not. That's what I'm trying to tell you." She was frantic, trembling, realizing her sole hope for control and sanity was slipping away. "You've got to help me!"

Twyla shook her head slowly. "Your travels are your own, honey, and I can't control any part of them." She offered the fermented smile of the Grim Reaper. "Sorry."

CHAPTER 42

Jane began the trek uptown in the vague direction of DSRR. Her anxiety was tangled with fear. December cold infiltrated her.

The city started to disassemble. She leaned against a storefront window.

The Manhattan images cracked into colored flakes, showering down around her before turning to dust motes lounging in a sunbeam stretching across the porch steps.

Lilacs.

"So what do you think, Jane, is this the balmiest December of all time?"

Jane stared at the man in the rocking chair. "I live here, but it's not my home, Russ."

"That's right, "the man replied, a pleased grin crossing his face. "Marie, come on out for a second," he called over his shoulder.

"I've just been here for a while," Jane said.

"Yes, you have. That's right."

A woman opened the screen door and walked onto the porch, wiping her hands with a dishtowel. "What are you two up to?" she asked.

Russ gazed expectantly at Jane. "Tell her what you just said to me."

Jane looked at Marie. "This isn't my home."

Marie nodded, a smile crossing her lips. "But you live here."

"I'm confused," Jane said.

She heard a blaring air horn and reached to cover her ears.

"I'm confused," she repeated.

Russ and Marie froze and their images became one-dimensional negatives—flickering black and white turning to gray smoke—disintegrating into luminous Manhattan color.

Jane feared she would never be normal again. She needed to calm her spiraling anxiety. Refuge was a gritty tavern. She stood on faded linoleum next to a stool at the bar. The scent of Pine Sol and stale smoke surrounded her.

A sleepy-eyed bartender with a smudged blue anchor tattooed on his forearm sauntered over to her. "What will it be?"

Jane hesitated. "A screwdriver."

He mixed the drink and placed it in front of her. "Five bucks," he said.

Jane fumbled in her purse and placed a ten-dollar bill on the bar.

The bartender walked to the register, tucked the ten in the tray and returned to Jane, placing five singles in front of her. He moved away. Jane downed the drink and pushed the five bills next to the coaster before walking out.

∞

On the train to Connecticut, despite the glass of wine she had in Grand Central before boarding, Jane could feel the alcohol's glow leaving her, allowing the anxiety to return and dart, ferret-like, in and out, up and down her spine.

She hadn't even called Carrie and told her about Jimmy.

At each stop, commuters leaving the train leaned forward against the arctic wind as they struggled away from the tracks and headed for their cars.

The conductor took her ticket and continued down the aisle.

Jane watched his back blur and whirl into a series of fluorescent pinwheels, spinning her over and over until she was righted in a swaying Ferris Wheel compartment overlooking flashing carnival lights. A single bar across her waist held her in place. Before she could reach out to Ricky sitting next to her, she stood in the farmhouse kitchen with Marie.

"I'm not clear," Marie said. "What is it you want to know?"

"Why do I think you're my aunt and uncle?" Jane asked.

"Because we are your aunt and uncle," Marie responded. "On your mother's side. Don't you remember your mother ever talking to you about us?"

A faint image was jogged loose. "Were you in the service?"

"Not me, but Russ was. We've seen just about the whole world."

"I'm so confused," Jane said.

"That makes sense," Marie replied. "Is Ricky coming over? He's real good for you."

Jane knew he would be arriving soon. She looked at her watch. "Yes."

"He's good to talk to," Marie assured her. "We love Ricky almost as much as you do."

Jane was jolted awake as her head banged against the train window next to her passenger seat.

"An-n-n-dover," the conductor called. "An-n-n-dover."

Minutes later, as she left the train and walked to her car, Jane heard a country-western singer crooning "Jingle Bells" over the railroad station speakers. The colored lights of the Depot Pub beckoned, but no matter how much fear was resonating through her, Jane couldn't allow herself to transform into her dead-drunk husband overnight.

"Jangle bails, jangle bails, jangle all the way . . ."

Southern belles were adding some Dixie spice to the chorus.

Jane struggled against the fierce wind until she arrived at the car.

"Oh what fun it is to ri-de in a one-horse open sleigh . . ."

She unlocked the car door and slid inside.

"Little Jimmy Dickens was singing 'Jingle Bells,'" the radio announcer echoed through the deserted parking lot. "All four-foot-eleven of him. Little Jimmy Dickens singing his heart out for all of you cold, freezing shoppers tonight. Wind chill is minus ten degrees, but it's warm inside here."

As she drove home, Jane watched the Depot Pub's colored lights vanish from her rearview mirror.

Ahead, the Texaco star, and above, the Bethlehem star, one nearly indistinguishable from the other.

CHAPTER 43

Later that evening, Eric's office smelled of damp wool and of embers glowing in a distant fireplace.

"I'm beyond frightened," Jane whispered, her eyes lowered. "I could hardly drive here tonight."

"Tell me."

Jane hesitated. "I've told you everything about the regressions, and about Jimmy's passing." She was a dark cat cowering in a blind alley. "But now, more than anything, I'm afraid of these regressions that seem to dominate me, these times when I'm somewhere else and I have no control over when and how I get there."

Eric studied her. He spoke quietly, but deliberately. "Jane, I've spent a lot of time thinking of our Sunday conversation. I'm trying to approach this from a different angle and I have a couple thoughts."

"What are they?"

"First, your anxiety level seems to be high and I think I should prescribe an anti-anxiety medication, short term, to make you more comfortable."

"What else?"

"I'd like to start you on an anti-psychotic regimen. I've seen a lot of very positive results with the appropriate therapy. Before you go, I'll give you a prescription and samples of both drugs to get you started."

"You don't believe a word I'm saying, do you?" Jane asked. "You think I'm delusional."

"It's not a question of believing you. I just think we should be looking for interim solutions while we work at solving the problem."

"You think I'm making everything up."

"I believe it's very real to you," Eric answered.

Jane hesitated. "Do you love me?"

Eric smiled briefly.

Do you love me?

"Of course, I do, Janey," Ricky said stretching his arms over his head as he sat on the front porch steps.

The lilacs. Again, the lilacs.

"You know I've loved you forever."

"What's wrong with me, Ricky? I'm afraid. What's happening to me?" She moved back and forth in the rocking chair, her feet skimming the gray planks. "I'm here, but I don't understand. It scares me."

"You know what happened, Jane. I need you to tell me," Ricky said. "It has to come from you."

"It's about Jimmy, isn't it? "Jane asked. The lilac fragrance was abandoning her. The air grew acrid.

"Yes," Ricky responded. "Of course it is."

"He's gone, isn't he?"

Ricky nodded. "Yes, that's right."

"He was just a baby," Jane said, her eyes glistening.

"Who was just a baby?" Eric asked.

Jane stared at the psychiatrist. "I don't know why I'm here, then there." She began to tremble. "I'm changing places in front of your eyes and you don't know it." Jane forced her hands together on her lap. "I was just talking with you when you were a medical student. Haven't I been quiet for a while?"

Eric shook his head.

Jane was silent.

"Who was just a baby?" Eric asked again.

Jane gazed at Eric. She still didn't respond.

Eric waited.

"But he was just a baby," Jane whispered at last. "He couldn't defend himself." The scent of lilacs was fainter still. Tears trickled down her cheeks.

"That's right," Ricky answered.

Jane remembered the perfect child on the cloud floating away from her, his arms outstretched, his fingers opening and closing, his eyes wide with fright and misunderstanding.

"Jimmy," she said, her heart torn in two.

"What about Jimmy?" Eric asked.

"He's not coming back, is he?" Jane asked.

"Yes, that's right," Eric answered, "your husband is gone."

"Yes, that's right," Ricky answered.

"The baby's not coming back," Jane mumbled.

"No," Ricky answered solemnly, "the baby's not coming back."

"The baby is not coming back."

"What baby is not coming back, Jane?" Eric asked, leaning forward. "Jane, please tell me."

"Mine, Eric, my baby is not coming back."

"Jane, I don't understand," Eric said.

"I have to go." She stood.

"Jane, please," Eric said, rising to his feet. "Please, Jane."

"And he'll never come back," Jane answered as she crossed the office floor and opened the door to the waiting room.

Eric followed her.

She lifted her coat from the hook, threw it over her shoulders, and reached for the outside door.

"Jane, it's critical that you not leave this way," Eric said, holding out his hand.

Jane paused. She was suddenly fearful that Eric might try to hospitalize her.

"Please. You're my last patient tonight. Stay and have some

coffee.

She didn't want to be in a hospital. No way that was going to happen.

She turned. She'd fake it somehow. "All right, Eric, I could probably use the caffeine."

∞

Jane sat for another hour, drinking coffee, making small talk, knowing the whole time Eric was quietly evaluating her. "I'm fine," she finally said and offered her best corporate smile. "It's time for me to go. And I thank you for being so caring, Eric. I do appreciate it."

"I want you to call me anytime if you're feeling the least distressed," he said. "That's what I'm here for. Can we meet tomorrow night at eight o'clock?"

Jane nodded.

"Good, here are the drug samples and the prescriptions." He handed them to her.

∞

An hour later, sitting in her living room, Jane listened to the phone ringing. She counted each ring, but never considered picking up the receiver. She was afraid it might be Eric instead of Ricky. Then abruptly, for no other reason except to stop the noise, she lifted the phone from the cradle. On the other end, a breathless Carrie said she only had a second to talk, but told Jane to make sure, to make absolutely certain that she came into work the next morning. "You won't regret it, baby doll," she concluded. "Trust me on this one."

Chapter 44

Jane opened her eyes on the train and squinted through the window at the sun reflecting off the fresh snow. No deer, or Christmas rabbits, or calico birds along the tracks, just rusted auto parts, frozen cardboard and bare bottles projecting from gray powder.

A war zone.

She shut her eyes.

∞

"New Yo-o-ork. Gra-a-a-and Central Station," the conductor called, "e-v-v-v-verybody off!"

Roused from her nap, Jane stood and reached for her coat on the overhead rack, then stepped into the line forming in the aisle.

Christmas music poured through the train station as people hurried by her. Red was everywhere, the population bleeding from the same pulsing wound. Jane looked down—she was wearing a navy sweater and slacks, and had forgotten she should be in a business suit.

And baby Jimmy was watching her from the ceiling. She didn't have to look. She knew.

After a cab ride uptown, Jane stepped out at the DSRR Building, pushed through the revolving doors and crossed to the elevator.

Once upstairs, she woodenly nodded at scattered employees as she passed. Inside her office, she removed her coat and hung it on the back of the door. Now what?

Carrie immediately popped in and closed the door behind her. Her smile was triumphant. "Hail to the victor!" she said.

"Sure, I'm a victor all right," Jane answered.

"Bye, bye, Mr. Brigg Shot," Carrie sang out of tune, "we hate to see you go. We hate to—"

"What are you talking about, Carrie?" Jane interrupted. She felt her tension and anxiety beginning to overtake her again.

"Briggs is in the process of getting canned," Carrie responded.

"You can't be serious!"

"I've never been more serious," Carrie answered, a smile continuing to sparkle across her face.

"How do you know?"

"Because Patty is in the middle of it, coordinating all the paperwork with HR." She offered a theatrical pause. "The two of us are a team. She's keeping me abreast of everything because she wants Briggs to go down too."

"I'm confused," Jane said.

"Aren't you thrilled?"

"Could be. Tell me more." Already Jane was feeling stronger, more confident.

Carrie took a deep breath. "Three nights ago, Howard was called to the women's lingerie department at Ashton's on Fifth because a couple was causing such a problem that the poor sales clerk needed a manager. Turns out an older gentleman, with his young girlfriend in tow, was attempting to buy a thousand dollars' worth of women's undies using his corporate credit card. Can you say MOR-on? He could only spend around five hundred dollars because the credit limit had been reached. The guy was ranting about how he had an unlimited credit line, that the store was a disgrace, and how he was going to sue, blah, blah, blah." She paused. "Howard said he could smell the liquor on his breath and alarm bells went off when he saw the name and company on the credit card."

Jane watched Carrie. "Yes? And?"

"So Howard left the couple at the counter and took the credit card and sales slip to his office to call Visa. Sure enough, the credit limit had been reached. Because it was a DSRR card, he made a Xerox copy before he returned it. Liquor Breath spent the five hundred on black lace anyway, grabbed the card, and left the store."

"I don't understand your point," Jane said.

"The point," Carrie said deliciously, "the point is that it turns out the old man was Briggs, and his young soul mate with the succulent *Scarlett!* lips, who he was intermittently fondling during his hostile interaction, was none other than Ms. MBA, the fair and lovely Lauren Fritz."

"Really," Jane smiled. "Now that's interesting." She was feeling much stronger.

"As you know, corporate policy states that the higher-ups may not have romantic relationships with employees. And those fortunate enough to maintain a corporate credit card are not entitled to use it to purchase personal items such as . . . " Carrie furrowed up her brow. "Oh, lace bras and see-through negligees, for example.

"Well, you know, it's our word against his," Jane countered.

"Almost," Carrie replied.

"What do you mean?"

"I mean a package with copies of the used sales slip, the credit card, plus time-stamped surveillance photographs showing Briggs and Lauren together, occasionally holding hands when they were taking a break from the fondling, was neatly delivered to each board member two nights ago. Yours truly used the magic of overnight delivery to make it happen. It's the least I could do for you. Here's your copy of everything." Carrie handed Jane a package.

Jane glanced through the envelope. "This is really true?"

"It is. And as we know, the board would have continued to look away from Briggs' personal escapades as they have in the past, including fraudulent credit card use, because he was hitting the corporate numbers. But when something has the potential to become a public scandal and those mighty captains of industry could get splashed, they have no choice but to react, especially because a few of their own affairs might surface." Carrie smirked. "Bottom line? I gave them five days before I went public. The board has no alternative but to react aggressively. John Briggs is gone, finito. He'll get a golden parachute, but will no longer be able to wander through girl-toy-land. He'll have to stay home with the old gray mare—and she ain't what she used to be." Carrie chuckled and winked at Jane. "Ain't this the greatest?"

Jane was momentarily speechless. "How do you know the board won't decide to defend him?"

"No worries. Patty said they're going to ax him—and very, very soon. Could be minutes, could be hours, but it will be before he has time to lawyer up."

"What will happen to Lauren?"

"Sayonara, baby. She should have kept her pants on. Grey Street will off her, and she'll lose her upcoming position here. You can't make a living hooking up with the client."

"Does Briggs know all this is happening?"

"No clue, according to Patty."

"Do you know if he's in today?"

"He is. I saw him fifteen minutes ago on the elevator."

"You're an amazing friend, Carrie," Jane said, giving her a quick hug as she walked to the door. "I really owe you," she called over her shoulder, the overnight package tucked under her arm.

∞

Patty looked up from her desk and smiled.

"Is he in?" Jane asked, nodding at the closed door.

"He is," she answered. "But who knows for how long. Go ahead. I'm not going to warn him."

Jane crossed in front of Patty's desk and tapped lightly on the door, then swung it open and walked into Briggs' office.

He was sitting at his desk studying a financial report. "I beg your pardon, Jane," he said, immediately standing.

"Please sit down, John, I need to talk to you," Jane replied as she closed the door behind her.

"I will do no such thing," he answered. "If you're not out of here in five seconds, I'll call Security." He moved to the door.

"I suspect Security might be calling on you," Jane answered.

Briggs halted. "And just what the hell is that supposed to mean?" He studied her.

Jane smiled, shrugged her shoulders and returned his gaze.

"Get the hell out of my office!" Briggs exploded, his face flushed. "Just who do you think you are? Get out!"

"John. I need a few more seconds. Let's talk about buying women's underwear with a corporate credit card. Ring any bells?"

"I have no idea what you're talking about," Briggs responded, his voice more controlled.

"Really?"

"I've had enough, Jane!" He strode back to his desk and picked up his telephone. "Yes, Security, immediately." He glared at her.

"You've had enough, have you, John? Too bad, I haven't. In my possession is a copy of your corporate credit card, a copy of the sales receipt showing the women's lingerie you purchased with that card, and lo and behold," she said, opening the envelope and holding up the enlarged surveillance photos, "these are from the store showing the two players in the transaction." Jane smiled. She placed the photos back in the envelope. "You look so content being half-loaded and fondling Lauren."

Briggs hung up the phone. "What is it you're after, Jane?"

"Only you, John. All I want is you."

He paused and offered a conciliatory smile. "If you want your job back, that can be arranged by the end of the day. You have my word. Lauren doesn't have your marketing skills anyway." He assessed Jane, his finger and thumb unconsciously rubbing against one Roman-coin cuff link. "You have my word that I wi—"

"John. John. John. It's too late for any negotiating," Jane interrupted. "Each board member has been notified of the colossal conflict of interest you're engaged in. Spending corporate funds for personal items—that's not allowed, John. And carrying on a relationship with a vendor, one who is soon to be a member of staff here, and who reports to you, can lead to sexual harassment claims that could cost the company millions of dollars."

"Certainly we can work this out, Jane."

"Really? Not with me. I have no power. I'm just the messenger."

A light knock and the door opened. "Mr. Briggs, Mr. Kirk is outside. He needs to speak to you," Patty said. "He says it's urgent."

"Arlen Kirk?" Briggs asked.

Patty nodded.

"I don't have an appointment with him today."

She shrugged. "He says it's urgent."

Briggs sat and scanned his office. "Give me a minute, Patty."

She nodded and closed the door.

He loosened his crimson assertive necktie. "I'd like to continue our conversation after this meeting," Briggs said. "Let's not forget we're good for each other. We're cut from the same cloth." Briggs' eyes continued to dart around the room as if looking for a backdoor exit.

"Trust me, there will be no need for a conversation after your meeting with Arlen," Jane answered. "And a board chairman doesn't like to be kept waiting." She stood and walked toward the door. Her fingers on the handle, she turned to Briggs. "Oh, and, John, one last thing." She opened the door halfway.

Briggs looked up.

"I wouldn't have slept with you for my job or a hundred million dollars. You're flattering yourself."

Arlen Kirk was standing immediately outside. Jane nodded to him as he passed her on his way into Briggs' office. As the door was closing, she heard Kirk's voice, "John, I'm afraid I have some bad news for you . . ."

CHAPTER 45

Jane wanted to talk with Carrie, to celebrate Briggs' demise, but her confrontation had been enhanced with adrenalin and false courage. After leaving his office with victory in hand, she was overwhelmed with anxiety again.

An hour later, she was at a table in a hotel lobby bar, a half-consumed martini resting in front of her. She had rejected Eric's prescriptions and the alcohol represented all she knew to control her apprehension and fear.

Jane stared, unblinking, at the front of the empty bar that stretched perpendicular to a twelve-foot glass window facing the street.

The view grew hazy and then burst into flame as if a match had been set to a pile of dried leaves.

Fresh air and the scent of lilacs drifted toward her.

She was on the back of the Indian, her arms around Ricky's waist. The motorcycle was easing down a graveled road that meandered around the perimeter of Russ' farmland.

"Let's pull over, Janey," Ricky called over his shoulder.

"Okay."

Ricky slowed the Indian to a halt. As Jane stepped off, her ankle slid against the white-hot chrome exhaust pipe, causing her to cry out.

Ricky quickly rested the motorcycle on its stand. "Let me see."

She stood still while he examined the burn.

"Not too bad, it could be a lot worse," he said. "It'll sting for a while, but I don't think we have to run back to your aunt's house unless you're uncomfortable."

"I'll be fine."

"Sure?" Ricky asked. He shoved his hands into the front pockets of his jeans.

"I'm okay," she answered.

"You don't act that way. You've been, how can I say it, kind of quiet for most of the afternoon. That's not like you."

Jane thought for another minute. "Ricky, I'm caught somewhere in the middle of a bad dream. I keep going in and going out. Sometimes I'm here, sometimes I'm in another place, another life. I don't know what to do."

"Janey, you're here with me."

"You don't understand! I'm not always here! How can I keep bouncing back and forth between two places? How can I be living in two different worlds?"

"Simple. You're not living in two worlds," Ricky answered.

"But I am! I'm frightened, Ricky. The other place is disintegrating around me."

"Look, Janey," Ricky answered, drawing her to him, then resting his hands on her shoulders. "This is where you are. This is your world. This is where you're supposed to be. There is no other place." He paused. "You've been through a lot, but it's getting better. Just remember, there is no other world."

"That's not possible," Jane answered.

"Of course it's possible, and it's also true."

"Am I acting, you know, like I'm crazy?"

"Not at all," Ricky answered. "And you're right where you're supposed to be, Janey. Right where you're supposed to be."

She watched, terrified, as Ricky's eyes burned to sepia, then rolled back into his head as the endless acres of corn fields slowly furrowed into flames.

"Ricky!"

A whisper hissing from the blaze, "You're where you're supposed to be, Janey."

The flames roared out of control, destroying the scenery, then subsided, leaving the mound of dried leaves that transformed into the front end of the bar.

Jane was still at the table, the martini unmoved.

She stared dead ahead, then slowly reached down and touched her ankle.

Nothing. No burn . . . no pain.

And yet it had just happened.

She wasn't in two worlds! The unburned ankle proved that the world of Ricky, Russ, and Marie didn't exist!

The shock overran her, demolished her. Not only was she now certifiable, she would never have Ricky. She would never survive. She began to cry, her forehead resting against the table.

A waiter hovered nearby.

It was over, it was over, it was so ov—

Wait.

Her tears halted and she lifted her head.

She had dismounted the motorcycle, singeing the inside of her ankle. True, but she had dismounted the motorcycle to the left, singeing her left ankle, and moments before, when she reached beneath the table to search for the burn, she had touched her right ankle.

Jane's fingers crept down her left leg, to her knee, to her calf. Slipping her fingers to her ankle, she touched the tenderness of burned skin.

She could feel the blood rush to her face.

Could it be possible?

"Oh my God. . . ." Jane felt her heart thundering in her ears as her hands trembled on the table in front of her. "Oh, my God, what if . . ."

What if . . .

What if . . . the current life of Jane McBride *didn't exist* and she was living in a long, irrational hallucination from which she had been gradually awakening.

Pure high-octane fear exploded through her spine, igniting her remains.

She was melting. God, she was melting while anxiety devoured what was left of her mind.

Where was she?

Before she completely shattered and disintegrated, Jane hurriedly rose and crossed to the front of the bar and out the door into the street. She looked from left to right, trying to figure out where to go, what to do.

Chapter 46

Outside the entrance to the Empire State Building, Jane studied the passersby the same way the homeless stared at their feet, or the curb, or their fingerless gloves—not processing what they were seeing.

The sunlight was shredding her.

But now she had a idea, a straightforward, simple plan. She would go to the top of the Empire State Building, to the Observatory, climb over the guard railing, and jump. If she survived, she would know her current life was not genuine, that she was existing in some bizarre unreality. If she died, it had to be better than what her current existence had become.

She bought the ticket to the top.

"Elevator to the Observatory," the operator said.

Jane stood, her back against the elevator wall, and watched the numbers climb.

"Observatory, everyone out," the operator said at the eighty-sixth floor.

As she walked into the sunlight of the deck, Jane could see for miles—buildings, bridges, water, more buildings.

The top of the fence around the Observatory was curved

inward, making it difficult to surmount. As she moved around the perimeter of the building, Jane saw a guard in each corner of the deck's walkway.

When they were looking in other directions, she kicked off her shoes and attacked the fence.

People screamed and Jane heard the footsteps of the guards racing toward her.

She managed to pull herself up and then swing a leg over the top of the fence's inward curve before her other foot was grabbed by one of the guards. "Get down, damn it, lady, you're going to kill yourself!"

She kicked free and pulled herself up and over, then slid down the outside of the fence. Sweet, pure air surrounded her. She stepped out onto the stone ledge. The silent city, exquisite colored bead work laced between glass tributaries, smiled invitingly at her, encouraging her to become one with it.

"Lady, for God's sake, don't do it," a security guard yelled out. "Jimmy, call the police."

She knew what it was like to float on a cloud, then slide to earth through the cornflower blue using a piece of it as a canopy.

She knew that if she just let go, the breeze would tickle her on the way down, and it would be cool, not frigid, and she would fall in a rhythm of life, her breath in and out, her hands opening and closing, her eyes blinking, open, shut, open, shut.

What could be better?

What could be more serene?

Nothing.

Jane took a deep breath, then stepped off the ledge into space and waited for the colors to envelop her, the glass tributaries to wrap around her like jewels.

Instead, she was left hanging overhead staring down at a flat poster of Manhattan. No breeze tickled her bare feet, car horns were silent, and exhaust fumes were unable to suffocate her. She couldn't hear herself breathe.

She looked down again. No city existed; no poster of a city

existed—just a movie that she didn't want to watch.

She began to hyperventilate.

She didn't want to see it!

She had no choice.

She didn't want to see it!

She couldn't escape.

She left Mass and was driving to Russ and Marie's for the baby's birthday party.

She arrived early. Marie and Russ were still at church. No one would be there except Jimmy and baby Jimmy.

She parked the car directly behind Jimmy's battered Ford and walked up the gentle incline toward the backyard.

As she rounded the corner of the house, he wasn't there.

She was immediately anxious, but then heard the familiar laughter that she'd left behind when she drove to church that morning—laughter imprinted so clearly in her memory, she would recognize it if ten thousand years had passed.

"Jane, watch this," Jimmy yelled from the patio. He held the baby against his chest with one arm, a can of beer in his free hand. He placed the can on the table next to him and clutching his son under the arms, tossed him in the air, catching him seconds later. "Jane, look how much fun he's having." He picked up the beer can.

"Jimmy, stop, stop," she called from the far end of the yard. "Stop it now!"

"Do us all a favor and relax for once in your life, Jane," Jimmy bellowed. "He's having fun."

The baby saw Jane and pointed in her direction. He smiled, and as he watched her approach, he tried to wiggle away from his father's grasp, but Jimmy wouldn't release him.

His face trembled and tears filled his eyes when he couldn't free himself. "Mama," he cried, struggling in his father's arms. "Mama!"

"Put him down, Jimmy," Jane called. "Put him down!"

"Any son of mine needs to be a man," Jimmy crowed. "You got to get tough if you want to play football!" He guzzled down

the rest of the beer and tossed the empty can at the metal trash barrel.

Jane was suddenly frozen with fear—locked in stop-action slow motion. She watched the can sluggishly careen around the rim of the waste barrel, each clang seconds apart.

"Watch this, Jane," Jimmy called, his voice muddy. Spit flecks slowly sprayed from his mouth as he struggled with the effort to throw his son in the air again.

Jane could see the strain on her husband's face, the broad arms flexing with the effort of flinging him higher than ever before.

She watched the baby gradually leave Jimmy's hands.

"Come to Mama," she called tentatively.

"Ma-a-a," he cried, his words muddled as the sky stretched between his body and his father's fingertips. Tears crept down his cheeks.

He resembled her. He was a part of her. "Jimmy," Jane called to the baby cresting in the air, hovering against the blue. Her legs were frozen.

"Ma-a-a-ma," the baby wailed, his fine hair adrift in the breeze as he began to descend.

Jane shoved away the crippling fear. "I'm coming, I'm coming." She ripped off her shoes and ran toward the patio.

"That's a big boy!" Jimmy roared as he reached up for his son just as his peripheral vision caught Jane's movement. He glanced in her direction, allowing the toddler to slip through his hands and smash into the steel mesh table, then twist and travel headfirst to the cement floor.

She was an instant too late.

The tiny face was locked in fear.

The blood splattered around her.

And as brightly as he shone, he was as quickly gone.

A pale green Royal Copenhagen candy dish—a keepsake birthday present for later years that had been resting on the table's edge—lay fractured in pieces encircling his body; a holy screen isolating a shrine.

As Jane leaned over, she noticed specks of blood resembling flecks of colored leaves scattered across the pale skin on top of each foot. The spots made her feel pockmarked and unclean. She reached down and using her forefingers, attempted to glide the spots of color from the tops of her feet. Sliding, slowly sliding, her forefingers bunched the dots of blood together, creating tiny pools above her ankles.

She gradually straightened, and then cautiously, painfully, pushed outward from beneath the misty veil that had engulfed her, at last to be judged in the bonfire of light. "Save me," she murmured, her voice weak, trembling. "Save me."

Gray Matter

CHAPTER 47

As she crossed down the side of one hill and up the next, Jane recognized the farmhouse in the distance. She headed in that direction, but made little progress, so instead sat in the grass and watched bees circle the Black-Eyed Susans. Gradually, she lay back, allowing the sun to stroke her and absolve her of all sins.

Jane knew that once she arrived at the farmhouse, an apple pie would be cooling on the window ledge. If she concentrated, she could smell the cinnamon on the breeze. As she inhaled and exhaled, listening to the rush of air in and out of her lungs, the simplicity of life surrounded her. Soon the fingers of the old woman who baked the pie would stroke her cheek, suggesting that she was special.

Jane touched her chin, her cheeks, then the lids of her closed eyes.

∞

Once at the farmhouse, she saw her Aunt Marie emerge

from the nearby orchard toting a tattered canvas bag overflowing with apples. "Russ needs another two pies for the Future Farmers meeting tomorrow night," she called. "Those kids eat like there's no tomorrow."

Jane moved in her direction. "Let me help."

"I'm good. How you doing, sweetheart?" Marie asked. She ran her fingers across Jane's cheek, studying her. "How you doing?"

"Let me carry those apples."

"Never mind. Come inside. I've got another pie cooling on the windowsill. We can have it tonight."

∞

After dinner, Russ settled in the living room with the newspaper while Marie and Jane sat at the kitchen table sorting through a mound of frosted glass fragments.

"All this is from Cape Cod?" Jane asked.

"Years and years ago when sea glass wasn't so hard to find. I look at it and have so many comforting memories," Marie answered. "These days a lot of people are on the beaches collecting." She held up a cloudy triangle. "I can usually tell the type of bottle the glass is from, but this one has stumped me for years. I can make out two letters, a capital 'D' and small 'a,' but that's all. I think there's another letter between those two, but even with this magnifying glass, I can't be sure."

"Let me try," Jane said. She squinted and saw the two letters, but nothing more. "No, I can't tell."

"One day we'll figure it out."

Jane hesitated. "I don't know what would have happened if you hadn't let me stay here."

"It's the way it should be," Marie answered. "We have one niece. If your mom was alive, she'd been pleased you're here with Russ and me."

"I'm grateful."

Marie smiled. "So are we."

The two continued to sort through the glass until Jane held up a narrow, sand-eroded bottle neck.

"Probably belonged to a chemist," Marie said.

"Blue," Jane replied. "The same color as the sky I fell through to get back here."

"Is Ricky coming over tonight?" Marie asked, disregarding Jane's remark.

"I would grab a piece of the cloud and fall down through pure blue, the same shade as this bottle neck."

Marie reached out and took Jane's hand in her own. "Sweetheart, that never happened. Trust me, you've been here with us the entire two months since the baby passed. I love you like you were my own daughter and I would never lie to you."

Jane shook her head. "Actually I've been working in New York City and I was twenty years older."

Russ walked into the kitchen, the newspaper folded under his arm. "Anyone feel like going into town? Get out of this place for a while."

"I was living somewhere else, but no one believes me."

Russ placed his hands on Jane's shoulders. "You weren't somewhere else, Jane. The baby's gone and it's time for you to understand that you never left here."

Jane stood. "I have to sleep," she said, blocking tears with the heel of her hand as she left the kitchen.

Russ and Marie stared at each other. At last he said, "No mystery. She feels safer asleep than awake." He shrugged his shoulders. "But her conversation worries me."

"The real challenge," Marie said, lowering her voice, "is whether she can lose a child and survive herself."

"She needs time, Marie. Poor kid." He shook his head and picked up a piece of frosted sea glass. "Is this what you two were talking about?"

Marie nodded.

Russ studied it through the magnifying lens. "I got a

capital 'D' and a small 'a.'" He squinted and changed the angle of the sea glass. "There's a letter between the two." He concentrated. "It's an 'o,' it's a small 'o' between the 'D' and 'a.' D-o-a. Must have been part of a bottle from Doan's Dairy, the big commercial farm operation outside of Boston."

∞

Jane gradually became conscious. She strained her ears and heard a baby whimpering a soft, preoccupied cry of need. Sitting up, then quickly rising to her feet, she followed the sound down the hallway to the living room. She switched on the light, but saw nothing except the furniture and Russ' folded newspaper on the rug next to the chair.

The night surrounding her was still.

As she moved back in the hallway, a sound drifted toward her again, but now she recognized the lonesome whistle of a distant train echoing from beyond the planting fields. She could visualize the headlight spearing the night, moving forward on a track leading away from all she understood, to new crossings, fresh towns and different lives. If she was aboard she could look back at the lights of St. Charles, or just sit, hugging herself with the realization that she had truly disappeared.

Jane concentrated on returning to sleep, but after ten minutes rose again and crossed to the bathroom. She was restless, but avoided the use of sleeping pills—concerned she might have inherited her father's addictive tendencies. She took two aspirin tablets and swallowed them with water.

As Jane stood with the medicine cabinet door ajar, she was ensnared in a crossfire between the cabinet mirror and the mirror on the opposite wall. Her image ricocheted back and forth, back and forth, growing smaller and smaller, until with her own eyes, she watched herself disappear.

Chapter 48

Dr. Ian Hammond had stated several times that her memory loss was protection from unfathomable mental anguish. Prior to her son's death, he claimed Jane's brain had been the equivalent of a supersaturated solution—fluid, but stable—and the one crystal of extreme grief, suddenly added, pushed her over the edge, turning a liquid, functional mind into a solid mass of denial.

Jane sat with Ricky in Dr. Hammond's office. "There's still so much I don't understand," she murmured. "I know you're a memory-loss specialist and a psychiatrist, but I'm still not totally getting it."

"Of course," Dr. Hammond replied. "That's normal."

"It's a process, Janey," Ricky said. "It takes a little time."

Jane glanced at Ricky and then focused on Dr. Hammond. "So what you've said is the death of my son triggered my mental exit from this world."

"In strictly black-and-white terms, yes. What I'm suggesting is that your entire memory was wiped clean due to a psychogenic disorder known as dissociative fugue. Your mind was unable to cope with the trauma of seeing your child's death, so it shut down, dismissing that image as well as everything before it." Dr. Hammond paused. "An extreme burn victim often has the same experience—the mind closing down, the memory lost—an alternative to recalling burning flesh. You hear much the same with severe car accidents."

Jane slowly shook her head.

"Sometimes it helps to have a graphic in mind." Dr. Hammond reached back behind his chair and lifted a pad of paper from his desk. He drew a straight line halfway across a blank page, then added a small eighth-inch dome before continuing the line until it ran off the paper. "The dome represents your two-month fugue period and the line running up to it is your long-term memory. When amnesia hit, you lost your memory of everything that went before in your life, spending two months that way." He ran his pen across the top of the dome and back over the line to the starting point at the edge of the page. "You had no idea who you were, Jane. You left your husband, Jimmy, who, of course, you didn't recognize, and you decided to live with your aunt and uncle, or two people who claimed to be your aunt and uncle—you weren't sure until you saw their driver's licenses. Oddly enough, you were able to continue going to school without a problem."

"Why did I use the name Jane?"

"Because it was your name though you needed your own photo ID to confirm it." He paused. "But we started you on the Proffera regimen and now you're back."

"Sort of back, Doctor, and I'm very upset." She shook her head. "My long-term memory has returned, but those two months in the fugue state—the time when I began living with Russ and Marie, are blacked out, with only a few hazy memories of what actually went on."

"I know," Dr. Hammond responded. "I understand."

"How can you understand if I don't understand?" Jane tried to control the anxiety in her voice. "During those two months, I was in another life stage, but I was twenty years older and active in the business world. It still seems incredibly real. I'd have brief episodes when I'd be pulled back to my existence here, but I'd end up back in that future life again." Jane shook her head. "I think what you've said is that Proffera's pull got stronger and stronger and was eventually able to deliver me home, so to speak."

"As a drug, Proffera initially had you on a sort of bungee cord," Dr. Hammond said. "You'd have a brief return here due to the medication beginning to integrate into your system, but then you'd bounce back to the other world, another quick trip here, a result of the Proffera, then a return to your other life, back and forth, back and forth, until the drug finally prevailed, the cord broke, and your memory was restored—except for the fugue period."

Jane paused. "I've also heard both Ricky and you say that the experience of thinking I was in another phase of my life, something that seemed so real to me, could be nothing more than some type of consciousness fabrication, or what did you call it, an ASC? Something that was happening in my own head."

"ASC, yes," Dr. Hammond replied. "Alternate State of Consciousness. Your state of consciousness changed and your perception of reality was inaccurate."

"I'm struggling with what you're telling me," Jane said.

The doctor thought a moment. "Honestly, Jane, no one is certain what happens to an individual who loses his or her memory because actual memory is a conglomeration of many specialized brain functions and biochemical reactions." He hesitated another few seconds. "You said that you were involved in a life elsewhere, that during the two-month fugue state, you were actually in another place." The psychiatrist shrugged his shoulders. "On one hand, there's quite a simple explanation. Your subconscious had to create a new life, a persona designed through fresh neurological mapping, simply to protect you."

"But even then I was receiving signals about my son dying."

Dr. Hammond nodded. "Even the massive, elaborately

constructed tower of denial could not stand upright, becoming less and less secure as you were increasingly able to acknowledge your child's death."

"You said, 'On one hand, there's a simple explanation,' Doctor," Ricky said. "Is there something else?"

Dr. Hammond ran his fingers along his jaw as if confirming he had shaved that morning. He didn't respond, absorbed in thought.

"Let me ask you this, have you ever heard of a condition like Jane's before?" Ricky asked.

"Yes . . . yes, I have, but only recently, and it's very uncommon. Ninety-nine percent-plus of all individuals who regain long-term memory have no recollection of what occurred during the brief amnesiac or fugue state. And really, Jane is no exception. She has very little recall of what *actually* occurred during those two months. She was a TV set that had changed channels. The main channel, the Jane real-life channel was still functioning, but she was watching something else. When she was here engaged as a student, living with her aunt and uncle in a relatively normal lifestyle, she believes she was elsewhere, or, back to the TV analogy, watching that different channel." He shrugged, then reached back for a file resting on his desk. "I've had several of my research assistants look into the medical literature, and I've found two cases similar to Jane's."

He paused, then continued, glancing at the file in front of him. "In the 1950s, an army recruit and radio operator named Rexford Wilker was stationed in Fort Benning, Georgia. According to this report, one afternoon as he huddled behind a boulder attempting to make radio contact during training maneuvers, he unexpectedly saw most of his platoon eviscerated by a single, inadvertently fired artillery shell, the result of an unconscionable internal error which eventually led to a series of courts-martial.

"Witnessing the devastation, Wilker, shocked, succumbed to a fugue state, blocking out the horror. Six weeks later, when he did slowly regain his long-term memory in a military hospital, he had no recollection of being transported there, or being cared for. As his memory gradually took focus, which, according to him, only happened when he was able to recall and cope with the carnage of his platoon, he claimed that during part of his memory loss, or six-week dissociative fugue, he had been in another portion of his army career, fifteen years in the future. During that period, he believed he was a sergeant in the jungles of Vietnam, where he saw more torture, horror and indifference to human life than he believed possible, all of which was a far cry from the military mission he had been trained for: to serve, protect, and respect. He watched his best friend and high school classmate die a brutal death, shot through both knees by a sadistic Viet Cong sniper. Wilker also was severely wounded and barely survived in the putrid jungles.

And when his memory returned or when the channel changed, however you want to describe it," Dr. Hammond smiled briefly, "and he realized he was really at Fort Benning, and that the year was 1954, he resigned from the army within six weeks—though he had no concrete intelligence indicating Southeast Asia would even be a future battleground. The Vietnam visualization had been too authentic, touched him too deeply, and he was convinced that scenario was what lay ahead of him if he continued his army career. So instead, he received his honorable discharge, returned home, married the girl next door, raised four sons, and lived happily ensconced as postmaster of his local post office in Breaux Bridge, Louisiana.

Jane and Ricky stared at the psychiatrist.

Dr. Hammond offered a momentary grin. "Fascinating, right? The other case we discovered also took place in the fifties and involved a husband-and-wife show business team called Jack and Jill. They were an opening nightclub act for big-name stars and from what I've read they did a little bit of everything, dance, jokes, audience participation—warm up the crowd—that type of thing. Jack was apparently getting involved with recreational drugs, and one night, under the influence, he fell off the stage and fractured his skull. His immediate condition was so grave that Jill was psychologically overwhelmed and her memory instantly vanished. She was hospitalized the same night.

Several weeks later, after confronting the fear of her husband nearly dying, she emerged from her fugue state in the hospital, with her long-term memory restored.

But in a social worker's office, this poor woman claimed she had no recollection of the time she was in the hospital and fervently believed that during that interval she had been transported fourteen years into the future—to 1965, when her husband was a full-blown drug addict. She had no training other than the entertainment act she'd done with him, and they lived in abject poverty, surviving on Jill's menial wages as a house cleaner. Jack was increasingly violent, unreachable, and living hour-to-hour for his next fix. The two were nearly homeless and Jill was on the verge of suicide."

"What happened?" Ricky asked.

Dr. Hammond shrugged. "Jill was absolutely convinced that vision represented her future and a place she didn't want to be. Once Jack had recovered from his stage fall, she divorced him and enrolled in college, received her teaching certificate and then taught high school drama for twenty-five years."

Dr. Hammond halted and looked at Ricky, then Jane. "So you see, Jane, your experience, though rare, is not without precedent. The mind's capabilities and devices of self-protection are miraculous, often far outside our realm of understanding."

The room was still.

"That's strange stuff, Doctor," Ricky said at last.

"So I'm not crazy," Jane added. "I guess that's a relief."

"No one has ever diagnosed you as being mentally ill, Jane," Dr. Hammond said. He hesitated a moment. "Enclosed with the reports on Rexford Wilker and Jack and Jill, was a generic white paper on a theory of dark matter and the human brain as it related to those folks."

Jane focused on the physician. "I've heard of dark matter before. A woman named Twyla, who was a past-life regression therapist in my other life mentioned dark matter more than once."

Ricky and Dr. Hammond stared at Jane for several seconds without speaking.

"I don't know how to answer that," Dr. Hammond finally conceded.

"Dark matter? What the heck is that, Doctor?" Ricky asked.

"It's part of a whole realm of biological study linked to astrophysics. As I understand it, dark matter is terminology defining some of the unused sectors of the human brain, areas that offer significant opportunities for heightened awareness and growth. Some scientists have a theory that the human brain is able to enter dimensions or corridors of time as a result of spontaneous biochemical reactions within the brain—reactions that are initiated by acute trauma and this dark matter." He shook his head. "The stuff dreams are made of."

Ricky hesitated. "I'm a hard science guy too, Doctor, and this trip-to-the-future talk, all this speculation, makes zero sense to me."

"Except for one thing," Dr. Hammond replied.

"What's that?"

"Jane believes it happened."

Briggs, Carrie, Twyla swept through Jane's mind. She looked at Dr. Hammond, then Ricky, and nodded. "It happened."

CHAPTER 49

Jimmy found Jane on campus and led her to a bench in the shadows of the Old South Church. “So you finally know who I am, huh?”

“I remember what happened with the baby.”

Jimmy shook his head. “Nothing I can say or do will ever take away the pain I feel.” He hesitated. “Please, Jane.”

“Please what, Jimmy?" She was annoyed. He was a professional victim whose best years had already passed. She glanced at her watch.

“We’re still married. You remember that now. We can figure this out. We don’t have to get a divorce.”

Jane stared at him. “You’re joking, of course.”

“I’ve stopped drinking.

“I would hope. Is this the fourth or fifth attempt?”

“This time I’m really going to stop.”

“No, you're not.”

Jimmy paused and lowered his voice. “You know the problem from day one, Jane, was that I loved you more than you loved me. That’s a tough way to go through life.”

She stood. “I’ve heard this all before.”

"Please." He reached up and tugged her sleeve until she was seated next to him again. "I guess that's what happens when a man and woman get together," he continued softly, "one loves more than the other."

Jane stared at him. Already, at his young age, the alcoholism was trashing his face. His cheeks were florid splotches and purple capillaries slithered across the bridge and down the sides of his nose.

"Know what I mean?" Jimmy asked.

Jane didn't respond.

"I always loved you more than you loved me," Jimmy repeated.

"I loved you, Jimmy," Jane said.

"But not anymore," he answered.

She nodded. "You're right, not anymore."

"You were the escape for me, Jane—beautiful, sensitive, brilliant. And then we suffer with a mutual tragedy and instead of growing together, making us both stronger, you decide to leave."

"I'm sorry, Jimmy."

He ran his hands on the front of his pants as if drying them—a nervous habit. "Even before the baby, Jane, you were cold and now you're a statue."

True. Her inaccessibility had been gradual until the baby's death had abruptly frozen her.

Jimmy sighed. "As an Irish kid, you learn fast that this old world will eventually get around to breaking your heart." He stared at her. "Is there any hope for us, Jane? I love you so much."

"I'm tired, Jimmy," she said, rising. "And you're not Irish. You're Polish."

"You're tired," Jimmy repeated quietly, sarcastically, disregarding the Irish comment. "Oh, I see, you're tired."

Jane began to walk away.

"You're tired. You've always been tired, Jane." His voice grew louder. "And I heard about that doctor you're going out with. You're still married and going out with someone else." All of a sudden, he was shouting. "You're a whore, Jane, a whore! Do you hear me?"

She stopped, turned and walked back several steps. "Here's my final gift to you, Jimmy: You should stop drinking, or if you can't do that, at least don't get behind the wheel of a car when you're drunk."

"Just what the hell is that supposed to mean?"

"Figure it out." She turned and moved farther and farther from the raving Fred Flintstone behind her.

Chapter 50

The chalk lines on the neighbor's baseball field, the puffy sky-written letters below the stacked cumulus clouds, all different shades of white depending on the vantage point.

Jane wished she was back in the cornflower blue, looking down, relaxed and oblivious.

"You going to see Annie tonight?" Marie asked. Her arm was laced through Jane's as they strolled across the meadow away from the farmhouse.

"Closing night. I wouldn't miss it."

"I think she's going to be famous someday. She's a wonderful actress." Marie paused and glanced at Jane. "You feeling better?"

"Sometimes."

Marie nodded and moved forward. "I was just thinking the other day about how much time we spend together. It's interesting how it all worked out and how much I've enjoyed it."

"And now you can't get rid of me."

"Never want to. You're the daughter we never had."

It was true. They were surrogate parents who loved her

unconditionally. And with the baby's death, conversation with Marie helped fill Jane's empty spaces and vulnerable moments. "I don't know why my mother was so weak."

Marie shrugged. "She had no coping skills, especially with a drunken husband and a hyperactive Jane. Of course, no one can handle an alcoholic, and you were just being a kid. When I realized she was sticking your head in the oven so the gas would make you sleepy, I knew it wouldn't be long before she unintentionally killed you.

"I don't recall her doing that."

"You wouldn't. You were little. I caught her in the act once and scared her when I explained the repercussions. She had gotten the idea from our mother and never considered death as a possibility." Marie shook her head. "My sister wasn't ready to be a wife or a mother. And, of course, your father was nothing more than a bottle of negative energy."

"Jimmy is a clone of my father. I should never have married him."

"We all tend to gravitate to the things that are familiar. When he graduated in Ohio and came up here to live, we knew what he was up to."

"I wasn't real good at taking advice, I guess."

"You grew up in a madhouse. I'm surprised you're not a drug addict or an alcoholic yourself."

"I wouldn't let that happen."

Marie nodded. "I believe it, and I'm proud of you."

∞

Annie lit up the stage. She was gorgeous, sexy, and wildly talented. That's true star power, Jane thought. Her friend sparkled and the crowd responded to every action, every piece of business, every aside to the audience. And when she stepped forward to take her last solitary bow, still wearing her ballerina costume from the final scene, instead of bowing, she deftly assumed the arabesque position.

Annie's pale cheeks and dark eyes created infinite beauty, and frozen on the stage, locked in the spotlight, she was surrounded by red roses thrown from the hands of captivated male cast members attired in tuxedos.

It was an image Jane would never forget—though in her mind, she envisioned the men to be wearing white ties instead of traditional black.

∞

"No, let's talk about you," Jane said later. "It helps me to keep my mind off the baby. You were brilliant tonight."

Annie ran her fingers around the stem of her wine glass. "You're so nice to say so, Jane. You know how much I respect your opinion."

"Believe me, I'm being honest. Anyway, you saw the audience's reaction." She thought a second. "Now tell me about the scholarship."

"Not too much to it. It's a two-year Schumann acting-writing program, obviously in Manhattan, that ends up with me receiving an MFA degree."

A local couple approached from a nearby table in the restaurant. "You were wonderful tonight, Annie," the man said. "You're going to be a big star and we knew you when."

"You're very kind," Annie said. She nodded and the two moved away.

"What about Kenny?" Jane asked.

Annie shrugged. "We've been together since our senior year in high school. Counting four years in college, that's a total of five. He'll come to visit me in New York and we'll talk a lot on the phone. It'll be fine."

Jane stared at her friend. "Distance kills," she said.

"Only if you let it," Annie replied. "And when I'm a big star, I'll buy an apartment in the city and Kenny and I will get married and live there. He can get a job and I'll be on stage. We've got it all worked out."

Jane lifted her drink. "To you; to success; to Kenny."

"And to you, Jane, for all that you've been through. You have such a beautiful soul."

∞

As the two stood under their umbrellas in the parking lot, Annie reached out and hugged Jane. "I'll see you in ten days at graduation, and then we'll have to get together before I leave for New York in two months." Her eyes were glowing with excitement. It was all ahead of her.

"I'll see you," Jane said.

CHAPTER 51

Jane glanced around the coffee shop. "I have a faint recollection of being here with you before."

"We stopped by a lot," Ricky answered as he slid a cup of tea in front of her. "You know, the price is right." He studied Jane, then reached across the table and took her hand. "It's been a tough road back, no?"

"You had never seen me until the day the baby died?"

Ricky shook his head. "Nope, we met in the hospital. I was one of the doctors attending you for the two weeks you were there."

"Then what?"

"You didn't recognize your husband, Jimmy, but I could see you didn't care for him. And we became friends, then even closer once you left the hospital. For me, it was love at first sight. And you told me you felt the same way."

Jane was silent.

"And, of course, now you're divorcing Jimmy."

"I am. As quickly as possible."

"Because of me?"

"No, because of him." Jane paused and studied Ricky. "I

do vaguely remember a few things that I think are from the fugue state; scenes that now seem hazy and unreal. I'm not sure whether they happened or not."

Ricky nodded. "Tell me."

Jane moved a forefinger around the top of her cup. The motion reminded her of the Lalique crystal bowl in the Connecticut home. "My life is so strange, Ricky. With this woman, Twyla helping me, I thought I was regressing into my past, when I was really returning here from some kind of unreal world that was out there."

"Where is out there?"

Jane shook her head. "I have no idea."

"Well, what's most important is that you're back," Ricky said. "The complete return of memory takes time. Who knows, the missing two months could reappear."

"I'll feel a lot better if they do."

"Any hazy, crazy memories with me?"

"Moments. Very brief moments, that's all—riding on the back of the motorcycle with you, that kind of thing. Then I'd flash back to the other world."

"What else do you recall?" Ricky asked.

Jane examined her hands resting on the table in front of her. "Dancing with you barefoot, occasionally wearing your college ring." She glanced at the ring on her middle finger, tape rolled at mid-circle so it wouldn't slip. "I remember being in bed with you across the street from some bar."

"Ah, my beautiful, struggling resident doctor's apartment. I think we spent more time at Jack Reed's tavern across the street than we did in the apartment—actually the rented room is a better description."

Jane looked away, over Ricky's shoulder. "I remember being intimate with you."

"You don't sound too excited about it."

"I can recall being in the backseat of a car. Why were we making love there?"

"Expediency. We couldn't go to your room in your aunt's

house and my apartment was thirty miles away." Ricky hesitated. "You still don't sound very excited, Janey."

"I was excited when it was happening," Jane answered. "I think I loved you."

"Think?"

"You know what I mean. Everything is so confused right now, Ricky."

"I know that," he answered, lifting the mug of coffee to his lips. "But all we have is time. And I do love you, Janey. Maybe I don't say it often enough." He stared at her. "I love you, I surely do." He paused. "But hold on a second."

Ricky stood and walked to the jukebox. He slipped a quarter into the coin slot and pressed two buttons. As he walked back, the music began:

Come, sweetheart, tell me,
Now is the time.
You tell me your dream,
I'll tell you mine.

He slid back into the booth. "Remember our song? We played it every time we stopped here."

"Each time?"

"Sure. You liked it. And I did too."

"The Mills Brothers, right?"

Ricky nodded as he watched her.

"It shouldn't surprise me," Jane said.

"No, it shouldn't." He thought for a moment. "And now here you are completing college," he said softly. "That's a very good thing, I think. We should be finishing up at just about the same time, give or take a credit or two. And based on everything you told me, you're a natural for the business world. I mean how many people can sell thousands of dollars worth of cosmetics door-to-door like you have?"

Jane smiled briefly. "I had to pay for college tuition, and don't forget I had the scholarship too. As far as selling the cosmetics, if you can convince women that the product makes them more attractive, nine out of ten times they'll buy what you're selling."

"I still think it's remarkable. I couldn't sell money to a bank."

"I'm sure you could, but being a psychiatrist is more important anyway."

Ricky shrugged. "Right now I'm not sure of anything, but I've passed the point of no return. A couple more years and it'll be official." He ran the back of his fingers across the side of Jane's face. "And you know what I was thinking?"

Jane shook her head.

"I was thinking about you and me. After being in medical school in Boston and then doing my internship and residency here, I'd like to go back to the Northeast. Not Boston again, but, say, maybe Connecticut or Rhode Island."

Jane hesitated. "Did we ever talk about that before?" she asked. "I mean about going to New England?"

Ricky nodded. "More than once, but I just thought about it again this morning.

"Maybe Connecticut instead of Rhode Island," Jane said.

Ricky grinned. "Well, that'll be fine."

Jane stared over Ricky's shoulder again. Dust motes floated in the ray of sun streaming through the coffee shop window.

"I love you, Janey," Ricky said. "You need to know I love you."

Jane continued to stare over his shoulder, unblinking. After several seconds, she returned her gaze to Ricky. "I know you do," she answered.

∞

Jane vaguely remembered hungering for his glance, his touch. She thought about the blurry and brief intimate moments . . . moments when she couldn't get close enough to him, times when she ran her fingers across his back and the perspiration from his brow slid against her breasts, moments that had convinced her she could never live without him.

He hadn't asked to make love since her memory returned.

That was smart. She was struggling emotionally. She didn't remember loving Ricky, and now she wasn't sure she felt anything at all.

Chapter 52

"You remember my conversation about Rexford Wilker, the army recruit, and Jill, of Jack and Jill, who shared similar experiences to Jane's? I reread the study, and had their doctors not taken extensive notes and made recordings during and following the return of their memories, we wouldn't be having this conversation today. Within weeks of their return to normalcy, both had completely forgotten the future they claimed to have been a part of."

"Why would that happen, Doctor?" Ricky asked.

"Got me." Dr. Hammond shook his head and stared at the two. "Their lives were permanently altered by their experiences in the future and the decisions they subsequently made as a result, but I have no concrete answers." He shrugged and closed the files. "Enough with all of that. We must work within the confines of what we understand." He focused on Jane. "What is abundantly clear, what we know for certain, is that by means of dissociative fugue, you were protecting yourself, shielding yourself from the tidal wave of pain your son's death represented."

Jane looked down. "I should have died instead of the baby."

"But you didn't, Jane. I don't mean to be harsh, but this is where we are, and we must go forward from this point." He paused and then added, "For your own well-being."

Jane nodded. "I know." But she didn't. "It's too unsettling, Doctor. The pain I feel as a result of the death of my child, and the alternate life I was leading that seemed so real—both are stronger than any nightmare I've ever experienced."

"Without being too intrusive, Jane," Dr. Hammond said, "I believe that a significant part of your continuing recovery will depend upon you being able to forgive yourself for your child's death." He spoke softly. "As I understand all the circumstances you have related to me, and though it's of little consolation, the death was not your fault."

Jane stared at the psychiatrist, her eyes glistening. "Maybe it wasn't my fault, Doctor, but the pain I have to live with, no matter whose fault it was, is relentless." She reached in her purse for a tissue. "Every day I wake up thinking of the baby. Every night I go to bed thinking of his death and how I could have prevented it. Then he dominates my dreams when I sleep. There is nothing else."

"But now you are discovering you have the strength to face the tragedy, Jane. That's one reason your memory returned. You're able to acknowledge that you will attack the pain instead of being victimized by it."

"What could be worse than a parent outliving a child?"

"Very little, but it doesn't change the reality, and that's what we have to focus on. For your own recovery, you must forgive yourself for Jimmy's death."

"The baby couldn't fend for himself. I hesitated when Jimmy was throwing him in the air. I waited too long and lost him. I was negligent."

"You were scared, and your husband was highly irresponsible. He's an alcoholic who was left to care for a toddler and he acted abysmally."

"I never should have left Jimmy alone with him. And that is my fault."

"You're human and you couldn't control everything."

She shook her head. "I knew that he was reckless, I mean, after all, I lived with him." She paused. "I never should have left him with the baby. And if I hadn't hesitated my son would still be alive."

The psychiatrist leaned forward. "I should have, I should have. You cannot punish yourself forever. You'll die broken." His eyes met Jane's. "If you can forgive yourself, you won't lose touch with your son. He'll remain in your dreams, your hopes. You'll feel him around you. And he'll know you're thinking of him as he is thinking of you." He leaned back. "I promise you."

Jane stared back at the doctor. "How could I feel him around me? He's not alive."

"It's a choice. It's acceptance, and it's far better than what you currently have," the psychiatrist replied.

"That makes no sense," Jane said, her voice a mere whisper. She stared at her hands, then away. After her tonsils had been removed at age nineteen, she recalled the depths of the anesthesia and the battle to regain consciousness. Her perception and awareness, blank from the drug, slowly became muddy, and like some prehistoric reptilian creature, she gradually emerged from a Permian swamp and clawed her way up the embankment, to gray tones, then sepia shades, and at last, vivid color.

But then she had wanted to return and participate in a life. Now she didn't. The pain was all-consuming.

"I've dealt with these situations before, Jane—acceptance, along with forgiveness for yourself, that's where you must travel if you are to survive."

She offered no response.

The three sat, encircled in the office, no one speaking.

"It's better than what you currently have," Dr. Hammond repeated at last.

An antique clock resting on a bookcase shelf chimed the half hour. The psychiatrist rose to his feet. "I think it's important that we stay on track with our sessions, Jane," he said.

She nodded, rising from her chair. "I'm trying, Doctor, believe me I'm trying, I really need to get this straightened out."

Ricky stood up and the three stared at each other, wagons circled, uncertain what would happen next.

A car screeched from the parking lot onto the street.

"Odd thing though," Dr. Hammond thought aloud a moment later as he crossed with Jane and Ricky to the door, "Rexford Wilker's high school classmate stayed in the service and died of sniper wounds to both knees while on patrol in Vietnam. And Jack, of Jack and Jill fame, died alone in 1965 due to an overdose, and without Jill, who was long gone and happily remarried. The only surprise was that Jack stayed alive that long." He smiled. "Sounds like Rexford and Jill met with the God of Second Chances." The psychiatrist nodded his head toward Ricky and Jane as he opened the door. "Life? Science fiction? Both?"

CHAPTER 53

Jane thought she could endure within the confines of a circle of light radiating from a solitary candle, and that she would have to look neither left, right, up, or down while she labored at merely existing. Safe within the flame's corona, she would be able to avoid the deep shadows.

But then her son would emerge from dark distances, sometimes with his arms open, searching for her. He was one, he was five, he was a teenager, or he was one again and laughing, or older again, thoughtfully watching her. Once he had his arm around a girlfriend, and another time he was wearing a football uniform, then later in the day he was leaning against a tree reading a book. She would wonder at his looks, his sensitivity to his surroundings, his love for her.

And each time she stopped thinking of him, she believed he would be gone forever.

Her sense of grief remained so overwhelming, so all-encompassing, that Jane now understood how her mind had closed down simply to survive.

And despite telling Dr. Hammond she was feeling better, she knew there was little hope. Her words were implying optimism, but she was really taking tiny steps backward. Soon she would end up wandering the planting fields and meadows at night, alone, disoriented, as she had done before. Perhaps Russ and his neighbors would search for her again, as they had several times during the fugue period, but never be able to locate her. It was only a matter of weeks, or days, or hours until the grief weighed her down, and succumbing to the pain, she withdrew to the swamp, to slip into the mire and blissfully hibernate, to never return.

Several weeks had passed since her memory reappeared and Jane was current in her classes. She was conceptually miles ahead of other students in marketing, business management, and advertising strategy, and could easily debate professors on business policy, revealing common-sense acumen beyond her experience and years.

It was instinctual.

She had ended the relationship with Ricky, handing him back his college ring—what was she thinking—were they teenagers going steady? He made her uncomfortable with his presumption of intimacy. She had no desire to be sexually involved with him, nor could she recall what had ever romantically stirred her in that direction. Perhaps he had arrived when the first blow of the baby's death had crushed her.

It didn't matter.

He had been enough of a psychiatrist to gracefully depart after hearing her pronouncement. She had been neither gentle nor kind, behaving as if it were the end of a bad business deal.

She didn't watch him ride away on the Indian, the wind streaming through his hair, an image she thought that one time she had worshiped. Instead, she walked up the steps to the farmhouse, crossed the living room and entered her tiny room with the crucifix hanging over the bed. As she closed the door, the motorcycle's engine was in the distance, screaming away from the farm until only a faint echo whispered through the fields.

Moments later, Russ yelled at a senseless deer that wandered too close to the house looking for food, then fired his rifle to scare the poor creature away.

Jane lay on the bed.

As she moved her head sideways on the pillow, the crucifix hanging on the wall behind her remained timeless. She remembered it as the same cross that was in the Irish boy's bedroom.

The child had passed and she had been responsible.

There were no coincidences.

Jamie, the handsome teenager she recalled sleeping on the dock, had the same shining green eyes as her son, Jimmy.

The college freshman her husband had nearly beaten to death, had matted, fine, bloody hair—the same as her baby's head after it struck the cement. Both names were Jimmy.

James, the waiter, twisted his neck to look behind him. The awkward, death-like angle of his head, similar to the baby's when he had landed on the cement, caused a panic attack, distorting Jane's hearing and her visual perception of Carrie. She had jumped up from the lunch table and run from the restaurant.

And the name Jimmy had continued to pursue her and encumber her, never allowing relief. The homeless man, Jimmy, whose laughter warmed her with its stop-start cadence, maintained the same laugh rhythm of her child, Jimmy. Look, laugh, pause.

Jimmy the cook at Flanagan's, Jimmy in the mall photographs, Jimmy on the ceiling of Grand Central Station, Jimmy the guard at the top of the Empire State Building—all clues, all memory fragments dragging her to a reality portrait she had desperately sought to avoid.

But it made sense now. All roads led home.

Jane closed her eyes. Nothing was real except the all-consuming love for her deceased son.

She was lost in the center of four hundred acres of corn, a phalanx of uniform rows, each the same, each different, all representing gradations of pain.

No one was awake but her.

No one was alive but her.

CHAPTER 54

The rivulets slid past on the window, pointed arrows aiming back home. Their message was clear—New York was empty, meaningless and she should return to the Midwest.

The Boeing 727 braked on the runway and U-turned before heading to the gate at La Guardia Airport.

The water streaks vanished, deleting the previous message.

The Manhattan life Jane had lived remained real enough, powerful enough, for her to search for conclusive evidence, yea or nay, that it had happened.

The big surprise was that Ricky still lingered in the back of her mind. He was gone, but the sense of being loved by him was unlike anything she had ever experienced before. She understood that now. Yet instead of simply basking in that affection, his presence had gnawed at her, leaving her conflicted and vulnerable, until she sent him away. Any personal joy would be unfair to the memory of her son.

From the airport, Jane took a bus into Manhattan and then a cab to The MacMillan House, a sparse hotel on the West Side she had discovered through a visitor's guide.

The ninth-floor room contained a Gideon Bible, a bed, and a telephone resting on the bedside table. The window faced a brick wall. At the far side of the room, a splintered stub of a yellow pencil—the type gamblers used at racetracks—rested awkwardly off the corner of the rug, as if it had been thrown in disgust by a chambermaid who had been one horse away from hitting the Trifecta.

The rain drummed on the roof and the water gurgled down a drainpipe next to her window.

She was missing two days of school, but had made it to New York.

Jane unpacked, and then rode the lurching elevator to the lobby. At the front desk, she inquired about a Manhattan phone book and asked for forty quarters in exchange for a ten-dollar bill. The hunched-over front desk clerk with tape-mended bifocals and a cardigan sweater handed her the coins, then pointed at the several New York City county White Pages piled on a table next to the pay telephone.

Jane lifted a wooden chair resting against the wall and carried it over to the table.

"Make sure you put that back when you're done," the man called, his watery eyes floating above his glasses.

Jane nodded and turned her back. She had begun her self-assigned New York City homework with Russ and Marie's telephone, using operator assistance to contact people she remembered in Connecticut and New York. She knew it would be nearly impossible to track down people twenty years *before* she had known them, but she was determined to try.

When she had begun in St. Charles, Jane had listed the most obscure names first, but Janet Hayes, the president of the Andover Country Club, Tom Turner, the president of the Barlow, Blake, and Turner advertising agency, as well as his employees Len Stein and Gene Dawson, couldn't be found. In fact, according to phone records, the ad agency didn't exist.

She even looked for the Versailles Club, where she had lunch with Briggs, but it wasn't listed.

She tried twelve more casual acquaintances plus each additional listing with the identical name, but had come up empty.

Halfway through her list, Jane had decided to attack New York personally, to get closer to the people possibilities, to search for actual places she remembered. She wanted to comb through the directories herself rather than trust the weary ramblings of information operators. And if she was lucky enough to locate someone, she could meet with that individual, or if a specific landmark she recalled was real, she would be able to confirm it with her own eyes, touch it with her own fingers.

Jane placed the Manhattan directory on her lap and taking a blind shot, looked up Get HIP-notized, the Greenwich Village store where she had bought her self-hypnosis kit. The closest listing was Get Higgins, an Upper East Side saloon.

She reached decades-old Cranford State through directory information, but learned that Robert Grassley, the author of her self-hypnosis book, was not a faculty member.

She continued to search the listings: DSRR, Carrie Binotti, Howard Dreyfus, Ashton's on Fifth, Lauren Fritz.

Nothing except three Howard Dreyfuses.

She called each of them.

Zero.

The clerk behind the desk eyed her, his elbows on the counter, his chin resting on the heel of his hand. "Watcha need all those directories for?" he called across the empty lobby.

"Job hunting," Jane answered over her shoulder.

Barbara Greenman and John Briggs were both on her list, but they had lived in Connecticut.

Jane turned to the clerk. "Do you have any Connecticut directories?"

"Yeah, over here. Whatcha looking for a job in Connecticut for? There's plenty of work right here in New York City."

"I'm not looking for a job in Connecticut," Jane replied as she walked toward the front desk, "just looking for some people."

"Yeah, all right, all right, I heard you," he answered, now surly that Jane was not more forthcoming or paying him any attention. He reached beneath the counter, lifted several directories and handed them to her.

"Thanks," Jane responded as she walked back across the lobby.

Six Barbara Greenmans; none an M.D. She called them all.

Nothing.

Three J. Briggs'. No Johns.

No luck.

Jane hung up the receiver. She was tired of phone calls.

She found herself thinking of Ricky again and pushed his image from her mind.

"Don't leave the Connecticut books over there," the clerk called, now overtly cross.

She stood and carried them back to the desk. "Thanks."

He nodded curtly, then placed the directories beneath the counter, now ignoring her.

Jane returned the chair to its original position against the wall and walked to the elevator, stepped inside, and waited for the door to close.

Moments later, she entered her room and sat on the edge of the bed. Her list was virtually at an end. Near the bottom of the page was the sensational G-clef murder of Carrie's blackmailer. It would have made the newspapers, and based on Carrie's description, had probably occurred while she was in her late teens or early twenties. If she could track down the homicide in a newspaper, it would have to mean something.

∞

Jane returned from the New York Public Library four hours later. She had examined all the microfilm covering New York City's most highly publicized homicides, but had found nothing to corroborate Carrie's G-clef story.

Jane stared out the window. Maybe she could save Annie. She dialed her friend's number in Illinois.

"Hello."

"Annie, it's Jane.

"Hi, Jane. Long time no talk." She chuckled.

"Hey, you know how I told you I was going to New York City? Well, I'm here for a couple of days and I was thinking, and this may sound off-the-wall, Annie, but I was thinking this city is such a competitive place that it's got to be really hard to make a living in the theater. Maybe you should reconsider coming here. I mean, there are a lot of local acting groups around Chicago, plus Kenny and you could be together."

"Jane, are you okay? I'd never give up the opportunity."

"But you don't know how tough it can be here, Annie."

"Maybe so, but I'm tough too." She hesitated. "You sound a little, I don't know, tense. Are you sure you're okay?"

Jane paused again. "Sure." She thought for several seconds. "Of course, I am. I was just nervous about a St. Charles girl being all alone here."

"Which is why you're my best friend."

"And you're mine. Just forget I called, Annie."

"We all have our moments. Let me know when you get back."

"Will do."

Jane placed the receiver in the cradle and stared at the floor.

She was a fool. She knew it. She could continue to try to reach the other phone numbers that hadn't answered when she called from the farm, or she could continue searching through more lists of duplicate names. But even if someone was willing to listen, how could she explain herself in a way that made any sense? And who knew if the people she was searching for even existed, and if they did, that they inhabited the same geography now as they would twenty years in the future.

She thought for a minute. Maybe she could locate, then visit some grizzled New York City detective and pick his brain about the G-clef homicide, assuming it had even happened, which now seemed to be more than doubtful.

No.

Jane began to comprehend her role. She could spend the rest of her life toting handfuls of coins to ever-changing public telephones, searching for tangibles in shadowy, psychological alleys that offered no foothold or termination point, or she could listen to the doctors and accept their practical explanation of memory loss based on their experience and existing medical literature.

To the world, conforming to the doctors' analysis would signal her recovery was beginning. Challenging their observations by insisting some fantasy of consciousness transformation was true would indicate she was still a mental case, jabbering on about life in another dimension, and maybe even a candidate for hospitalization.

She was trapped and unready for either option.

Jane walked into the bathroom for a glass of water. It was rust colored so she emptied it into the sink.

She studied herself in the mirror. At least she was young, not a burned-out middle-aged commuter married to a drunk. That was never going to happen.

Which was good.

Which was very good.

She thought of Ricky, then chastised herself for not concentrating on her son's memory. She needed to be more vigilant of the memorial guidelines she had devised for herself.

She could never forget that she could never forget.

She stretched her arms over her head and yawned.

∞

At 3:15 that morning, Jane suddenly sat up in bed, the sheets held to her neck. She'd almost forgotten what it was like to wear his ring and feel his fingertips pressed against hers.

CHAPTER 55

"I don't know what you're looking for here in Andover," the cab driver said, studying her in the rearview.

"Just visiting," Jane said. "But ready to go back to the train station."

She had searched. Her home didn't exist. The country club and shopping mall were farmland, and no Flanagan's was on Main Street. In fact, there was no Main Street—the primary boulevard was Midland Avenue.

Jane stared out the window at the rain. "Yes. Just visiting, and it feels like I've never been here before."

The driver glanced in the rearview again and nodded. "Know what you mean."

Jane studied the back of his head. He had no clue what she meant.

∞

Back in Manhattan, she couldn't locate the DSRR building, and the existence of the Waldorf Astoria, Grand Central Station and the Empire State Building proved nothing—they had been around for decades. On the West Side, she was unable to locate the theater where she'd seen the musical with Annie in the chorus.

Jane rested against a phone booth. After all her detective work, all her phone calls, all her agonizing, she realized if there was ever a speck of truth to the future life she recalled, she would have stumbled on something beside the landmark buildings.

And Twyla, Carrie and Briggs, his necktie white-on-white, were now paper dolls attached to the tail of some faraway kite. They were slipping away, leaving no fingerprints, no shadows, no trace.

She walked down Seventh Avenue. In the gutter, a Three Musketeers candy wrapper pinwheeled down a tiny stream and lodged in the drain. On the opposite sidewalk, a spotted, unleashed mongrel with yellow teeth exposed in a silly grin, shook himself repeatedly while running sideways. Behind the dog, pink, green, and blue neon bled through the post-rain overcast and then disappeared again.

Jane began to realize that her behavior was sad, and in its own way, disturbed, because in her rare guiltless moments, those brief seconds when she forgot she was responsible for her son's death, she had considered attempting to move on, or as Dr. Hammond had instructed, to forgive herself and learn to accept she would never hold her child again.

And . . . she had been loved by Ricky. Maybe she still was. The sense of being wanted by him was unlike anything she had ever before experienced. It now infiltrated her, filling every corner, coloring every breath she took.

That thought now jockeyed with her son, Jimmy, for priority position. She made a mental effort to shove it away.

∞

Jane reached the downtown block in forty-five minutes. She had walked instead of phoning because she had never known Twyla's last name.

Leave, Jane thought.

No, she had come this far.

She stared across the street at what she thought was Twyla's building. Four floors of dark windows gazed back. Jane was unsure of anything. She couldn't even recall the number of floors the building had contained.

She paused, uncertain. Why had she visited Andover that morning? It was odd. She couldn't quite remember.

Jane dismissed the thought and cautiously crossed to the building's entrance. Inside the vestibule, she scanned the names next to the apartment buzzers. No initial T appeared for a first name anywhere. She studied the two name tags for the second floor where Twyla had been located. The first read "L. Smyth," the second was blank. She thought it had also been unmarked when she had visited Twyla for the regressions.

She decided to ring L. Smyth first. A man's harsh voice answered almost immediately. "Yeah, who is it?"

"I'm trying to reach your neighbor and—"

"Then buzz her."

Her?

"I've tried and there's no answer."

"That means she ain't home. Try again later."

"Do you happen to know her first—"

"See ya," he said.

Jane heard the intercom click off. She pressed L. Smyth's buzzer again.

He didn't respond.

And again.

No answer.

She pressed the blank second buzzer.

No answer.

She tried one more time.

A man's annoyed voice answered. "Who? What?"

"You don't know me, but—"

"What are you selling?"

"Nothing, nothing at all."

"Then you must be from that church." He didn't take a breath. "Look lady, I got neither the time nor the energy and you just pulled me out of bed."

"I don't mean to—"

"Then don't."

The intercom went dead.

Jane dropped her hands to her sides and turned away. She walked out to the street.

It was over.

She knew it.

But what was over? She wasn't sure. It was hard to figure why she had even come to New York City. Probably to locate Briggs and Cara, she thought. Was it Cara or Carrie? What did they look like?

On the opposite side of the street leaning against the wall stood a figure she thought she recognized.

Her son, Jimmy?

So quickly, so subtly.

He was talking with a young woman and she heard the familiar laughter, now more mature, that had left her life long ago, yet remained laughter imprinted so clearly in her memory she would recognize it even if ten thousand years had passed.

The young woman departed.

His eyes caught hers.

"Jimmy," she said,

He resembled her. He was a part of her.

"Jimmy," she said, her eyes filling.

He was in his twenties, dressed in a sports jacket and

jeans. He smiled at her, then very slightly shook his head. "Don't cry."

Jane could read his lips. She was locked in place, just as when he had been thrown in the air. "I can't help it if I'm crying. I can't help it."

"Please, don't," he said again.

"I can't help it!" she suddenly screamed.

An elderly woman who had stepped out of a cab approached her. "Are you all right, dear?" she asked, leaning on a walnut cane. "Can I help you, dear? Would you like me to call someone?"

"Jimmy, Jimmy, why are you doing this to me?" Jane shouted over the woman. She tried to move toward him, but could not will her legs forward. "Jimmy, come here. Come to Mama."

He was backing away, still watching her.

"Jimmy."

A cluster of pedestrians crossed in front of him, and after they passed, he was gone.

"He's not there! He's not there! Why did you have to interfere?" she screamed at the old woman. "Why did you do that? Why didn't you mind your own business!"

The woman walked slowly away.

Jane couldn't control her pain and covered her face with both hands. "Jimmy." She had prayed to have him delivered safely to her, and then had neglected to protect him beyond his first year, instead transporting him from his birthday to his death day.

She couldn't bear to ever see him again.

She couldn't live without ever seeing him again.

With her back to the railing, Jane slid down and sat on the stoop adjacent to the apartment entrance, her face still covered with her hands as she quietly wept.

"Are you okay, Miss?"

Jane looked up at a policeman. A small group stood behind him.

"I'm fine. I'm fine," she answered. "I've had a tough day, that's all." She still couldn't control the tears.

The officer gave her a long look before he turned around. "Okay, folks, it's over. Let's give her a little breathing room." He turned back. "You want to go somewhere? Hospital? I'll get a car down here."

Jane shook her head. "No, no. Just let me rest. I'll be fine."

The policeman nodded, still watching her closely. At last, he said, "Okay. Call 911 if you need help. I'll be around this area and will keep an eye out for you."

He left.

Still the tears. Tears for all Jimmy could have been.

Minutes passed.

Jane gradually grew weary from the effort of crying and allowed her hands to slide to her sides as she struggled back to her feet.

She glanced across the street again and slowly began to understand. Her son, Jimmy had been there for a reason. He was letting her go, to be free to explore, to carry on. She knew that's why she had seen him. She was sure that was his message.

Because he loved her too.

But letting go would mean she was guiltless and that would be untrue and tarnish his memory. And she was afraid to be free. He might disappear forever.

"Please don't cry," he had said.

Jane lifted her head.

She was so guilty. Guilty beyond all hope.

"I should have . . . I should have . . . you cannot punish yourself forever. You'll die broken."

Dr. Hammond's words.

She ignored the voice, knowing all the while that ounce by ounce, the accumulated weight of the guilt and pain was driving her into the mindless, eternal haze of the swamp again.

"If you can forgive yourself, you won't lose touch with

your son. He'll remain in your dreams, your hopes. You will feel him around you. And he will know you are thinking of him as he is thinking of you."

"It's not true," Jane said aloud. "And anyway, I want more. I want him alive because I'm dead without him."

"I promise you." Dr. Hammond's echo.

"I can't do it," she screamed. "I can't do it!"

"And he will know you're thinking of him, as he is thinking of you."

"I can't!" Jane cried. "Do you hear me, I can't! I can't! I can't!"

"I promise you."

Silence.

"I can't," she whispered.

Jane looked downward at the glistening pavement still damp from the rain, sparks of mica flickering at her, and for a moment, instead of considering what she was, she thought of who she might be.

She gathered her courage to glance across the street again and he was there, now wearing a gray overcoat, his hands in the pockets.

He walked to the curb and quickly crossed, weaving his way through a line of cars, moving forward until he stood in front of her.

"Ricky." She believed and disbelieved.

He gently touched her face with the back of his fingers. "You know, Janey," he said after several moments, his voice muted, "sometimes angels fly too close to the ground and die."

Jane stared at him, then downward. "I came back here looking for that other life, that dream."

"There is none, Janey. We make our own dreams."

She looked up again and wrapped her arms around Ricky's neck, then rested her head against his shoulder. "I'm so sorry, Ricky," she murmured.

"Other angels can live," he whispered.

"How?"

"They're born and they live."

"How?"

"The timing is right."

Jane knew that much to be true. She lifted her head and looked across the street and saw her son smile, then turn away and slip into a crowd.

She felt the shackles that enveloped her begin to loosen.

No child would ever be as special as Jimmy, but instead, each exceptional in their own way. She would never let her firstborn leave her, but what if she could allow herself to continue with a life—one with its own distinctive moments and bright horizons? Her son would remain a vital part of her until all the constellations drifted away, but what if she was able to move forward and instead of being trapped in the passages of the maze—lost in the middle of acres of eight-foot corn—she could float away?

New York had been nothing more than a vision of denial, elaborately constructed for protection and survival in the face of a monstrous tragedy. Dr. Hammond and Ricky had both told her so, and now she understood and was ready to let it slip away. She barely remembered why she had returned to the city. Her old friends and enemies alike, once thriving in multi-dimensional structures she had designed and erected, had quietly disappeared.

Water under burned bridges. They were gone.

"Did you follow me?" Jane asked at last, her eyes touching Ricky's.

"What's more normal than a psychiatrist-to-be doing a little stalking of his own?"

Jane was silent.

"We need a new beginning, Janey," Ricky said.

"My room is uptown."

"I know," he answered.

Jane slipped her arms from Ricky's neck, to his waist, and remained standing, her head resting against his shoulder. "I'm ready," she whispered.

He nodded and ran his fingers through her hair. "Then we should go now, Janey. It's time."

"I know," Jane answered, a brief smile touching her lips. "It's about time."

DARK MATTER

Epilogue

"Anybody phone while I was upstairs at Rita's?" she called, parting the window curtain and peering down on the street where the young woman with auburn hair rested her head against her boyfriend's shoulder.

"Negative. Some woman buzzed us," he answered from the back of the apartment. "Didn't know who she was looking for, but she dragged me out of bed."

A pause.

"Hey, baby, how about hip-hopping back here into the bedroom?"

"Hold your horses, I'm looking out the window."

"The hell with the damn window."

She chuckled to herself. He did make her laugh, and that's why she put up with a young-buck cowboy claiming to be from Fort Worth, who lived with his mother in Yonkers.

On the street below, she could see the two begin to walk

hand-in-hand away from the building.

"Come on, sweetheart, you're wasting valuable time. Hell, I'm starting to get cold all by myself in this bed."

She watched until the couple disappeared around the corner.

"You mad at me from the other night, baby? You shouldn't be. That guy deserved to be punched in the mouth. He's lucky I didn't kill him for what he said to you."

No response.

"Hell, I'm freezing to death in here. These satin sheets make me feel like I'm getting mugged by a damn coffin."

She let the curtain slip into place, then moved across the living room and down the hallway, unsnapping her navy western shirt with the two intertwined red roses embroidered across the breast.

"If you're mad from the other night, the least you can do is give me a second chance. A second chance is the very least I should get."

She entered the bedroom, unloosened her belt and let her jeans fall to the floor. "Of course I'll give you a second chance, honey," Twyla murmured, "everyone deserves a second chance."

Ted Alexander grew up in Vermont and Long Island, New York. He won a Shubert creative writing fellowship, completed his master's degree, then joined a rock band and toured America for five years. He later worked as an account supervisor and media director for two Manhattan advertising agencies, followed by a career in publishing. He is currently a columnist for the Asheville *Citizen-Times* in Western North Carolina, where he lives with his wife, Portia.

Visit the author's website at TedMAlexander.com.

Praise for *The Fall of Summer*

"This is a very impressive debut . . . No cardboard cutouts here. These are real people and Alexander makes us care about them. One looks forward to Alexander's second novel, due out next year."

-*Kirkus Reviews*

"There's tenderness and wisdom in Ted Alexander's novel, as there is in his well-regarded column in Asheville's *Citizen-Times*. He promises another book, *After & Before*, in 2015. I'm on the waiting list for another great read."

-Suzanne McLain Rosenwasser, author,
Manhasset Stories: A Baby Boomer Looks Back

"Alexander's debut novel immersed me in fascination, wonder . . . I did not want it to end."

-*New Atlantic Independent Booksellers Association*

Available at the author's website at TedMAlexander.com/Books.

Also by Ted M. Alexander

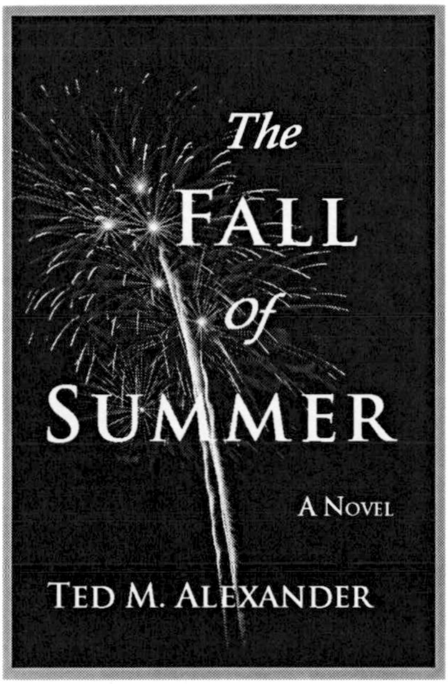

President John Kennedy is dead. Vietnam looms on the horizon. But days are long and time is cheap in Hardscrabble, a sleepy Long Island town reluctant to awaken.

DJ Elders, a high school senior, finds himself stumbling through the no-man's-land between adolescence and adulthood. Suddenly a striking beauty with a hot body and mysterious background shows up. DJ notices. She smiles. He falls. And tragedy leads to homicide as the once-tranquil town of Hardscrabble blows up around him.

In a heartbreaking and humorous testament to the enduring power of friendship and youth, *The Fall of Summer* is a bittersweet glance back to a simpler time, when the Beatles had just hit American shores, the Yankees couldn't lose a pennant, and life's promise was still within reach.

Lightning Source UK Ltd.
Milton Keynes UK
UKOW04f2110241015

261328UK00001B/15/P

9 780991 423705